I0538520

COUNTERACTION: WEREWOLF APOCALYPSE

THEM POST-APOCALYPTIC SERIES BOOK THREE

M.D. MASSEY

MODERN DIGITAL PUBLISHING, AUSTIN, TX

FREE BOOK OFFER!
Get your FREE novella now at
MDMassey.com

Modern Digital Publishing
P.O. Box 682
Dripping Springs, Texas 78620
THEM Book Two: Counteraction/ M.D. Massey. — 1st ed.

Dedicated to the sheepdogs, who keep the wolves at bay.

Then Ulysses tore off his rags, and sprang on to the broad pavement with his bow and his quiver full of arrows. He shed the arrows on to the ground at his feet and said, "The mighty contest is at an end. I will now see whether Apollo will vouchsafe it to me to hit another mark which no man has yet hit." On this he aimed a deadly arrow at Antinous, who was about to take up a two-handled gold cup to drink his wine and already had it in his hands. He had no thought of death—who amongst all the revelers would think that one man, however brave, would stand alone among so many and kill him? The arrow struck Antinous in the throat, and the point went clean through his neck, so that he fell over and the cup dropped from his hand, while a thick stream of blood gushed from his nostrils. He kicked the table from him and upset the things on it, so that the bread and roasted meats were all soiled as they fell over on to the ground. The suitors were in an uproar when they saw that a man had been hit; they sprang in dismay one and all of them from their seats and looked everywhere towards the walls, but there was neither shield nor spear, and they rebuked Ulysses very angrily. "Stranger," said they, "you shall pay for shooting people in this way: you shall see no other contest; you are a doomed man; he whom you have slain was the foremost youth in Ithaca, and the vultures shall devour you for having killed him." Thus they spoke, for they thought that he had killed Antinous by mistake, and did not perceive that death was hanging over the head of every one of them. But Ulysses glared at them and said: "Dogs, did you think that I should not come back from Troy? You have wasted my substance, have forced my women servants to lie with you, and have wooed my wife while I was still living. You have feared neither God nor man, and now you shall die." They turned pale with fear as he spoke, and every man looked round about to see whither he might fly for safety...

~from Homer's Odyssey, Book XXII, translated by Samuel Butler

I snapped off a round from my suppressed .45, sprinting like hell for the front yard of yet another McMansion. The deader I shot dropped, even though it looked like I'd barely creased his skull. Sometimes the little ones would go down like that. He had been a front-runner. I figured if I took him out, it'd get us out of visual contact with them—at least for the moment. Maybe the rest of the group wouldn't be so quick to pick up our trail.

We'd been running for hours because that pissant of a punter Pancho Vanilla had led us right into a trap, on our way to rescue my girl Kara and a bunch of settlers from the werewolf pack that roamed the IH-35 corridor. The plan was to get them back and take them to the Facility, a sort of underground secret lair for mad scientists that the CIA and the Army had created before the bombs dropped and the dead started walking. Only one of those mad scientists still remained, and she was on our side, so the Facility was an empty house just waiting for some new occupants. All we had to do was rescue a few dozen people from a pack of werewolves and find a way to get them halfway across the state of Texas, safe and sound. *Piece of cake.*

But now we had this huge deader herd on our tail, thanks to that sorry slaving son of a bitch Jimmy. I'd nicknamed him Pancho Vanilla because of his complexion and the sombrero he'd been wearing when I first met him. He wasn't the sharpest tool in the shed, but he was mean and crafty, and damn it if I hadn't let him lead us into those shamblers. Currently, we were trying to ditch a couple hundred of them in the wide streets and fenced backyards of an upscale neighborhood in southwest Austin. It wasn't going so well, and frankly I was bone-ass tired and ready for a nap.

Be that as it may, my young charges weren't faring much better. We'd been running and gunning since Pancho led us into a deader herd that'd probably been in a holding pattern since the last time he and his crew came through here. Once that herd had gotten wind of us, there was no shaking them. Food had been scarce over the last few days since we'd hit Austin city limits, since the very deaders who were now chasing us had once been part of the local citizenry. They'd likely stripped the shelves of every corner gas station and supermarket bare before they kicked the bucket and turned.

So, the kids were running on empty. At least they weren't making me look bad, what with me gimped up and all. Bobby, a twenty-something werewolf I'd saved from a group of slavers a while back, was physically doing fine, but mentally I could tell that the constant running was taking its toll. And Gabby, a young teen who'd latched onto to me after I'd saved her from a herd of deaders, was looking damned tired, although she'd never complain about it. Gabby and I had both had our DNA altered with werewolf genes and some other crazy shit that Gabby's adopted aunt, Captain Perez, had cooked up in her lab. Dr. Perez had worked at the Facility before the War, and she'd been involved with all manner of experiments done to try to cross supernatural and human DNA. Gabby had received the treatment years ago to help her survive in our post-apocalyptic world. Me? I'd gotten juiced because I'd been bitten by a deader, and probably would've turned if they hadn't given me the Doc's serum.

But the serum hadn't quite taken in me the way it had with Gabby. She'd been treated years before, so her body had been given ample time to adapt and mutate, and she was running with the full treatment: faster reflexes, improved endurance, and an upgraded immune system and healing capacity. I'd only had it in me a few weeks, and since I'd gotten the treatments, the deader venom and my now-boosted immune system had been locked in an epic battle within my body. It was slowly robbing me of whatever energy I might have had while operating in near-starvation conditions.

On the plus side, at least we had plenty of water. Most folks didn't have a clue how to tap their water heaters in an emergency, so about every third house had a small supply of portable water to drink. *Thank the Lord for small favors.*

We pulled up short in a driveway next to a Mercedes Sedan that'd probably cost more than I'd made in my first four years in the Army. Gabby squatted next to Bobby while I peeked over the hood of the car and through the glass to look for any movement. Not seeing anything at the moment, I ducked back down and glanced over to them.

Gabby wiped her brow with the back of her hand, angling her silenced .22 away from me as she spoke. "You got any ideas about how we're going to get out of this, *cabron?*"

I glanced over at her. "Watch your mouth, kid."

She rolled her eyes, a typical teen. Bobby snickered. Gabby knew I wasn't serious; there were much more important things to worry about in a paranormal apocalypse than polite language. I shrugged and ducked back down. "If I recall correctly, this neighborhood backs up to the Colorado River. If we cross, we might be able to shake this herd and get some rest. But with the rains, the river is probably high. We need a safe way to get across."

Bobby raised his hand.

"What, Bobby?"

"Um, Scratch—I don't know if you're aware of this, but werewolves sink."

This time, it was my turn to roll my eyes. "I thought you liked to surf?"

He nodded enthusiastically. "Oh, I do, most definitely—but I have to wear two life jackets when I go out. If I lose my board, it's Davy Jones' locker for me. Glurg, glurg, glurg..."

Gabby chuckled, cocking an ear before ducking down further and groaning softly. "I think I hear something. *Pinche* deaders are coming our way again!"

I nodded and surveyed the area. This house had a *porte-cochère* that led to an enclosed driveway. The wrought-iron gate was closed and looked solid. I nodded toward it.

"Bobby, you boost Gabby over and follow right behind her. Stay down and try to find a way to get inside that house— quietly. I'll try to lead the herd off and circle back around after I've lost them."

It was a testament to how tired they were that neither even bothered protesting. "You got it, boss." Bobby nodded once at me and headed to the gate with Gabby in tow. Once they were over the gate and out of sight, I took off running past the front of the house and into the street. The low moaning sounds that Gabby had heard quickly become a virtual symphony of the dead during the few seconds the kids had spent in the relative safety of the backyard.

The soundtrack of my life. I sprinted down the road.

As I rounded a corner past another McMansion, I was forced to pull up short as I observed a dense herd of deaders coming down the street toward me. In another situation, we could have just holed up in any old house and waited for them to pass. But a herd this large could easily break down doors and climb over each other to crash through windows, just by the sheer weight of their numbers. Since the deader venom running through my veins made me halfway invisible to them, I banged on the side of a nearby car to get their attention and then took off down the street, away from where I'd left the kids a few moments before.

I hadn't even covered another block when I felt a sharp pain in my right foot, probably from stepping on a rock. One thing they'd never mentioned in the old Westerns is that running in moccasins is only comfortable on natural ground. The human foot was just not designed to pound the pavement, no matter what an entire generation of "born to run" advocates thought. My dogs were barking, and that was no lie. However, I either had to deal with a stone bruise tomorrow or become zombie chow right now. I happily chose the former, ignored the pain, and trucked on.

Even so, a few blocks later I was starting to tire and decided it was time to shake these assholes. I hooked a left down a side street, only to find I'd entered a cul-de-sac. Even worse, there was a small group of deaders milling around in the street. *Shit*. I decided just to barrel through so I could jump a fence and get away from the main group while still leading them away from Bobby and Gabby.

As I ran, I drew my suppressed .45 caliber Glock in my left hand and my tomahawk in my right, and barreled straight into the crowd of Z's, chopping into skulls and firing into eye sockets to make a path as I zigged and zagged toward the driveways on the other side of the cul-de-sac. Only one managed to grab me, getting a lucky—yet firm—grip on my shirttail and practically dragging me to a stop. I tried to tug out of his grasp, but deaders were strong, much stronger than the average human. Out of options, I quickly spun and chopped off his hand at the wrist with three strikes of my tomahawk.

Once free, I started moving again, breathing hard as fire consumed my lungs. *Shake it off*, I thought and kept running, literally shaking the thing's already stiffening hand off my shirt on the move. I glanced back over my shoulder in time to see the vast herd heading straight past the cul-de-sac. *Crap!* I holstered my silenced Glock and drew its match, sighting down the barrel and taking the time to attempt a headshot on one of the lead Z's. *No sense in wasting good ammo.* My accuracy was off because I was breathing hard, so I hit its shoulder. Still, the report of the round was enough to draw the attention of the herd as a whole, and they started shambling after me in earnest.

Taking a moment to get my shit together so I wouldn't fall and shoot myself, I holstered the sidearm and choked up on my tomahawk, then took off on a dead run for the closest driveway. I bolted around the side of that house, dodging an abandoned Big Wheel and vaulting over a discarded trash container to reach the fenced backyard. I slammed the side gate shut behind me and headed for the back fence, hoping that the tail end of that herd wasn't waiting for me on the other side.

As I vaulted the fence, I saw that the way was clear ahead. But I wasn't three steps into the green belt behind the house before I heard the first deaders crashing through the wood fence behind me. *It's going to be a long afternoon*, I thought, running off into the brush.

[2]
GROUND

Roughly 45 minutes later, I'd lost the deader herd and circled back around. With one final look behind to make sure I'd ditched them all, I jumped the same gate where I'd left the wonder twins and headed toward the back of the house. True to form, the kids had found an entry, and there was a handwritten note on the back door that said "Speak, Friend, and Enter." A smiley face had been doodled at the top, which I suspected as Bobby's handiwork. I removed the sign, then softly and carefully opened the door and snuck into the house, shutting and latching it behind me with as much stealth as I could manage in my current sorry state.

As I walked into the house, I whistled softly and got a reply from the next room. That turned out to be the kitchen, where Gabby and Bobby tossed cabinets and drawers with care. They had stacked several cans of food in the middle of the room, along with a few boxes of dry goods and a tin of potted meat. They turned to look at me as I walked in, and I gestured for silence. Both nodded and went back to their search, so I decided to make sure the house was clear above and below.

I stalked my way through the house with my tomahawk in hand, figuring I wouldn't tempt fate with the suppressed Glock. So-called "silenced" weapons tended to be a lot louder than most people thought. You could still hear a pretty loud report from them even under the best of conditions. I'd risked it earlier when we were in danger, but saw no sense in chancing it now. All it could take was one curious, moaning deader to cause the herd I'd just lost to circle back—and I didn't think I could run one more mile in my current state.

With dreams of sleeping in a real bed dancing through my head, I snuck through the bottom floor of the house looking for signs of life, and determined that people had been living here recently. There were food wrappers scattered here and there, along with indications that someone had recently used the downstairs toilet, perhaps within the week. Bedsheets were rumpled in two of the bedrooms as well; all told, it made me a little jumpy.

I decided to check upstairs next, listening for movement as I made my way up. What I heard and saw was a barely audible whine coming from behind one of the doors, along with a shadow that moved back and forth under the door as I watched it from the staircase. I took a peek around the corner at the top of the stairs and saw that the doors to the other rooms were open. I cleared those rooms first. Then I decided to see what was behind door number two...

As I approached, the whining grew slightly louder and more insistent. With one hand on my Glock, I opened the door a crack and was greeted by a dry black nose attached to a white snout, and the overwhelming stench of dog poop and urine. The nose sniffed at me through the crack a few times, completed its assessment with a gruff *woof* of approval, then backed away from the door.

I'd owned American Bulldogs before I deployed to

Afghanistan, and figured this for one based on the snout and the attitude. But as I cracked the door further, I realized that this was no standard bully. I knelt down in the doorway and held my hand out, not making eye contact but looking the dog over instead.

"Hey there, fella," I cooed softly. "Somebody forget about you up here?"

He whined and started edging toward me. I stayed still and let him sniff me out, and soon he was nudging my hand. I gave him a small scratch on the head, still unsure of where we stood. He licked my hand, and I patted him softly on his head and neck. Apparently, we were cool. I gave him a once over.

"You're a good looking fella, aren't you, boy? Oh my, someone paid a pretty penny for you, didn't they?" He whined a little and began nudging my pockets. "You hungry, boy? I bet you are. Thirsty too, I imagine." I stood up, and he sat down on his haunches, all eighty pounds of him. The poor guy was a little lean, but not in bad shape despite his isolation. There was a bowl sitting on the floor that I assumed had once held water, so I took out my water bottle and emptied it into the bowl.

He whined and looked at me.

"Go ahead, boy, it's okay."

He lapped the water up enthusiastically. Once he finished, I headed back downstairs and into the kitchen with the dog in tow. When we walked in, Bobby noticed the dog first.

"Where'd you find the mutt?" he asked.

Gabby turned before I could answer, and her eyes widened. "Oh my gosh, he's so cute!" Before I could stop her, she had the dog in a bear hug, and soon after he was licking her face off. She giggled as she petted him and received a prolonged bath by licking. I sighed inwardly, relieved that the dog had been socialized properly, despite being raised in a zombie apocalypse.

I looked over at Bobby. "He's no mutt. I'd say he's a full-bred Dogo Argentino, and a good-looking one at that."

Bobby crinkled his nose at me. "A dojo-what-o?"

"Dogo Argentino. They were bred in Argentina for protection and hunting big game. They're a brave, fiercely loyal breed —and expensive. I figure this guy's owners locked him up here for safety while they were out foraging, and they just never made it back."

Gabby started pushing the dog away, as he was still licking the skin off her face. "Stop that!" She giggled again. "Stop it—I mean it!" She finally got him to quit and looked up at me; I knew what was coming before she opened her mouth. "Can we keep him?"

I raised my hands in protest. "Gabby, I don't think that's a good idea—"

"Oh c'mon, Scratch, he's harmless. And half-starved, too!"

"Gabby, harmless is one thing that dog isn't—that's not the point. The point is, we don't know if he'll be a liability or not. Where we're going, I'm not sure if it'd be wise to bring a dog along."

"But look at how well-behaved he is!" She leaned in and whispered softly to me behind her hand, gesturing with her head in Bobby's direction. "And besides, we already have one mutt following us everywhere we go."

Bobby piped up from across the kitchen in a loud whisper. "Hello—werewolf ears. I can hear you whispering about me, and it's not cool."

Gabby giggled as the dog licked her leg. Feeling guilty over the events of the previous few days, I relented. "Fine, but he's your responsibility."

She smirked at me and cocked her hip. "Yes, Dad."

I didn't know what to say to that. I just mumbled something

to the effect of, "Be sure you get him something to eat and take him out to pee once it gets dark."

I went off to clear the basement, with those two jokers chuckling softly behind me.

[3]
TABLE

After clearing the basement and finding nothing but a lot of expensive and useless electronics, I decided to check out the garage to see if there might be something we could use to help us get across the river. I'd have even settled for a couple of foam noodles and an inflatable pool float if it'd help us avoid another run-in with that deader herd. If I had to, I'd put Bobby in some water wings and drag his ass across, lifeguard style.

When I opened the garage door, it became apparent that the former owner had been an outdoors type. There were fishing rods and golf clubs arranged in tidy rows along the wall, as well as a complete set of clubs in a bag leaning against a workbench. Apparently they'd been into fly-fishing as well, with some very nice fly rods and a neatly maintained set of plastic apothecary drawers full of flies and the various components needed for making them.

Bingo, I thought to myself as I began looking around the rest of the garage for something that might have been relatively water-worthy. A search turned up bupkis, but I remembered seeing a second, detached garage on my way into the house. I headed out the back door and snuck over to the side garage door, keeping an eye on the last few straggling deaders still wandering the street in front of the house. None had made it up the driveway, so I was safe for now.

I tried the door, but it was locked. *Crazy white people,* I thought, *locking their stuff up during a zombie apocalypse.* Like anyone cared about their Barry Manilow record collection during times like these. I knelt down and gently worked my knife blade in between the door and the jamb, wiggling it and levering against the latch until I heard a slight click and the door popped open. I eased it open slowly and duck-walked into the garage.

Inside, all was silent and covered in dust. I looked around and saw little of interest, and almost walked right back out again. Then, I looked up in the rafters; lo and behold there was a very serviceable fiberglass canoe up there, along with a couple of Day-Glo orange and pink kayaks. A further search revealed some paddles and life preservers as well.

It looked like we had a way out of here if we could just hold out quietly until we were sure that the bulk of the Z's had passed. I decided to head back to the house to tell the kids what I'd found, and took a quick peek around the door before heading out. *Shit.* There was lone deader, right at the fence, sniffing around and moaning softly.

I looked her over while she had her head turned away. She was short, slightly built, and wearing a faded and tattered sundress along with one strappy sandal on her left foot. Her right foot was a mess of gangrenous tissue and gore, and I was pretty sure she was walking on bone in places. She must've walked a long way to get here—probably a straggler from that big deader herd.

I wondered if I should put her out of her misery, but weighed the benefit versus the risk and found none. So, I decided to get comfy and doze off for a while here in the garage.

So much for that real bed, I thought. I looked out one last time and saw Gabby looking for me from the doorway. I signaled to her that all was fine. Then I locked the door and grabbed a wadded up tarp for a pillow and a few old patio furniture cushions for a pallet, and took a nap.

A few hours later, I awoke to a thumping noise at the garage door. I slowly cracked my eyes without moving a hair, and saw there was a deader bumping into the door, over and over again. How he had gotten into the yard, I hadn't a clue, but there was no way I was getting out of there without taking him out. I remained still until it was completely dark, perhaps another ninety minutes or so. Then I belly-crawled over to the door, hopefully completely out of his line of sight.

With the blade held in an ice pick grip in my right hand, I eased my left hand over and unlocked the door as silently as I was able. As the door latch clicked softly, the deader began moaning louder and banging against the door with more force. I needed to take him down quick before he brought the whole neighborhood of goons down on us. I timed his door-bashing and opened the door just after he bounced off it and began to lean toward it again.

As I had anticipated, the deader lost his balance and stumbled through the doorway. I was on him in an instant, burying my Bowie knife to the hilt in the top of his head. I let go of the knife and grabbed him, ignoring the odor as I lowered him to the floor as quietly as possible. I then froze for a good five minutes and listened for any sound or sign that the other deaders had heard the ruckus. *Nothing. Phew.*

With some effort, I dislodged my knife from the deader's skull and cleaned it on his pant leg. I sheathed the blade and skulked across the yard and back over to the house. Sneaking in through the back door, I plopped myself down at the kitchen table. Gabby, Bobby, and the dog were already enjoying their evening meal.

Realizing that I was famished, I grabbed two full water bottles and a small box of Shredded Wheat off the pile that had accumulated on the table in my absence.

Gabby nodded at me. "Glad you could finally make it. I thought I was going to have to go outside and kill that deader myself."

I shrugged, so Bobby chimed in, never one to let a lull in a conversation go to waste. "Sorry, but the dog ate the potted meat. I was going to fight him for it, but I felt sorry for the mutt and decided to let him keep it." The dog cocked an eye at Bobby from his place on the floor next to Gabby's foot and sighed.

"Probably for the best, considering the number of stragglers that are still left out there." I grabbed a box of steel-cut oats and a metal pot, dumping the contents in and covering them with a half-bottle of water. I found a clean but dusty dinner plate next to the sink, wiped it off on my sleeve, and used it to cover the pot. With any luck, by morning the oats would be soft enough to eat.

Gabby scratched the dog's head absentmindedly while she chewed her lip. She glanced at me and cocked her head. "So, *viejo*, any idea of how we're going to get out of here without attracting that whole herd of deaders again?"

I nodded as I chewed my Shredded Wheat, wishing for a nice cold quart of milk and a big bowl of sugar. "There are canoes in the garage—all we need to do is get them to the water without drawing that herd." I paused to stifle a yawn. "I have a plan, but let me think on it overnight. I'm too tired right now, and I'd rather look at the problem with fresh eyes in the morning." Gabby merely nodded and yawned as well; she was too exhausted to press me for more info.

I slugged more water as I chewed and then shook my head.

"I can't believe you gave the dog the potted meat. There's a full bag of dry dog food in the basement."

Bobby perked up. "Please tell me it's Natural Balance. Ol' Dick Van Patten sure could make some tasty dog food. Yum."

Gabby and I both looked at him like he was crazy. Bobby returned an unapologetic look and shrugged. "What can I say? Most humans can't eat dry dog food, but werewolf jaws, bro. Just means more for me."

[4]
STREAM

The next morning found us packing things up before dawn. I had convinced Bobby that we needed to get the canoe down in the dark so we could be ready to move before first light. I'd also sent him back to get the gear and weapons we'd stashed during our flight from the deader herd the day before, which he'd been hauling since my mule had gotten spooked by a deader ambush. So, when I woke Bobby up the next day, he was pissy and slow to get going, both from healing inadequately and from the lack of sleep.

Gabby, however, was as chipper as Mary Poppins. I figured it had to do with the dog. She'd already found him a toy: a stuffed squirrel with a squeaker that I'd made her remove. The dog had already shredded it, but he'd seemed to enjoy doing it, so I considered it a win all the way around.

The plan was simple; we'd load all our shit into a single canoe, then Bobby and I would portage it the few hundred feet or so from the back wall to the river. Based on the map I had, the last stretch of houses in this neighborhood backed straight up to the Colorado, so I anticipated just a short hike and quick canoe ride to the other side. There was a large city park almost directly across the river from our current location, and I intended to hit it for some rabbit, squirrel, or even deer meat. I figured we could all stand to eat some decent protein, the dog included.

Night vision aside, it was still a bitch lugging the canoe over the back wall. Doing it without noise caused us yet more grief, but somehow we managed. Getting the dog over was less hassle than I thought it would be; as soon as Gabby climbed the wall, the dog vaulted his front paws up then scrambled his hindquarters over to follow her, with nary a bark or a whine.

Once Bobby and I jumped over, we picked up the canoe and started off in what I determined to be the general direction of the river. The area was thick with juniper cedar, so it was slow going, but we forced our way through. About a hundred feet in, Bobby let out a yip and disappeared from view, dropping his end of the canoe to crash onto the ground with a bang. I lowered my end to see what had happened, but Bobby was nowhere in sight.

I edged forward and parted the branches that were obscuring my view ahead. As it turned out, we were on the edge of a short bluff that led down to the river's edge. I looked over the side, where Bobby picked himself up, dusting himself off roughly fifteen feet below.

He waved and smiled. "I'm okay, I'm okay!" he shouted up to us. I frantically motioned for him to stay quiet, but he kept mumbling to himself about how werewolves were tougher than they looked or some such.

A few seconds later, the dog started growling and staring in the direction of the subdivision. I turned to Gabby and yelled, "Climb down, now!"

"But what about Ghost?"

I threw my hands in the air in frustration. "Oh, so the dog has a name now? Great! Gabby, that dog can take care of himself. Now, climb down the freaking ledge!"

Gabby hesitated for a few moments and then started picking out a route down the cliff. The dog went to the edge, looked down at her, then at me. I shook my head. "Don't look at me, buddy—you'll have to find your own way down." He let out a short, almost silent bark and took off along the bluff toward the west.

Wasting no time, I frantically dug through our gear until I found a length of rope. I tied one end to the canoe and yelled, "Bobby, catch!" before throwing our packs and gear down the cliff.

As I worked, the moans behind me were getting louder. Meanwhile, Bobby ran back and forth like Mario dodging barrels in Donkey Kong. To be honest, he was doing a great job of intercepting our gear and keeping the mission-sensitive stuff from getting bashed on the rocks; werewolf speed did have its advantages. I particularly worried about the optics on my rifle, and said a silent prayer that it would avoid taking a tumble. There'd be precious little opportunity to sight it in later, at least without drawing some undesirables down on us.

As I threw the last bag down the cliff, I spotted movement out of the corner of my eye. I drew the suppressed pistol and snapped off a quick headshot to take out the nearest deader. Keeping the Glock in my right hand, I grabbed the rope with the other and kicked the canoe over the edge of the bluff, bracing myself to take the load.

I started slowly letting out the rope, instantly regretting the fact that I hated wearing tactical gloves. As the rope burned the skin from my palm, I ignored the pain and kept letting out rope with one hand, pausing every so often to fire one-handed at the deaders with the other. Within moments, it was clear that I'd soon find myself surrounded, so I let the rope go and hoped the fall wouldn't pierce the hull of the canoe.

Turning to fire again, I snapped two more shots off as the

slide locked back on an empty chamber. I hit the slide release and holstered the weapon, then sprinted about thirty feet in the same direction the dog had gone. I wanted to get some distance from the deaders converging on my position before heading over the bluff.

As I prepared to climb over, I yelled to Bobby, who was getting ready to clamber back up to help me. "Bobby, load up the freaking canoe and get it in the water! Now!"

"Alright, alright already. Make a little noise and bring the zombie herd down on our heads, and everyone has a heart attack. Sheesh." He sulked off to do as I asked, but thankfully Gabby was already loading our gear in the boat. An eighty-five-pound ball of white fur, teeth, and muscle paced back and forth between her and the deaders on the ridge above. How the dog got down the cliff was anyone's guess, but nothing those animals could do surprised me.

I scrambled down the ledge a few feet, only to feel a cold, stiff hand clamp around my wrist. "Son of a bitch, this is just not my day!" I growled, grabbing my Bowie and waiting for the thing's head to pop over the cliff's edge. As soon as the Z showed its face, I stabbed it through the eye with a vicious thrust, and then hacked the hand off at the wrist with a couple of hard chops of the sturdy blade, since it was still hanging on post-mortem-mortem.

Knowing that more deaders would be right behind, I sheathed the knife and continued to climb down the cliff. As soon as I hit the bottom, I ran after Gabby and Bobby, who'd dragged the canoe down to the river's edge and halfway into the water. They both waited for me and stood around wondering what to do, while deaders walked off the cliff and landed with loud smacks and crashes, up and down the shore. I could hear them hitting all around us, and knew it was only a matter of time before enough of them were crawling and limping our way to be a serious threat.

I waved at them frantically, yelling at the top of my lungs. "Go! Go! Go already!"

Bobby leaped into action, steadying the canoe while Gabby hopped in and scrambled to the front. As I ran up behind them, the dog obediently jumped in and followed her. "Bobby, get in the freaking boat already!"

I pushed us off and jumped in the canoe, right as half a dozen deaders hit the muddy shore of the river and began wading in after us. Gabby had already started paddling, so I took mine up as well and steered us toward the opposite side, breathing a deep sigh of relief as the deaders' moans faded behind us.

[5]
STRANGER

Once we crossed the river, the size and quality of the homes we passed went from McMansions to truly freaking palatial. The water was high, which allowed us to paddle up a small tributary that must have been dredged out to provide local residents with boat access to the river. We were still in a residential area, but I knew based on my map that this little creek would take us closer into the park and green belt, so I opted to keep us paddling for a short while longer.

Soon the canoe came to an area where it bottomed out, and I signaled for them to disembark. We unloaded our gear and quietly stowed the canoe and paddles in some brush along the creek. Then, I took a compass reading and we headed off to the north.

Sure enough, we were soon in a densely wooded area with only the barest remnants of park maintenance to be found. I signaled everyone to stop and rest and listened to our surroundings for a good fifteen minutes. The moans of the dead from across the river had faded off, and all I could hear was the wind through the trees, some birds chirping, and the movement of small mammals and reptiles through the brush at various points around us.

I nodded and pulled out my water bottle to take a swig. "Alright, I think we're clear. But let's stick to hand signals and use speech only when necessary. We have no idea what we're going to find out here so let's stay focused and aware. Gabby, you're on point with... Ghost. Keep that .22 handy and take any small game you see."

Gabby nodded and headed off while Bobby waited for orders. "Bobby, you take up the rear guard and make sure no one's on our tail." I stood up and let Gabby take the lead.

Bobby saluted me with mock seriousness, and I ignored him and headed after Gabby. Within a quarter mile, she'd bagged two squirrels and a rabbit, which would be enough meat to feed us all with some left over for the mutt. Deciding we'd better eat while we had the chance, I had them stop near a shallow depression with plenty of foliage for smoke dispersal, and made a small fire while Gabby cleaned and dressed the game.

An hour later we were tucking into roasted squirrel and rabbit when someone shouted from the ridgeline above us. "Stop, in the name of Dame Sweetlove! You are poaching game on royal land, and any attempt to escape or resist will result in your demise!"

I looked up and found us surrounded by a bunch of pimply-faced kids in full Ren fest regalia. I estimated their ages between fourteen and seventeen, tops. Most were carrying what appeared to be handmade longbows, as well as either long swords, short swords, or axes on their hips. As I took in their strange appearance, I didn't know whether to laugh or applaud them for getting the drop on us. One thing I did know was that they could've attacked us from concealment, but they didn't. So, they weren't slavers. They posed no real threat to us, since

Bobby could go through the lot of them without even breaking a sweat. I decided to play along and see what they were all about.

The dog began growling, and one of them made to draw and aim his bow at Ghost. I whispered to Gabby, low enough so only she and Bobby could hear. "Gabby, settle him down. Bobby, don't do anything rash. I don't think we're in danger here, so let's see where this leads."

Bobby looked at me doubtfully and snorted while stuffing the last bits of his meal down his gullet. "Boss, whatever you say. But if one of these punks tries to stick me with one of those toothpicks, I'm going to teach them the meaning of medieval."

"Noted, but let's cooperate for now." I raised my voice to a suitable volume for human ears and raised my hands at the same time. "We mean no harm, and had no idea we were encroaching on someone's land. We've been on the run for days and just escaped a large deader herd on the other side of the river. So, we stopped to hunt something to eat."

An older boy stepped up out of the trees. "Nothing comes through here on two legs but the odd dead one or the slavers. I see not the look of death on your visage; you must be slavers." He motioned to three of the younger boys. "Squires Darren, Valiant, and Pip: take their weapons. But be gentle with yon lass, as she is likely their captive." He walked up to Gabby and took a more or less graceful bow in front of her. "Never fear, milady, you shall not be harmed."

Gabby smirked and rolled her eyes. "Yeah, well don't hurt my dog either, or we're going to have words."

The young man smiled as he stood upright. "On my honor, milady."

Bobby snorted loudly, which drew some angry looks from their group. "Bobby, stow it," I whispered under my breath. "They could be useful."

He smirked and gave me a "What, me?" look, then zipped

his lips and tossed the imaginary key. Once the boys had taken all our weapons, they led us off into the trees. Unfortunately, one of them was having issues with the gear bag containing the Stoner and the Light .50, which gave Bobby no small amount of amusement.

Bobby reached a hand out to him. "Hey, sport, you want me to carry that for you? Wouldn't want you to strain your jousting arm, you know."

The leader called back to him. "Speak not to the prisoners, Squire! They may be planning mischief or worse." Their leader sent another "squire" back to help the first with our gear.

Bobby shrugged. "Suit yourself, then."

Before long the group had walked us roughly two miles to the edge of another upscale residential area, mostly sticking to deer trails and doing a decent job of leaving no sign of their passage. I was impressed. Anyone who could sneak up on all three of us might be worth getting to know. And, I had a sneaking suspicion that these people weren't going to be friendly with the Corridor werewolf pack, so I figured they'd at least be good for some intel, or maybe even some assistance on the chance they didn't try to kill us.

As I considered what my options would be if they proved to be hostile, we marched another mile or so into the neighborhood, which mostly consisted of rather sizable homes along the river. Along the way I noted several barricades that had been erected between the houses, mostly out of abandoned cars, trash cans, and lengths of wooden fence, reinforced with brick and stonework. It was crude, but good enough to keep stray deaders out. Before long we ended up at the driveway of a huge mansion that was, unsurprisingly, built in the style of a castle.

Bobby whistled softly. "Holy crap, boss. Wonders never cease. Which do you think came first, the castle or the nerds?"

One of the boys shoved Bobby from behind. "Quiet! You are

about to enter the court of the Lady, Dame Sweetlove. Show some respect."

Bobby looked back over his shoulder with an amused expression. "Yeah, about that Sweetlove thing—"

I cut him off before he could make the situation any worse. "Bobby, I said stow it!"

He waved a hand in the air and spoke back to me over his shoulder. "Whatever you say, boss, but you gotta wonder—"

"Later Bobby. Please, let's show our hosts some respect."

Gabby snickered and muttered under her breath. "If you say so, but if one of these *pendejos* hurts Ghost, I'm going to clobber him."

W e were marched inside the large, castle-like home, through a foyer into an entryway with a rather impressive grand staircase, and then down a hallway into another room. I guessed it had once been a home theater to rival any small town movie house for size and splendor. There were some homemade flags hung on the wall at the other end, along with a small makeshift dais. And there on a rather throne-like easy chair reclined a young lady in her mid-to-late twenties, wearing a formal evening dress that had been obviously modified to look like period wear from the fourteenth century.

In truth, she was rather stunning in an Anne Hathaway sort of way. She had a nice figure from what I could see, along with long wavy hair that she'd styled in a rather wispy and tastefully wind-blown manner. She had full lips, blue eyes, carefully plucked eyebrows, a pale complexion, and an amused expression that told me she wasn't as into all this pomp and circumstance as the boys who had brought us here were. And, she was wearing a very serious looking Colt .44 Python on her hip.

On her left was a skinny middle-aged man, also dressed in period attire, but wearing more of the Merlin look than the

Robin Hood get-ups the boys were in. On her right stood a rather serious-looking giant of a man. He was wearing a chain-mail shirt and buckskin breeches, with a steel great helm tucked under one arm and an equally serious-looking longsword at his hip. I got the impression that both the armor and the sword weren't just for show.

Without a doubt, the whole situation was weird as hell. But in eight years of surviving the apocalypse, I'd seen things that were a hell of a lot weirder. Crazy cults, slavers who worked for Them, inbred Nazi rednecks—even cannibals. You name it, I'd seen it. These people were acting kooky, but they seemed to be more or less harmless. As far as the adults were concerned, I suspected that it was all just an act. But even if it wasn't, in a paranormal apocalypse you had to take whatever friends you could find, kookiness be damned.

The older boy who was the apparent leader of the group who had brought us in knelt in front of the young lady's "throne." He spoke while looking down at the carpet, like any good vassal would in times of yore.

He cleared his throat and spoke up. "Milady, we found these folk poaching game on your lands. We suspect them to be slavers, although I also think that the young lady is their captive. I promised her that no harm would come to her."

She nodded and rubbed her chin with one hand, brooding in momentary silence. Then she waved him away. "Sir Matthew, you and your men may leave us. Chancellor Tuck will record your bravery in the annals, rest assured."

He nodded and stood. "As you wish, Milady." He turned sharply and motioned for the remainder of the boys to follow him out. The tubby one who'd been carrying my bag of goodies looked around, confused for a moment, then he simply dumped it on the ground and ran out after the rest. I supposed he was tired of lugging it around. Frankly, I felt surprised he'd even made it back.

After they'd left and shut the door behind them, the young lady stood up. I noticed that the man-at-arms moved his hand closer to his sword, but the good Lady Sweetlove seemed unperturbed at our presence.

She tapped her foot in impatience and nodded at us. "You don't look like slavers."

I scratched my chin, which admittedly was overdue for a good shave. "We're not. I'm a hunter from the safe zone to the west, and these are my apprentices."

She laughed, a loud, tinkling laugh. "There are no safe zones."

I shrugged. "Well, there was one out there until a few days ago. Then the Corridor werewolf pack came through and either killed or kidnapped almost everyone I care about. I'm here to get whoever's still alive back."

She seemed to consider that for a moment. "Your people, you mean."

I nodded. "Yes, the people I was supposed to protect."

"A suicide mission, no doubt."

I tilted my head. "Could be. But I have plans to even the odds."

She leaned over to confer with the older man, who was apparently her advisor. They whispered softly together for a few moments, and then she spoke up. "We are not in the habit of killing our own kind. And, I for one would love to see the ranks of the Corridor pack thinned. In the past we maintained an uneasy truce with them, but lately they've been getting more and more aggressive."

I cocked an eyebrow at that last bit. "A truce, with the werewolves? I didn't think that to be possible."

She grimaced. "Believe me, they weren't my first choice for

neighbors. However, we scavenge widely and barter with them frequently. So, they find us useful and up until recently they've left us alone."

"Alive in the shadow of evil. Doesn't sound like much of an existence, living in constant fear of attack."

She tilted her head slightly. "To an extent, they fear us as well. But I will admit, it is a delicate situation." Then she seemed to perk up slightly, as if remembering where she left her car keys. "Oh, but where are my manners? I haven't even gotten your names."

"I'm Scratch Sullivan, and this is Gabby and Bobby." Gabby elbowed me in the ribs. "And, um, Ghost the dog."

The old man gasped slightly, then caught himself. He leaned over to Dame Sweetlove and began whispering furiously in her ear. She nodded and raised a hand to silence him. "I am, as you may have gathered, Dame Sweetlove. The knight to my right is my champion, Sir Reynard. And my advisor, Chancellor Tuck." She gestured at each man in kind.

"We're honored to meet you all."

"The honor is ours, I'm sure. Now, let's get the immediate business over with so we can enjoy ourselves while we are able. As you can imagine, a domain such as this one does not remain secure on idle threats alone. I have rules that must be followed, not only to keep my subjects in line, but also to maintain a certain reputation among our neighbors. If I allow trespassers to steal from my lands, I'll be seen as a weak ruler, and likely something will attempt to unseat me."

I smiled without humor. "You're referring to the wild game we killed in the park."

"In my park, Mr. Sullivan. And that is an infraction that I cannot ignore."

I nodded. "I take full responsibility."

She sat back down on the throne and steepled her fingers.

"That's good, because tomorrow at dawn you'll face a trial by combat with Sir Reynard here. Staves and waisters only, of course, but there is still some risk of serious injury. Reynard here has killed dozens of vampires and untold legions of the undead. He has never been beaten."

Bobby snickered and coughed into his hand. "Cough, bull-shit," is how it came out.

I winced slightly but kept a neutral expression on my face. "We'll be happy to adhere to the laws of your domain during our stay here, and we thank you for your hospitality."

She tilted her head regally. "Sir Reynard, Chancellor Tuck —please see that the young ones are fed and allowed to bathe. I wish to speak with Mr. Sullivan alone."

Reynard immediately spoke out in protest. "Lady Sweet-love, I do not think that would be wise—"

She raised her hand to silence him. "Enough! I'll not have you question me in my own court. Now, see to it that they are fed and allowed all the comforts we can offer, and then return to me after their needs have been met."

Reynard bowed stiffly. "It shall be done."

Tuck gave me a dirty look and followed after him.

Gabby leaned into me and grabbed my shirt. "Scratch, you're not seriously thinking of going through with this, are you? I mean, that guy is wearing armor!"

I smiled and patted her shoulder. "Trust me, everything is going to be alright. Get something to eat, keep Bobby out of trouble, and I'll find you two later on."

"But, Scratch—"

I gently pushed her in the direction of the doors. "Go, I said. It'll be fine."

Bobby was already making a beeline to the door. "Is this going to be some kind of Medieval Times meal, with roasted chicken and all that? I went to the one in Dallas once, and that food sucked. But hey, I'll roll with it. Beggars can't be choosers, right?"

He strolled off down the hall following Reynard and Tuck, with Gabby and Ghost not far behind. She gave me one last look of concern, then headed down the hall after them.

Once everyone else had left the grand hall/media room, Dame Sweetlove rolled her eyes at me and stood up. "Oh for heaven's sakes, finally I can get some decent conversation." She sat down on the edge of the dais and patted a space next to her. "Please, sit."

I walked over and sat down on the dais, a respectful distance apart. She made a face and stuck her tongue out at me. "Well, you're no fun. Don't tell me—big bad wolves stole your girl?"

"Yep, guessed it in one." My girlfriend Kara had been abducted by the Corridor werewolf pack, along with the entire population of the settlement where we'd lived. Over the last few weeks, I'd been sidetracked on my quest to rescue them by everything from slavers to a rogue militia, to getting bitten by a deader. But I was close now, and nothing was going to stand in the way of getting Kara back safely. "Now, my turn. You were what—a school teacher? Fencing coach? Scout leader? Or something to these boys before the shit hit the fan."

She rolled her neck out and shrugged. "What do you want me to say? I was running a LARPing group for my little brother and his friends. You know, something fun to do between doing cosplay at cons and Ren fests. Plus, it gave me a way to bond with my little bro. Then, the whole world went to hell, and I happened to have the boys with me when things went sideways. We were out in Plantersville at the fairgrounds when it happened, the night the bombs fell."

She looked down and rubbed a fold of her dress between her fingers. "Austin and Houston were both a hot mess, so we waited it out at the hotel. Once the dead starting showing up, I got us the hell out of there in the van we'd rented, and we hid at a farmhouse with a retired couple. They were nice. But when the zombies started showing up there, they didn't last long."

"And your brother?"

She looked off at the wall. "He was one of the first that we lost."

I shook my head in sympathy. "I'm very sorry to hear that. I lost some people during those first few days as well."

She wiped a tear from her eye and smiled. "Yeah, well, I imagine we all did. At least I got to spend some fun times with him right before it happened. Besides, this world—" she gestured around her, "it just wasn't meant for children."

I leaned over to pat her hand. "Yeah, but I gotta say, you seem to be doing a heck of a job keeping these kids alive."

She looked at me and blew her nose in a scarf that she'd pulled from her dress somewhere. "Sorry, seasonal allergies. Plus, I always cry when I talk about Brian; that is, when I'm not being Dame Sweetlove." She wiped her nose and tucked the scarf away under her leg. "So, what's your story?"

"Well, I was a Ranger in the Army. Went to Afghanistan, got hurt, and came home. I was still living the war in my head, so I built a cabin out in the sticks on the family ranch to just get away from everything and get my head right. Just when I started feeling better, the world went to shit. Lost my parents in the initial surge. Upside is, got no time for PTSD when there are zombies to kill. And it turns out Uncle Sam's money wasn't wasted on me after all. I guess I'm sort of made for this shit."

She frowned and nodded. "You probably think it's stupid, right? The whole make-believe thing? But how else was I supposed to keep these kids from freaking out, but by pretending it was all just a game?"

I squinted and shook my head. "I don't think it's stupid at all. In fact, I would say that you're damned smart to play it the way you did. People need something to believe in to keep them going in tough times, kids especially. In the battalions it was believing that the guy next to you had your back, and that completing the mission was all that mattered. I can't imagine what it must have taken to keep these kids together and keep them alive. Besides that, from what I've seen they've picked up some pretty decent survival skills. They didn't get those from playing make-believe."

She tilted her head from side-to-side. "I taught them a little. I'd done some survival courses for fun when I was in high school. Girl Scouts was too tame for me, and cheerleading and all that happy horseshit—forget it. But Reynard and Tuck helped me out a lot, too."

"They friends of yours?"

She shook her head slightly. "No, at least not at first. Just a couple of guys who happened to be at the Ren fest that week-end, who saw that I needed some help. Reynard had a thing for me— he'd been hitting on me all weekend. I think that's why he stuck around at first. And Tuck—well, Tuck is just a good guy."

"Whatever their motivations, I think they'd have taken advantage by now if they weren't honorable men."

She laughed. "Oh, it's been tense, believe me. Tuck has it worse for me than Reynard ever did. Those two have a rivalry going that you wouldn't believe, each one waiting for me to pick one of them. It's infuriating, like I'm the last woman on earth or something."

I chewed my lip and considered my next words carefully. "What do you think is going to happen when these boys all grow up?"

She tossed her head back and rolled her eyes. "Oh gosh, don't even remind me! Little Matthew was nine when this shit all went down—nine! Now, he looks at me in a way that seriously creeps me out. I know he doesn't mean any harm, but I don't know what I'm going to do when the rest of them start looking at me that way."

I tapped my foot against the dais. "Well, I can't make any promises, but once I get my people back, we're heading to a safe place. We have plenty of room, and we could use more people we can trust to rebuild."

She looked at me with a combination of hope and skepticism behind her eyes. "That's a lot of maybes and ifs. But when you roll back through here—if you roll back through here—I'd be tempted to consider your offer."

"Fair enough." I stood up and brushed my hands on my pants. "Well, I guess I'd better see how Gabby and Bobby are doing."

She smiled and crinkled her nose at me. "I bet Gabby is getting all sorts of attention right about now."

"Yeah, but she's into older men." She gave me a weird look, and I quickly held up my hands in disgust and confusion. "What? No, not me! God no, the kid is like a daughter to me. But Bobby, though, I think she has a bad crush on him."

She nodded. "It's easy to see." She held out her hand. "My name's Anna, by the way. But Sweetlove actually is my last name."

I shook her hand and smiled. "No wonder you're so tough."

She groaned and arched with her hands in the small of her back. "Oh, you don't know the half of it!"

I began walking out and paused, looking back over my shoulder. "Anna, how did you know that you could trust me?"

She chuckled and ticked off each point she made on the fingers of her left hand. "Let's see. A full grown man with two kids in tow. Both well-fed, and free of any signs of abuse. By all appearances, they both think you hung the moon. And, you didn't kill any of my boys when they surprised you."

I nodded once. "Seems legit. Now, about this trial by combat thing—"

"Oh, Reynard is going to try to take it to you, no doubt about it. He was an ARMA champion in longsword and sword and buckler. And Reynard probably sees you as a threat, a challenge to his leadership here, I think. Or, he might just be bored and spoiling for a good fight. Sorry, but you should expect to have a fight on your hands." She smirked and shrugged. "Rules are rules. No hard feelings, you know."

I shrugged. "I suppose I understand. Just don't hold it against me if I damage your champion."

She laughed. "Oh, I do like you, Scratch. But good luck with that."

The next morning I got up early to stretch and mentally prepare. I knew it was just going to be a matter of who took the worst beating first, but nerves could always do a number on a fighter before a match. I did some deep breathing exercises and visualization techniques to calm me down, the same stuff I used to do for panic attacks after I came back from the 'Stan.

The LARPers, as we were calling them, had put us up in decent digs the night previous. As it turned out, the castle house had an entire sub-basement that was designed to withstand a nuclear apocalypse. It had been made for fortification rather than comfort, however, which was a surprise to me considering the opulence apparent in the rest of the mansion. Anna had explained that it had belonged to a friend of theirs, someone who had been heavily involved in LARPing and other similarly geeky activities. He got killed early on, but before he died he'd given them keys to the place and provided all the access codes as well.

And truly, this place was a fortress. Even in the house above there were iron bars on the windows, reinforced doors, and the remnants of a security system that was utterly useless now. Anna openly lamented the fact that her friend had neglected to consider alternative and emergency power sources. They'd scavenged some solar panels and rigged a rudimentary system, but it was barely enough for a few LED lights at night and to keep the emergency backup batteries on the keypads charged up. For safety's sake, they locked themselves in at night and only used the keypads in emergencies. But, once someone shut the doors to the vault, without power there'd be no way to access it from outside.

At any rate, they seemed to be doing okay. Reynard kept the boys busy with lessons in swordplay and archery, and with hunting and scouting. Tuck took the role of their schoolteacher; apparently he'd been some kind of engineering geek before the War. And both allowed Dame Sweetlove to maintain her position as queen and leader of the entire operation. I had to hand it to them; they were decent men. But I think they also knew that she was the natural leader of the group, and I doubted either of them wanted the responsibility of making the tough choices.

After breakfast, Bobby and Gabby came back to the large guest room where the LARPers had placed us the night before, with the dog at Gabby's heels. Gabby was clearly upset, while Bobby appeared to be excited at the prospect of seeing me take on Reynard. The dog didn't look to be interested in much, except taking a nap.

Gabby plopped down on the bed across from me and gave me a hard look. "So, I guess you're still going through with it? Even though we aren't obligated to follow any of their stupid rules?"

I shook my head. "That's not the point. The point is that we're trying to make some allies, and sometimes when you're trying to get an in with the natives, you have to concede to their whims and wishes. Besides, this is the only way I'm going to get the respect of their entire group. Remember, we have no idea how many of the settlers are left alive. If we're going to start over after we get them back, we're going to need more able bodies."

Bobby nodded and his face grew uncharacteristically serious for a moment. "Yeah, and besides that, Gabs, those teenage boys out there have been training to scout and fight since they were kids. By the time they become full-grown adults in a few years, they're going to be a group of badasses. I honestly would rather have them as friends than enemies. I mean, if it was up to me." He coughed and looked off to the side, as if embarrassed to have shown some sense for a change.

I nodded. "Bobby, you're starting to think like a leader. Good for you." The kid blushed and pretended to mess with his kit on the bunk behind him. I looked at Gabby and grinned. "The truth is that I'd like to see if we can create an alliance with them. Or, even better, if I can convince them to come back to the Facility with us. That is, if we return from the Corridor alive."

Gabby harrumphed. "First, you have to make it past 'knight boy' down there."

I stood up and tousled her hair, and she shook off my hand with a lot less anger than she probably wanted to display. "Trust me, kid, I have this under control. But speaking of which, you two need to pay close attention to this match today. The type of people who manage to survive in a world like ours will always have unique survival skills. Sometimes it's knowing how to fight, sometimes it's knowing how to hide, sometimes it's knowing how to run, and sometimes it's knowing how to use violence to get what they want. Reynard survived because he knows how to handle himself, and believe me, you're going to come across people who have the same skills in the future. Watch how he fights, and learn from what you see today."

Bobby turned around, and his face lit up. "Oh, believe me, I wouldn't miss this for the world. Getting to watch you kick that guy's ass medieval-style is going to be the highlight of this whole trip."

I smiled as I tightened up the laces on my mocs and made sure my pants were tucked into them properly so they wouldn't get in the way. "Well, at least someone in this room has faith in my abilities."

Gabby frowned. "It's not your abilities I'm concerned with, *viejo*. It's your health. What if you have one of those attacks again?"

Granted, she had a point. I was still pretty worn out from everything we'd been through over the last couple of weeks, as well as from the constant war my body was waging against the Z-venom. But, a soldier fights the battles he's faced with, not the battles he chooses. "I haven't had one of those episodes in a few days, Gabby. Trust me. I can handle Reynard."

She shook her head and looked at me like I was an idiot. "*Del dicho al hecho hay mucho trecho.*"

Bobby looked at me in confusion. "What'd she say?"

I chuckled softly. "'Easier said than done.'"

———

THE MATCH WAS to be held in the training yard directly behind the castle house. Whoever had built this house was definitely a trip. Instead of the typical pool and cabana house that you'd expect to see behind a mansion, there was a large patio of smooth limestone blocks surrounding a smaller circular area covered in crushed red granite, approximately ten meters across.

Positioned around the yard were several wooden pells covered in layers of carpet, with duct tape or rope to secure the material to each post. There were also archery butts, and cross-sections of logs set up for knife and axe throwing. Apparently, this guy knew how to have a fun time. I wondered to myself if girls like Anna had been impressed with this sort of thing before the world went to shit. I also wondered how the guy had ended up getting himself killed.

If I had to guess, I'd have said that it probably had to do with treating survival like a sparring match. Warfare and survival were a far cry from sparring with your friends, that was for sure. Afghanistan had taught me that. And, I was counting on the fact that old Reynard still had a bit too much of the reenactor in him to be any good against a seriously ruthless son of a bitch like myself.

When I walked out into the yard, Reynard was already there warming up with a wooden sword. He was wearing breeches, a wide leather belt, combat boots, and a loose leather jerkin. The waister he was warming up with was a monstrous thing, roughly the size of William Wallace's great sword. His muscles flexed and bulged in his arms as he swung it around, thrusting and parrying, then using footwork to dance around and follow up each movement with flawless precision.

Without a doubt, this guy knew his shit when it came to period weaponry.

Anna was sitting on a raised dais off to the side, this time dressed in a white lacy get-up that showed an ample amount of cleavage. She may have been worried about all the attention she got from the boys, but she damned sure wasn't above using it to her advantage, that was for certain. She nodded at me as I walked out into the circle and began pacing about the area. I ignored her; although I didn't blame her for enforcing her own rules, I needed to keep my mind on the fight, and she was a distraction. I was still human, after all... well, more or less.

Matthew came running up to me from some log benches across the way. All the other boys were sitting around on one side on the benches, watching Reynard warm-up and chatting excitedly amongst themselves. As he strode up, he did a quick bow, and when I didn't respond he stood up.

"Dame Sweetlove says I am to be your second for this match."

I stuck out my hand. "Well then, I'm honored." The kid looked at my hand, hesitated for a moment, and then shook it with no small amount of vigor. "Sir Matthew, tell me about the rules."

He looked around thoughtfully and then gestured to some racks off to the side. "You are allowed to choose the weapon of your choice. Sir Reynard almost always fights with a sword, and although he's warming up with the Zweihänder, he'll most certainly fight you with a standard longsword. I suggest a weapon with some amount of reach—perhaps a polearm, or something to give you some protection like the sword and shield."

I nodded to show I was listening. "Please, continue."

He cleared his throat and went on. "The match is fought exclusively inside the ring. If either of you steps completely out of bounds, the bout will be stopped, and you'll be brought back inside. This is merely a safety precaution and not a stipulation against running to evade an attack, although it is considered poor form to step out of bounds—"

I gestured to interrupt him. "How do I win?"

"Well, normally when we practice, it's to the first touch. But in this case, you're fighting a trial by combat. So the match ends when one person concedes or when one or the other contestant cannot continue."

I chuckled. "So, I could just throw down my weapon at the beginning of the match and claim forfeit?"

Matthew looked at me in horror. "Why would you want to do that? Besides, if you did so you'd be declared craven, and they'd place you in the stocks for a week."

I smiled. "Alrighty then. So, I get to choose my weapons. I can't concede the match outright, at least not without serious repercussions. And, the fight continues until one of us can't go on. Anything else I should know?"

Matthew looked over at Reynard as he considered my question for a moment, and then he looked me in the eye. "Be wary of his tricks. He is fond of feigning fatigue, and then he sucks you in to finish you off with half-sword techniques. He's also a bastard when it comes to grappling, and likes to throw his opponents hard to the ground. I once saw him knock a man out in just such a manner. Remain on your guard at all times."

I slapped the kid on the shoulder. "Thanks for the advice, Sir Matthew. You are indeed an honorable man." He cracked a slight smile, nodded, and then walked off behind me to take a knee at ringside.

I looked around, stretched my arms, and yawned. Then I sauntered over to the weapons racks to see what I could find. Although Matthew's advice was sound, I knew that this would be no picnic if I had to fight Reynard's fight. He was used to fighting guys who fought the way he did, and likely beat them with a combination of superior speed, power, and guile. So, I intended to fight him in a way that allowed him to use none of his skills in the manner to which he was accustomed.

Stalling for time while looking through the racks, I waited until Reynard selected a wooden longsword, just as Matthew had predicted. Now that I knew what I'd be fighting against, I chose a pair of sturdy gladius-style short swords of sufficient weight and length. Typically, most shorter practice weapons were made tip heavy, both to produce grip strength and to strengthen the wrists and shoulders. I intended to use that to my advantage, because while Reynard undoubtedly was using a practice weapon that was as close to his everyday carry as possible, it meant that his narrow longsword would be lighter and hit with a bit less impact than the thicker short swords I'd chosen. I assumed that he chose that sword because he likely intended to wear me down, in an attempt to humiliate me in front of Anna.

Me? I had no such intentions, and planned to introduce this guy to the down and dirty blade fighting methods of Southeast Asia. I grabbed the two swords and spun them in my hands to get the weight and feel of them, and then strolled out to the mark that had been placed on my side of the ring. Tuck walked out to the center, and instructed our seconds to inspect the other fighter's gear and attire. The kid who walked over for Reynard was the chubby boy who'd carried all my firepower back yesterday, and he looked me over with more scrutiny than a pissed-off TSA agent. He gave a curt nod to Tuck, then jogged back over to his own side. Matthew inspected Reynard's waister, patted him lightly to check for hidden weapons, and then nodded to Tuck and ran back past me, presumably to wait until it was time to drag me out of the ring.

Tuck backed out of the way, looked at each of us in turn, and then shouted, "Begin!"

[9]
CONTEST

R eynard practically sprang to the center of the ring, so I moved quickly to meet him halfway and then started circling away from his probing thrusts and slashes. He was spry for a big man and wasted no motion whatsoever. Me, I merely backed away from his cuts and thrusts and used the ring to the best advantage possible. I knew I couldn't run forever, but that wasn't the point. The point was to see how Reynard moved and to wait for him to commit to a powerful attack.

While I was still sizing him up, he leaped forward and began to attack with a series of two-handed cuts that came at me from different angles. And man, was he fast; almost superhumanly fast. In fact, outside of practice with Gabby, I'd never seen a human move as quick as this guy.

Thankfully, my serum-enhanced perception speed and reflexes were working just fine, so I took one more step back, and then flipped my left-hand sword around into a reverse grip. I rushed forward into his next attack, using the flat of the sword like a tonfa to block his weapon and allow me to get in close. I used the handle of the sword in my right hand like a fist load and punched him right in the mouth... once, twice, three times as I wrapped my left arm around his arms and stepped on his lead foot to keep him from backing up on me.

Soon he realized that this sword fight had turned into a grappling match, and he got wise and head-butted me in the face. I whipped my head sideways to take it on my skull and to avoid losing some teeth. Reynard took that opportunity to smash his shoulder into my chest and disengage from me. I took the blow and rolled away, coming up to my feet and moving my swords in circles as I sidestepped around him and watched him bleed.

The people around the circle were silent at first, and then they all let out a collective gasp. There was a sort of whispered chattering going on around us, but I blocked it out and continued to focus on the task at hand. Reynard began probing again, but more cautiously now, and I think he'd finally figured out his mistake in using a lighter weapon. Sure, it was quick, but unless he poked me in the eyes or the throat, it was fairly useless against someone who was willing to ignore its sting.

I got tired of waiting and decided the press the attack. I came in with a classic *krabi-krabong* double sword attack pattern, slashing first with one sword and then with the other in a left-right, right-left manner, using all my power to either break his waister or crash through his guard. He parried just as I knew he would, with a high two-handed block using the flat of the blade. As he brought his sword up again to block, I changed my attack at the last moment and struck both his wrists with a vicious forehand strike that caused him to back off quickly and roll away.

I continued to press the attack and managed to step on his sword as he dove away from me, briefly trapping his hand against the ground and bending his sword near the middle. I used that opportunity to crack him over the head with the flat of my weapon, avoiding the edge as I didn't want to fracture his skull. In response, he launched off the ground and barreled into me, snatching my near leg with his free hand and driving his shoulder directly into my waist to lift me up and relieve the pressure from his hand. As soon as that hand was free, he released his weapon and continued to drive me forward off balance.

And then, we were wrestling again. I briefly tried to get my sword into the space between his neck and my body, in an attempt to use it for a choke, but before I knew it I was on my back and he was coming around to side control position in order to secure an armlock. I rolled to face him and covered up, and he gave up on securing the arm and started dropping knees like jackhammers to my head and body. I waited for an opening and tied up his near leg, sacrificing a rib or two in the process. We ended up in a scramble as I drove into him with my own single leg to take him down on his back. However, the sneaky bastard turned that into an almost textbook *tomoe-nage* throw, placing his knee on my gut and grabbing my shirt by the shoulders to throw me over him and onto my back.

I rolled with it and stood up, only to feel his hands wrap around my waist from behind. I decided to avoid using a Krav Maga technique to strike him, since I knew he'd be tossing me on my head before I could get off a decent stunning elbow to his. I based out and dropped my weight forward, capitalizing on his forward momentum as he grabbed me from behind. I continued driving forward and tucked into a Russian roll, diving for his leg between my legs as I tucked under him. This had the net effect of keeping him from doing a suplex on me, and it allowed me to go for a nasty kneebar or perhaps even a toehold at the end of the movement.

I was banking on the assumption that he hadn't had much experience with leg locks, and I was right. As I came out of the roll, I ended up on my back with my legs wrapped around his upper thigh and his ankle behind my right shoulder. He landed face down lying in the opposite direction, and as tight as I had the lock there was no way he was getting free. I slowly began arching my back and hips and applying pressure to his knee joint.

I could hear him grunting and felt him struggling to break free, and I was afraid I was going to have to pop his knee. "I'll break it!" I yelled in warning. "Yield! Tap you sorry bastard, or you're going to spend the rest of the apocalypse in a knee brace!"

Finally, he slapped the ground forcefully and calmly exclaimed, "Yield, I yield!" I turned him loose and rolled away, ready for another attack should he be the dirty-fighting kind. He wasn't. He turned over on his back, flexed his knee a few times, and then stood up with a grin on his face. With a shrug, he walked over to me and extended his hand in congratulations.

I looked at his hand with caution, then shook it. He cracked an even wider grin and spat some blood out to the side. "Thought I had you when you gave me your back. Was sure it was going to be lights out once I got you in the air."

I laughed. "I knew what was coming and didn't like the idea of getting a rapid neck adjustment. Besides, concussions aren't my thing. Good fight."

He nodded and grabbed my wrist, then turned us to face the dais, where Dame Sweetlove was looking on in shock and amusement. Reynard growled the outcome as he raised my hand into the air. "Sir Scratch wins by submission, and by rights is absolved of his offense!"

The boys and Bobby went nuts, shouting and cheering. Gabby, not so much. Within seconds, the boys had stormed the ring, and a few even made an attempt to lift me on their shoulders, but I turned out to be too heavy for them. So, they satisfied themselves with crowding us both and peppering us with commentary and questions for the next fifteen minutes. Eventually, Dame Sweetlove called an end to it and announced that we'd all eat a meal together before we'd be allowed to depart in peace.

As we walked back into the castle house, she leaned over and whispered in my ear. "I didn't think you could beat Reynard. He's proven himself to be unstoppable for the last eight years."

I merely shrugged. "I guess it was just my lucky day."

[10]
REVELERS

After the excitement had died down from the match, we all went back inside and enjoyed a feast with Dame Sweetlove and her subjects. The food was pretty good; roast wild pig, fresh tomatoes and other garden veggies, and some candy bars that someone had been hoarding for just such an occasion. I guess they were pulling out all the stops, being as they didn't normally get friendly guests, and also because I didn't kill their best fighter. It had been an honorably-fought match, and he acquitted himself well, so I guess everyone saw it as a win all the way around.

Later after the meal, Anna's boys took Bobby and Gabby outside for a friendly archery contest. Gabby beat their best archer, the chubby kid with the sour face who'd had to haul all my gear back. His name was Christopher, and he turned out to be an okay kid. After she had beaten him, I think him and half the LARPer's wild boys ended up even more in love with her than they were before. Which I had mixed feelings about, but then again there wasn't much about the sort of father-daughter relationship I was developing with Gabby that wasn't perplexing these days.

After watching the kids play for a bit, Anna, Reynard, Tuck and I went back inside to discuss adult matters. Anna was interested in what I could tell her about things outside of the Corridor, and Reynard and Tuck expressed an interest in where we were from and how the hell we expected to take out the Corridor pack.

We sat down at what was once the kitchen table to enjoy some cheap but very serviceable Scotch, and then we got down to brass tacks. Anna spoke up first. "Scratch, tell me about the settlements, and this place you say you're heading to after you get your people back."

I cleared my throat and sat up a little straighter. "Well, before the werewolves came, we had a good thing going. In fact, I wished I had appreciated it a lot more back then." I explained about how the wolves had attacked our settlement, and the relative peace and quiet we'd had before they came.

Reynard chimed in. "Sounds inviting—almost like a normal life."

I nodded. "It was, and frankly I miss it. Used to bitch about being around all those people all the time, and couldn't wait to get back to the Badlands when I was there. But now if I had it to do all over again, I think I'd just have settled down and stopped hunting entirely."

Reynard nodded. "Anna filled us in on your story last night. Sorry to hear about your wife."

I winced at that. "Well, she isn't my wife—not exactly. But we're the closest thing to it, I suppose. The way we argue, well, you wouldn't know the difference."

Tuck sipped his drink and nodded. "My wife and I used to argue like cats and dogs. What I wouldn't give for just one more spat like that."

That elicited more than a mild reaction from Anna and

Reynard. Anna was first to the trigger. "You never told us you had a wife, Tuck."

He scowled. "Hell, Anna, you can just call me Mickey. No need to keep up the show here among friends. And I think I might have mentioned it once, but we were trying to avoid getting killed by a herd of shamblers at the time, as I recall. It wouldn't surprise me if that small bit of info slipped your mind."

Reynard sat back and nodded in silence. "Well, since we're all about transparency here—" He held out his hand to me across the table. "Name's Colin. Reynard was just my reenactment stage name."

I shook his hand again. "I wasn't always Scratch. My folks called me Aidan."

He laughed. "Well, that's a good Irish name if ever I heard one. How'd a dark-skinned beauty like yourself end up with a Mick name like that?"

I shrugged. "Half-Mexican on my mom's side."

"Damn it if that don't beat all. You speak it?" I nodded in the affirmative. "Well hell, ain't that something." He paused and sipped his drink again. "Well, I for one am glad to know you. Ain't that right, Mickey?"

Mickey tipped an imaginary hat at me. "Indeed, I am. And if there are any single women in that group of settlers you're heading off to rescue, I might just go with you."

Anna placed the back of her hand on her forehead and pretended to swoon. "Oh, I do declare, Mickey, you do so wound my heart!"

He smirked at her. "Yeah, well, I think Colin and I both figured a long time ago that neither one of us was your dream date."

Colin sat back and crossed his arms, and as he did, I noticed they were scarred up something fierce. "Hey, speak for yourself, Merlin. I'm still hopeful." He winked at Anna, but based on her facial expression I was pretty sure he was barking up the wrong tree. Still, you can't fault a guy for trying.

Anna piped up with a little too much squeak in her voice. "So, Scratch, you were going to tell us about this safe house you have?"

I decided to rescue her and go with it. "Well, it's not a safe house—it's more like a massive extended bomb shelter. Think 'Cheyenne Mountain' but Texas style. I can't say more right now because honestly there's a lot more riding on us making it back than our health and safety."

Mickey leaned in with a twinkle in his eyes. "You sound like you're talking fate of the world stuff."

I pursed my lips and exhaled with force. "Well... Alright, I'll tell you. But don't be mad at me for cheating, Colin. I didn't exactly beat you fair and square."

He tipped his chair back on two legs and crossed his arms. "You a 'thrope?"

"No, not exactly." I pulled up my sleeve and showed them the Z-venom lines. Anna's jaw about hit the table, while Colin nearly fell out of his chair, and Mickey looked like he was going to shit a brick.

———

MICKEY SPOKE UP FIRST. "You're infected. How are you not shuffling into walls and craving brains?"

"Well, it's complicated."

"Uncomplicate it," Anna responded.

So, I told them the story of how I met the Doc and Gabby and Bobby, and how I had gotten captured by the militia, and how I'd gotten infected. Then I told them how Bobby saved me, and how the Doc's witchery saved me even more, and then some. "But, it's still affecting me. Feels like I'm getting better all the time, but I also don't think I'm completely out of the woods, either."

Colin just sat back and rubbed his chin during the whole telling of our tale, while Mickey and Anna would interject a question or two here or there to clarify a minor detail. When I finished, I slapped my hands on the table. "So, that's the story."

Colin grunted. "So, you say this super-serum stuff can make humans like Them, but without wanting to drink blood or eat human flesh?"

"Yeah, more or less. As far as I can gather, it affects different people in different ways. Gabby has quite a bit more spunk than me, but she had the treatments when she was just a young girl. I've only had it working in me for a matter of days, and most of that I think has been spent on keeping me from going deader."

He tapped his fingers on the table, beating out a rapid rhythm that reminded me of a TV show, but I couldn't remember which one. "What you're saying is, if you survive the infection you could end up just as resilient and quick as a vamp or a 'thrope."

"So they tell me."

He threw his hands up in the air. "Well shit on a stick in winter and call it a fudgesickle—what the hell are we waiting for? I've been training those boys in my *fian* to be silent death since—" Colin paused for a moment, and a tormented look briefly crossed his face. "Well, since things went sideways on us. Can you imagine what they'd be like if they had superpowers? We'd be unstoppable."

Anna didn't look as convinced. "What about the girl, Gabby? She seems a little maladjusted to me. Is that a side effect of the serum?"

I chuckled. "Aw, hell no. That's just puberty, I assure you. But don't tell her I said that. No, that kid is as human as a child can be, after having been raised among all this crap. I mean, look at the boys in your merry band—do you think anyone would consider them well-adjusted if we wound the clock back ten years?"

She grimaced and looked down at her hands, which I noticed had been doing a fair bit of fiddling and wringing. "No, I suppose not. What about the boy, Bobby?"

Not wanting to give away secrets that weren't mine to share, I shook my head. "He—hasn't been through the treatment yet."

Mickey whistled sharply and smiled. "Hey, I'd do it. Maybe for once I'd be more than just the brains of this outfit."

I held a hand up as if to placate him and shrugged. "Nothing wrong with being the smart one. Lord knows the world's short of those types these days."

Mickey screwed his face up and squinted with one eye. "Yeah, but a fat lot of good that does when you're fighting were-wolves. And, I can foresee a time in the very near future when that could be the case. That is, if you fail in your venture, of course."

I sighed and held up both hands. "Well, I'm not taking offense. I have a plan, but I didn't say it was a good one. My primary goal is to ensure that those kids make it back alive. Then it's saving the settlers. Because the truth is, the settlers chose to live in danger. These kids, they're just tagging along because they have no one else to follow."

It was Anna's turn to pat my hand this time. "I know the feeling. It's a big responsibility, is it not? But I suspect that if you tried to leave them behind, they'd be hot on your heels the minute you were out the door."

"You got that right. I already tried it, and it didn't stick." I swiveled my head and took them all in, one at a time. "Tell me, how do you guys do it?"

Colin spoke up first. "What else are we going to do? Go out and become slavers? I for one would rather try to preserve some of what's left of humanity, and look toward the coming of a better day."

Mickey raised a finger off the table. "Ditto that."

Anna lifted her Scotch halfway to her mouth and then thought better of it. "Personally, every time I look at one of those kids I see my little brother. No way I could leave them alone in this mess if there's hope for something better. No way, no how."

I took a deep breath and looked each of them in the eye. "Then you're just the type of people I want with us, helping to force these sons of bitches out of Texas so we can build a new world. You can bet your asses that I'm going to be back through here to take you to meet the Doc. And believe me, she'll be thrilled to have more subjects—I mean, people—to juice with her supernatural serum."

They all looked at each other, and something passed between them. Anna nodded and slapped her hand on mine. "Count us in."

MAN

Despite the urgency of the situation, we decided to stay one more night to rest up before the big push into north central Austin. Also, to be fair, we wanted to give Anna's guys some time to prepare. She'd offered to loan us two scouts to guide us through the city into the werewolves' territory, at least as close as they thought would be safe for them to go. At first I'd refused, but Anna insisted that it would be a good experience for the boys, and Colin agreed, so that settled it.

As it turned out, they had a couple of kids who served as their weaponsmith and armorer. I spent some time in the shop with them, repairing the handle on the katana I'd found at the pawn shop, rigging the sheath for shoulder carry, and honing the blade until it would shave the hair off a gnat's ass.

Their weaponsmith helped with the work, and when we finished it, he wrapped the cast aluminum handles in leather and wire, securing it to ensure that the blade wouldn't come loose. I spent some extra time gluing it all together with epoxy and sealing the space between the blade and the crossguard to make sure no blood would get inside the handle and rust it up. A blade like that wasn't likely to come along again any time soon, so I wanted to be certain it was serviceable and ready for action.

After dinner, Colin and I shared a growler of homemade cider and talked shop. We laughed and talked shit while the younger kids played. Gabby, Bobby, Matthew, Anna, and Mickey looked at us like we were nuts.

"What's the craziest way you ever killed a zombie?" he asked me with a twinkle in his eye.

I thought for a moment and grinned. "Skilsaw. It was a few months after the shit hit the fan. Got surprised by one hiding in an old tool shed when I was scrounging for supplies. Sumbitch came at me from the shadows, and the saw just happened to be near at hand. Good thing it was charged up—I was just going to hit it with the blade, but I accidentally hit the trigger, and it split the damned thing's skull right down the middle. Got Z brains all over me, too. Nasty."

He snorted cider out of his nose and slapped the table. "Wait, wait, wait—I got one. Rest stop bathroom. A little short one came at me in the john, caught me with my pants down. So, I leaned back and kicked him into the stall door. Coat hook punched through the back of his head, and the little bastard just hung there, trying to reach me but not knowing how to get himself off that damned door."

I laughed. "So what'd you do?"

He took a swig of beer and wiped his mouth on his sleeve. "Finished my dump and left. For all I know, he's probably still there!"

We both busted out laughing, and then I realized no one else thought it was funny. Meh, gallows humor. You don't start getting it until it gets you. The conversation reminded me of the days before the War; I used to go to the theater on Friday after-noons to watch action flicks because it was mostly empty and crowds still freaked me out back then. I'd be the only person in the theater laughing when someone got their arm broken or their kneecap blown off.

It's not that I'm a sadist. I just thought it was funny to see the bad guy get his due.

Colin wiped the tears from his eyes and looked around. "Aw, you guys are no fun." Anna gave him a dirty look; one of those looks that said, "Honey, not around the kids." I'd seen my mom give my dad that look plenty of times before the War.

He rolled his eyes and grabbed the growler. "C'mon Scratch, let's take this party somewhere else."

How could I refuse? I followed him out the dining room and into a hallway, then up the stairs to a reinforced steel door. He unlocked it and walked through to a parapet up on one of the castle house walls. It was about twenty feet down to the ground from where we were perched. He leaned out over the wall on his elbows and let out a long, slow breath. He handed me the growler.

"This isn't my first rodeo, you know."

I took a swig and handed it back. "I figured as much. What were you, SWAT? HRT? SEALs?"

He shook his head. "None of the above." He turned to look me in the eye, amused. "Would it shock you if I said I was killing these things before the War?"

I leaned back against the wall and thought about that for a moment, recalling something Wendigo Donnie had said to me when we last visited. "No. No, that wouldn't surprise me at all. In fact, not much surprises me anymore."

He grunted. "The thing is, there weren't as many of these things back then. Just a few, here and there. You'd get a little outbreak, guys like me would go in and take care of it, and then we'd go back to our normal, happy lives." He gestured with the bottle out over the parapet and belched loudly. "Not like this. Hell, never like this."

I let that sink in a minute and spoke just to break the uncomfortable silence. "Were you with the government? Christians In Action or something?"

He made a sound like a buzzer. "Wrong again. Nope, I got mixed up in some seriously screwed up supernatural shit. Thought I was a hero. I—thought wrong."

"Well, I believe there are a dozen or so people downstairs who consider you a hero, that's for sure. I wouldn't discount the value of their opinions at all, my friend."

He remained silent. "They're the only thing that's kept me going. You know that? I made the biggest mistake of my life, right before things went pear-shaped, and it cost me dearly. It was just coincidence that I was at that Ren fest where Anna and the boys were. I was looking for someone there, trying to make it right."

"And?"

He grimaced, took a long slug, and handed me the bottle again. "Never found who I was looking for, but I ran into Anna and the kids and saw they needed help. The rest is history."

"Anna says you were an ARMA champion. That true?"

He chuckled. "I was, but that's not where I got my training." He shook his shoulders out and smiled. "Oh, but that's a story for another time. A dark tale, that one. And we're supposed to be celebrating. Besides, that's not why I brought you out here. I need to ask you a few questions regarding this place you told us about. It's not bullshit, is it?"

I swallowed a slug of cider and sighed. "Good stuff. And no, not by a long shot. I'd never have believed it if I hadn't seen it with my own eyes, but it's as real as I am. The serum, everything." I took another swig and offered the jug back, but he declined. "Would you consider trying the serum? I think you'd be damned near unstoppable with that shit in your veins."

He lifted his shoulder in a half-shrug. "Meh, I don't need it.

You say that serum put a little of the supernatural in you and the girl? Well, me—I was born like that."

I inclined my head. "You don't say. Care to explain how that is? Not trying to pry or anything, but after eight years of fighting this war, some things are just now starting to come to light. A little info goes a long way, I'm finding."

Colin raised his chin and grinned. "You know, you might have some of it too, and not even know it. In fact, I'd almost bet my hat on it." He chewed his lip for a moment, lost in thought. "Alright, so you've heard all the legends and myths, right? I mean, every nation and people had them."

"Sure. The Greeks had their gods and monsters, the Irish and Welsh had the fae, the Norse had their pantheon, plus the elves and so forth. I could go on and on. You're saying that stuff is real?"

He extended his fingers and wiggled his hand, palm down. "Sort of. Those things have been coming across for millennia, preying on mankind and meddling in our affairs. From what I've gathered, humans have always had champions who fought against Them; call it a cosmic balancing act, if you will. And in each culture, there has always been a warrior tradition among those champions, with one generation training the next.

"Except sometimes, it skips a generation, or two—it's hard to say why. Maybe these champions only show up when they're needed, or maybe it's all a genetic anomaly, or perhaps it's an evolutionary event when one is born. At any rate, sometimes there's no one there to pass on the knowledge, and the champion is walking around without even knowing what they are, or what their purpose is—"

I set the jug down loudly. "Okay, now you're just dicking with me."

"No, I swear! Look, I've seen some things that would make

your head spin. I mean, you think you've seen some monsters? You don't know the half of it."

I snorted. "Well, this guy I know is a wendigo. That's some damned weird shit."

He snapped his fingers. "See, that tells me something. Some of these things are attracted to champions from their own cultures. I've never figured out why, and no one has ever been able to give me a straight answer on it, but we tend to be drawn to fight monsters from our own people's legends."

I nodded. "I do have some Native American on my mother's side."

"Yeah, I figured as much. Hell, most Americans are mutts anyway, so you get a champion from that stock, and no telling what kind of crazy is going to pop up around them."

"This is messed up, Colin. Really messed up."

"Yeah, well—try dealing with this crap when you're fifteen. That's how long I've been at it."

I shook my head sadly. "That's a long time to be fighting a war."

"I know. Makes me hurt for my boys." He tilted his head toward the door. "They didn't deserve to be born into this shit, not a one of them."

"Any of them—you know—got the juice?"

He laughed. "Not that I can tell. My mentor had a way of knowing, but he never revealed it to me. If someone does, it'll start showing as they enter their middle teen years. Excessive aggression around supernatural creatures, uncanny skill with weaponry—that sort of thing."

"So, is that why those 'thropes haven't run y'all off yet?"

"Pretty much. They're afraid of me. We Irish have our werewolf myths, and with me being of the Celtic warrior tradition, I'm not afraid to tangle with them. They learned that early on, so they leave us alone."

I exhaled slowly. "I killed one barehanded, just a few days ago. Bobby said he didn't think it could be done. Not by a man, anyhow."

"Well, most of these second generation werewolves have never met a real champion before." He must've seen the concern on my face, and raised a hand in a placating gesture. "Relax, I already know what the boy is—it's not hard to tell. And he's correct. Only a champion could kill a 'thrope in mortal combat."

I sat there for a moment, soaking it all in; it was a lot to take. "And what Bobby is—that doesn't bother you?"

"Not really. In our legends, werewolves were sometimes good and sometimes evil. They're the most like men of all the supernatural creatures."

"I'd trust that kid with my life."

"Well, it's obvious he trusts you. And it wouldn't be the first time a werewolf followed a human." He stretched like a mountain lion and yawned loudly. I took it as a sign that it was time to wrap things up.

"Food for thought. Anything else I should know?"

He leaned back against the ledge and rubbed his chin. "Without a doubt, never trust any of the supernatural creatures, except perhaps wolves who see you as their alpha. Once a wolf accepts you as their alpha, their loyalty is absolute. Well, unless you show them weakness, but even then sometimes they'll protect a solid leader. But the rest? You can't trust them, ever. Their way of thinking is so alien from ours—well, you just never can predict what they're going to do."

"Reminds me of the old Irish and Welsh legends of the fae."

"That's exactly right. For our purposes, every single one of these things is a type of fae, so to speak. They're all connected, and they all come from the same place—across the Veil—and even though they have their factions and inner turmoil, they'll never ally with a human, ever. And especially not against their own kind."

"'Thropes being the exception."

"Yes, and only under the circumstances I described. Watch yourself when dealing with Them. I assure you that they cannot be trusted."

The next morning, Colin assigned two of his wild boys to guide us through the city. I had the maps that Donnie had given me, but I didn't trust him, especially not after what Colin had said the night previous. So, for added insurance, the boys would take us as far as they cared to go.

Despite the benefit of having them along, I planned to send them home as soon as things got hairy. Protecting the two teens who were already under my care was cause enough for worry, and the last thing I needed was some dead kid on my conscience. Besides, I could see how Gabby might cause some friction among the three boys while we traveled. She was probably the closest thing to a potential girlfriend that any of these boys had seen in years. No sense tempting fate on that end, either.

We said our goodbyes, and Anna and Tuck gave us some provisions to replace those we'd lost in our flight through Southwest Austin. The night before, I'd talked Gabby into making the hard decision to leave Ghost behind. Much as I liked the mutt, he'd be a liability where we were going. She'd hugged the dog and told him to stay. Ghost had whined, but held his ground.

Before we left, Colin had taken me aside and spoke with me privately while the kids bid farewell to each other. "Look, about what we discussed last night—it's not common knowledge around here. So, I'd appreciate it if you didn't say anything to the boys about it."

My brow furrowed as I spoke. "You mean they don't know about your past?"

He looked around to make sure none of the kids had wandered over before replying. "No, and I'd like to keep it that way. Things are weird enough for these kids without them getting the idea that I'm their magic talisman."

"You're thinking of leaving them. Alone."

He scowled. "It's not like that. You may not understand this yet, but eventually it's going to start to make sense. I have business that I've been putting off for some time now, in order to train these boys properly so they can survive. But if what you told us is true, then once they're safely ensconced in your batcave, I'll be able to start catching up on things I've set aside for too long."

I rubbed my chin and nodded. "Well, if it means that much to you, we could use another fighter when we face the pack."

He clapped me on the shoulder and smiled. "When the time comes, I'll be there. Trust me. I'll know when and where to find you."

"Are you telling me you're psychic or something? C'mon, Colin. Now the bullshit is getting deep."

He chuckled and picked his teeth with his thumbnail. "Let's just say I have a few tricks I haven't told you about, and we'll leave it at that." He turned his head and gestured at the small crowd gathered in front of the castle. "Looks like they're waiting on you."

I smirked and flipped him the bird. "Fine, be a cryptic asshole." Then I leaned in and extended my hand. "When the time comes, I'll be counting my kills. Care for a friendly wager?"

He paused and squinted. "Top kill count cleans the other guy's gear. Plus, they get their pick of the loser's weapons."

I kept my hand extended because I didn't intend to lose. "Shake on it?"

He shook my hand and picked his teeth again with the other. "See you in, oh, say three days?"

———

WE MADE good time after leaving their demesne, or domain, or whatever the hell they called it. The boys Colin sent were Sir Matthew, his oldest and most experienced fighter, and Squire Christopher, another of his stalwarts, as he called them. They spent the first half-hour trying to chat Gabby up, but she had good bush discipline and kept it zipped while scanning the woods. After a while, they got the picture and realized they were making fools of themselves. Soon, both boys were trying to out-do each other in terms of seriousness and mission focus. I had to hand it to Gabby; she sure had an instinct for handling boys.

About an hour after leaving the castle house, Matthew picked up someone's trail. He squatted and pointed it out to me. "Human, medium build, packing light. Looks like he's favoring his left leg."

I motioned Bobby over, and he sniffed the ground near the tracks Matthew had found. Bobby nodded and looked up at me with a gleam in his eye. "It's Pancho. I'm sure of it."

Matthew gave him a skeptical look. "Seriously? You can track by smell?"

Bobby shrugged and gave a sheepish grin. "I made him pee himself the last time we saw him. Must've leaked out his shoe or something." Matthew turned his nose up at him and walked several steps down the trail in an attempt to find more tracks. Bobby looked at me and mouthed "Sorry." I motioned that he shouldn't be worried about it. He made a coarse and very childish gesture at Matthew's back and stood up.

Matthew called us over to look at something else he'd found. "Scouts from the Pack have been this way recently." He pointed at two sets of rather large paw prints made by something on two legs and not four.

Gabby noticed what we were looking at and strolled over to me. Of course, she'd heard the entire conversation. "Scratch, if the Pack finds him before we do, we're screwed. That *pendejo* is going to tell them we're coming."

"And we'll lose the advantage of surprise." I turned to Matthew, who'd been joined by Christopher. "Gentlemen, where do you think he's headed?"

Matthew looked ahead and scratched his nose. "If he keeps heading in that direction, he'll end up in Kill Valley. We'd planned to skirt around it—we never go there."

Bobby's ears perked up. "You mean Death Valley, right?"

Christopher chimed in. "No, Kill Valley. As in, 'kill or be killed.' That place is a death trap. There's a bloodsucker who claims it as his territory, and he controls an entire legion of undead there. Nobody who goes in there comes out again, and especially not at night."

I looked at Chris. "This vampire, is he one of the pretty ones, or a nos'?" Chris looked at me in confusion, so I elaborated. "Meaning, one of the ugly ones."

He bobbed his head. "Definitely one of the ugly ones."

"Do you two know if he trades with the slavers?"

Matthew inclined his head. "Most assuredly. We stopped their traffic from coming in from the south, but they still come through from the north and west. He takes slaves in trade for goods and safe passage."

I turned to Gabby. "What do you think the odds are that Pancho has done business with this nos' before?"

She gave me a rueful look. "I'd say, good to certain. We have to catch him before he gets to the Pack and rats us out."

"Correction: *I* have to find him before the Pack does. You guys are staying here."

A look of consternation crossed Gabby's face, but before she could speak, I pulled her aside and spoke quietly to her. "Gabs, before you get all pissed off that I'm leaving you behind, I want you to look at those boys for a second." She glanced over, and both of them quickly averted their eyes and pretended to watch for movement from the trees. "I'd say you have two serious admirers there. Now, knowing what we know about their cocka-mamie, Knights of the Round Table sense of honor, what do you think would happen if you went running off with me into this Kill Valley place?"

She thrust out her lower lip and scowled. "They'd follow us in."

"Yes, that's right. And they'd get themselves killed. Are you willing to live with that?"

She looked at the boys guiltily. "No, I suppose not. Can't you just send them back?"

"They're hormonal, not stupid, Gabby. Although I daresay, there's not much of a difference."

She barked a laugh. "So I've noticed. Why doesn't Bobby act that way around me?"

I rolled my eyes. "You really want to have this conversation right now?" I looked over at Bobby, who I knew was listening. He turned beet red and abruptly walked off down the path.

Gabby continued staring at me intently.

"Fine. One, because he's older and no longer at the mercy of his hormones. Two, because you're too young for him. And three, because he probably sees you more like his younger sister than a potential mate."

Gabby crossed her arms and fumed. I really wasn't in the mood for giving her "the talk" about boys, partially because I didn't have time, and partially because I'd never been a dad, never had sisters, and had no idea how to go about it. So, I improvised. "Look Gabs, you're a heck of a young lady. And frankly, in a few more years I think guys like Bobby are going to be falling all over themselves for you. But for now, he just doesn't look at you that way. My advice to you is to not be in a rush about all this stuff."

She continued to fume, arms crossed and closed off to me. "Fine. I'll stay here and babysit the boys."

I sighed. "Thank you. I'll tell Bobby. Now, let's ask the wild boys if they can find you guys a safe place to hole up until I get back."

———

MATTHEW AND CHRISTOPHER took us to an old cinder block shed that had been built by a utility company in days long past. They told me that it was one of the safe houses they used on scavenging trips into the city. It was surrounded by a still serviceable chain link fence topped with barbed wire, which would serve to keep the dead out, and it had a solid steel door and no windows. *Perfect.*

I instructed Bobby to make them stay put until I got back, giving him explicit instructions not to come after me. He'd see to the safety of the boys and Gabby.

"How long you think you'll be gone, boss?" he asked, with more than a little concern in his voice.

"I'll likely be back before nightfall. But if something holds me up, stay here and don't let Gabby or the Knights Who Say 'Ni!' to follow after me. Chances are good if I get held up, I'll find somewhere to hide for the night and head back come morning."

He grinned at the Monty Python reference and nodded. "If you say so."

"I do. See you in a few." I waved at Gabby, who still pouted, and nodded to the boys, who were too immersed in an argument over the benefits of chainmail versus boiled leather to pay attention. I left them to their nerd talk and headed out toward the spot that Matthew had marked on my map, which appeared to be a residential area that bordered the old Mopac Expressway.

According to the boys, we were currently on the outskirts of the city proper, north of the Colorado River near the 360 bridge. We'd stuck to the greenbelt and skirted the residential areas to get this far, but the boys told me I'd be leaving the areas they patrolled shortly, so I could expect to start running into deaders soon. My map had a safe house marked near there, with a note that said 'power station near highway.' I assumed Pancho was headed there, probably to get supplies and wait to see if the wolves would show.

I followed the greenbelt and passed up several large homes in what was formerly a desirable area of town to live. Now, it was populated by random groups of the dead, who I occasionally spotted through the trees as I flitted along silently, avoiding their attention. Before long, the greenbelt ended, and I paused just inside the trees at the edge of the residential area to get the lay of the land and consult my map.

I was just a few streets over from the highway, and had the choice of either sticking to the neighborhoods or cutting across a retail shopping area that bordered the freeway. I decided to stick to the backyards and long-neglected green spaces between the houses, now overgrown with weeds and vegetation. These afforded me some cover from the small pockets of dead that wandered the area.

Twice I had to put down a deader who was in my way, both times by stealth and without attracting the attention of any others in the area. I finally made it to the expressway, which was littered with abandoned vehicles along with the odd shambler. I vaulted a fence and several segments of traffic barriers to sprint, car to car, across eight lanes of highway separated by a railroad track in the middle.

I took out a deader with my tomahawk in drive-by fashion on the way across the first side of the highway, but otherwise made it to the tracks without incident. An abandoned freight train, stranded on its tracks, provided me with some cover as I crossed over. As I reached it, I found I'd attracted the attention of some of the shamblers, but they had a difficult time with the fences and barriers. I'd be long gone before they managed to navigate them.

After a similar experience on the other side of the highway, I made it over the last barrier and into a graveyard that neighbored my destination. I hunkered down behind some trees and looked around; the only dead around me were six feet under. I snuck north toward the safe house and observed it from a distance for a good fifteen minutes.

A flash of movement in window rewarded my efforts. I couldn't be certain, but it looked like Pancho.

Gotcha, *you little bastard,* I thought as slowed my breathing. I waited several minutes to make my move and snuck around to approach the buildings via a blind spot created by some trees and foliage. After vaulting the chain link fence surrounding the power station, several more minutes of sneaking brought me to a position outside the building, hidden under a window. I heard movement inside, and managed to pinpoint the sounds to the other side of the building.

Perfect. I managed to pry open the window without making too much noise and climbed into an office. I crept to the door and drew my silenced Glock. Standing next to the door and hugging the wall, I slowly turned the knob.

BLAM! Shikt. BLAM! Shikt. BLAM! Shikt.

Three shotgun blasts pierced the door, leaving gaping holes that revealed only darkness behind. Based on the size of the holes, Pancho or whoever was on the other side of the door fired a 12-gauge loaded with buckshot. The last thing I wanted to do was take a load of double-aught to the chest. I backed into the corner of the room and slowed my breathing, keeping the muzzle of the .45 trained on the doorway.

Minutes passed in complete stillness. Suddenly, the door exploded open in a shower of shredded door frame and wood splinters. I saw the barrel of the sawed off pump coming through the doorway first and knew Pancho or someone was right behind. It was such a rookie mistake; the first thing you learn about clearing rooms is to avoid flagging your position with your barrel. I was already squeezing the trigger when Pancho stepped through.

I pulled twice and placed two shots in his torso. One looked like it shattered the bone in his upper arm, while the other hit him in the lower abdomen. I moved right behind the shots I'd fired, checking the barrel with my free hand and clocking him across the jaw with my pistol. I could have easily killed him. But I didn't want him dead yet, although he likely soon would be with these injuries.

He dropped like a sack of potatoes.

I kicked the shotty away, dragging Pancho over to the desk and frisking him. Once I had removed all his weapons, I started patching him up with strips of his own clothing so he wouldn't bleed out before I got the intel I needed.

Minutes later, he came back around. "Oh, holy hell. You son of a bitch, you gut shot me."

"Do unto others before they do unto you. Tell me what I need to know now, and I might kill you quick."

He moaned and turned his head sideways to vomit. "Oh, Jesus, it hurts. Why'd you have to do that?"

"You mean shoot the person who was trying to kill me? Oh, I don't know. Self-preservation? Common sense? Just plain old orneriness?"

He laughed, and then winced and stopped. I had bandaged his arm and put it in a makeshift sling while he was out, but it still had some wiggle. Those bones were splintered pretty good. You don't appreciate how much a broken bone hurts until you shatter a long bone. Pancho was in a world of hurt, in more ways than one.

"Ah hell, Scratch, what'd ya expect? A warm welcome? I saw you sneaking around out there, and knew it'd be you or me. Guess it turned out to be me, didn't it? But I owed you for killing my little brother. I couldn't give a shit about my cousin, truth be told. But my brother? I couldn't let that lie."

"If you'll recall, Jimmy, you and your brother and cousin were about to rape someone. They had it coming. Then, in retaliation, you attacked us and shot Gabby. You had it coming, too."

He shook his head and sighed. "There's always some dumb sum' bitch like you messing with guys like me. Man tries to mind his own business, have a little fun and blow off some steam with his friends, and you come along and screw it all up by killing people. A little rape never hurt no one."

"I'm sure that woman and her child would disagree. As would all the other women you raped who I wasn't there to save."

He laughed. A short, bitter laugh. "Boys too. Don't forget them."

I nearly shot him again on principle but restrained myself. Instead, I drew my Bowie knife and held it up for him to see. "Now, I need information that you have. This can go slow, or it can go all night. I got the time. So, tell me what I need to know and I'll see to it that you don't suffer any more than necessary."

"Piss. Off."

I shrugged. "Have it your way." I dug the knife under the dressing into his gut wound and began to dig around. He screamed like a banshee and arched his back off the table, which I knew had to hurt his broken arm as well. I withdrew the blade and backed off. "Ready to talk?"

He wheezed in short little breaths. His stomach and chest

moved in rapid, terse movements to match his breathing. "Alright, alright. You know I'm not that tough. Shit. Ask."

"Good call. The wolves—do they know we're coming?"

He groaned and held his side with his good hand. "You mean have I spoken to them? Hell no, hadn't the time. Been running from you and shamblers since we parted ways."

"That's not what I asked." I gestured with the knife. "Again, we can do this the hard way—"

"Alright! Yes, they probably know your stupid ass is going to try to take them on. Shit, you're an idiot, you realize that? They have numbers, they're damn well invincible, and they'll smell you coming before you see them. What the hell do you think you're going to accomplish by going on the warpath now?"

I laughed. "That's funny. Going 'on' the warpath. Hell, son, I never left the warpath." I stabbed the Bowie into the desk as close to him as I could without nicking him. "Now, you spoke about numbers—what kind of numbers do they have?"

He shrugged with his healthy arm and winced. "Maybe fifteen, sixteen wolves? And don't forget that creepy vamp who looks like a movie actor. Even the alpha, Van, kowtows to him. That thing is scary as hell. I'm telling you, anything that scares Van is bad news."

"I'll take that under advisement. What about fortifications?"

"Nothing much—fences mostly. They have some blood-sucker working for them that keeps the dead away. They're werewolves—they don't need much else."

I nodded. "Now we're getting somewhere. Where do they keep the prisoners?"

He chuckled. "Missing that fine piece of ass, huh?" I chambered the knife high in an icepick grip, and he cringed. "Shit, man, stop already! I'm dead as a doornail, no need to speed up the process." I lowered the knife and he relaxed. "There's a small hotel across from the campus where they house everyone.

Like I told you before, they have nice digs. We got to stay there and sample the wares on occasion." He flinched away from me as I reacted with a glare. "Not trying to be a smart-ass, just telling the truth."

"Patrols. How many and how often?"

"Hell, it changes all the time. These wolves, they aren't stupid. Trust me. You're in for a world of hurt."

I tongued my cheek and smirked. "Trust you? I trust you like I trust a rattler on meth." I grabbed the shotgun and racked it several times, catching each shell as I did so. I checked the tube to make sure it was empty and then slid one shell back in, leaning it against the desk. "Here's how it's going to work, Jimmy. I'm going to leave this here, and it's up to you how you use it. You can try to fight your way out of here with one shell, or you can end your misery. Up to you. Me, I could care less at this point."

He grimaced with a spasm of pain. "Gee, thanks. You're a real generous piece of shit."

I nodded. "I am at that." I turned and walked toward the door.

Jimmy started yelling at me as I walked away. "Scratch! I'll see you in hell, you son of a bitch!"

I turned and replied over my shoulder. "Yeah? Well, when you get there, do me a favor and tell 'em I got more coming after you."

With a clear conscience, I left him bleeding to death and walked out into the afternoon sun, feeling better than I had in weeks.

[14]

SHED

The sun was getting awful low in the sky by the time I left Jimmy to his fate. I doubted he'd use the shotty; he was too chickenshit. He'd probably find a way to crawl off and survive. Cockroaches like him were like that. I had time to get away from here before the smell of blood brought in a rev' or a nos', but not enough time to get back to the kids before dusk. So I headed toward the direction I'd come from and looked for a suitable place to hide for the night.

Instead of hiding in the houses, I decided to check out the train that was stuck on the tracks. I considered the rail cars, but decided that I didn't like the idea of getting locked inside. I chose instead to lock myself inside the cab of the front engine. It was high off the ground, relatively secure from most deaders, isolated, and I'd have an unobstructed 270-degree view of my surroundings as well. I headed inside, cut the fireman's seat up to make a makeshift bed and pillow from the seat foam, and settled in for the night.

Several hours later, I awoke to the sound of scratching on the window glass. I opened my eyes to see a nos' staring at me through the glass. I had my .45 trained on him under my blanket, so I wasn't concerned about the thing coming at me. But its behavior was strange, and I was curious as to why it hadn't attacked.

We stared at each other for several seconds, then it spoke. "Huuuumaaan. Where are my slavessss?"

That explained a lot. Apparently, this nos' thought I was a punter. No sense changing his mind about that. The ruse might be useful in getting us through his territory alive. I decided to see where this went. "Not here. We ran into a deader herd southwest of here, and they took out our crew and cargo. I'm the only one left."

The thing blinked once and continued to stare me down. "Maybe I should take you for my meal, instead."

"Not unless you want trouble with the wolves. They're expecting us, and I have intel on equipment they need for their project."

The nos' hissed at the mention of the Corridor pack. Apparently, they weren't on the friendliest of terms. "If it were not for Piotr, I would have nothing to do with them."

Shit, I thought. *Who the hell is Piotr? The vamp?* I decided to play dumb. "I don't know him. The only one I deal with is Van, and he says they need some equipment we located for him a few days ago. He'll be pissed if I don't show up. You can count on it."

This nos' was a weird one. He stared at me for another minute, maybe more, during which time I was sure he was going to come through the glass at me. I held tension on the trigger of the Glock, and it's a wonder I didn't accidentally snap off a round at him. Finally, he spoke. "On your way back, bring me a slave from their brood. Or die. It is your choice." He moved away from the window so fast, it almost looked like he vanished.

I popped up and sprang to the glass, spotting the thing running like a scalded dog north, where I assumed its hideout and hunting grounds were located. I'd have to ask the boys if they had a precise location on where this nos' slept, once I got back to them. I sure wasn't going to get any more sleep, so I sat in the engineer's chair and scanned the night for more threats until dawn.

———

As soon as dawn broke, I headed back for the camp where I'd left Gabby, Bobby, and the LARPers the day before. I took the same route back through the neighborhoods, avoiding a few lone shamblers and making it to the greenbelt without a hitch. But no sooner had I entered the concealment of the woods did I run into Bobby, hauling ass in the opposite direction.

"Bobby, what the hell are you doing here?"

"When you didn't show up last night, I figured you might need some help. So I left Gabby with the LARPers, and I started tracking you down. Did you find Pancho?"

"We can discuss that later. Right now I want to know why you disobeyed me and left Gabby and those boys all alone."

He shrugged. "Gabby can handle herself. You've seen it. She may be small, but she's tough."

I shook my head in disbelief. "Sonuvabitch, Bobby—are you out of your mind? She's only twelve years old. And those boys, they might have some skills, but they're only humans, not paranormals. What do you think is going to happen if the Pack runs across their trail?"

He hung his head in shame. "I didn't even think about that, boss. Sorry."

"I know you didn't. Look, you have a lot going for you, but planning ahead is one skill that you lack. From now on, listen to me. If you don't understand why I want you to do something, ask."

He nodded in reply. I didn't chew his ass too badly because I didn't want to deal with him looking like a whipped puppy all morning. Even so, I was pissed, and he knew it. I decided to just let it go.

"Alright, there's nothing we can do about it now but head back, and hope that Gabby and her merry band haven't gotten into too much trouble in our absence." Without another word, I started running back in the direction of camp, Bobby close on my heels. We took off at a steady pace and ran downhill whenever the opportunity arose. Moving fast, we attracted a few shamblers. Still, I punished the kid by sending him back to deal with them whenever we happened to get a deader on our tail.

By mid-morning, we were back at the camp. The boys were conspicuously silent as we jogged up, and Matthew averted his gaze. "Matthew, where's Gabby?"

Without looking at me, he pointed inside the shed. Curious, I walked up behind him and gently turned him around to face me. One eye was almost completely swollen shut, and he sported the beginnings of a shiner to end all shiners.

Bobby whistled, shaking his head. Matthew just looked at the ground and blushed, making the black and blue mess of his right eye stand out even worse. Christopher made a funny face and smirked, but with one look from me, he waddled off to find something to busy himself with on the other side of camp.

"What happened?"

Matthew tried to hang his head even lower, if that were possible. "I deserved it. We were shooting at butts, attempting to redeem ourselves after the sound thrashing the lady provided us at archery yesterday. She proceeded to beat us again, and I accused her of cheating. She struck me." I began to speak, but he held up his hands. "I am aware that it was poorly done. I have tried to apologize, but she will not speak to either of us."

Christopher spoke up from across the camp. "And I didn't even do anything!"

I stifled a chuckle, then did my best to look serious before Matthew looked up at me. "Um, maybe you should just avoid her for a day or two until she gets over it."

He nodded. "I suppose you're right. But how shall I redeem myself in the lady's eyes? It seems I've besmirched her estimation of me beyond repair."

Oh, woe is me, I thought. "Trust me, Matthew, she'll get over it." I paused to think about how I wanted to phrase my next few words and leaned closer to whisper so they wouldn't carry. "Gabby—she's going through a tough phase right now. Just leave her alone, and this will have blown over before long."

He looked up at me with renewed hope. "You're sure of this?"

"I'm sure. Let's break camp and see if we can't make some time today before I have to send you boys back to Colin."

He gave me a funny salute that somehow reminded me of something from *Men In Tights* and then dashed off to help Bobby and Christopher break camp. I had to fight to avoid releasing a chuckle that would crush the poor kid's confidence. I understood why Anna, Colin, and Tuck had raised these boys as they did, but damn it if they weren't both annoying and amusing to be around. I could only imagine how they'd react to seeing *The Princess Bride* or Monty Python's *The Holy Grail*. It might break their psyches entirely.

I walked over to the little cinder block hut and knocked on the doorframe. "Mind if I come in?" I felt like a sitcom dad, walking in to soothe my T.V. daughter's wounded heart. It felt a bit ridiculous, but I couldn't help but feel responsible for her. And guilty, too, for letting her get involved with my shit. But, what's done was done.

Silence. Then, a small voice echoed from inside. "Sure,

why not."

I walked in and sat on a cot across from her. The little shed still had all the pipes and apparatus it had come with, but someone from Colin's group had equipped it with the barest amenities to make it more livable. I wondered how many other safe houses and way stations they had like this in the Corridor; that knowledge might be useful in days to come.

It was common for caravaneers and scavs to have dozens of hideouts and safe houses like this one peppered all over the map. Often, they'd keep the best ones to themselves. It was only when you got to know someone well, like I knew Sam Tucker, that they'd let you in on their sweetest hiding places. I reflected that I wouldn't mind adding a few choice spots like this to my own map, if only to have a backup plan should things go south with the wolves. I made a mental note to ask the boys if they could share some intel with me before we parted ways.

Gabby was playing with her knife, flipping it up in the air and catching it using a variety of grips. Between her finger and thumb, between her middle and index fingers by the blade, by the butt balanced on her palm, snatching it mid-air and flipping it between her fingers; she had a seemingly endless number of permutations of this game. I watched her for a few seconds, then spoke up.

"Matthew sure has a heck of a shiner." She nodded. "Did you have to hit him that hard?"

She snatched the knife from the air and did a half-shrug. "He asked for it."

"Yeah, that's what he said. He feels really bad about it, you know."

She frowned and looked at me like I was nuts. "Seriously? I mean, I laid him out with that punch. I figured he'd be pissed that not only did I beat him twice at archery, but that I also kicked his ass for real."

I tilted my head and smiled. "Well, boys have a way of forgiving the faults of girls they're interested in, and I'm pretty sure Matthew has a thing for you."

"He's almost as old as Bobby. Aren't I too young for him?" She stated it sarcastically.

I grunted. "Bobby's older than he looks, remember?"

She looked down at her knife, staring as she flipped it between her fingers. "Yeah, I forget sometimes. He just seems so young, you know?" I had the feeling she was hinting around at something, and then it clicked.

"Gabby, how old are you, really?"

She bobbed her head. "I dunno, fifteen or sixteen, maybe. It's easy to lose track of time, living underground."

Secrets and lies, I thought, *and I was always the last to figure it out.* "The serum, it slowed down your growth, didn't it?"

She nodded. "The Doc and my Uncle Tony told me that I had to act the age I looked and that no one could know. Otherwise, they might think I was a 'thrope, or something else. It would make people suspicious. So, I had to act younger."

"And Captain Perez, she told you to hide this from me?"

"It was my choice. I didn't want you to think I was a freak."

I let out a small gasp of exasperation. "Gabby, c'mon. You're traveling with a werewolf and a guy who's just one bad day away from becoming a full-on deader. You have nothing to worry about."

She smiled, slightly. "Yeah, you guys are kind of weird."

"We are at that." I sucked on my lip and squinted at her. "But Gabs, this keeping secrets thing, it has to stop. Half the time, I feel like everyone is holding out on me, and that you and the Doc are just leading me around by the nose."

She turned to look at me, curiosity and maybe a little shame written across her delicate features. "Scratch, I'd never hide anything from you that could hurt you. I swear it."

I tilted my head. "And I believe you. But I don't have the same opinion of Captain Perez. And, I'm a little suspicious of your story about who your uncle is and what he did before the War. A lot of it just doesn't add up."

When we'd first met, Gabby had told me that her uncle had disappeared under mysterious circumstances right before I found her. Yeah, I wasn't buying that story anymore. Too much of what the Doc and Gabby had first told me had turned out to be half-truths or lies. I figured there was a story behind this "uncle" of hers as well. My money was on him being a spook, but time would tell.

Gabby started to protest, but I raised my hands, and she stopped. "Now, I'm not judging you—I mean, in this world, this age, we all have to keep some secrets. All I'm saying is, when you're ready to tell me your whole story, I'll be here to listen."

She stopped twirling her knife, then spun it one last time through her fingers and slammed it into the sheath at her waist. "Deal. But if that *cabrón* tells me I cheated again, I'm going to break his jaw."

I looked out the doorway at Matthew's mangled face, just as he winced while covering the last coals of the small campfire they'd built. "Yeah, I don't think you have to worry about that."

That morning, the boys led us back on the same route I'd taken the day before. We snuck across the highway at the same point and ended up at the cemetery near the safe house where I'd left Pancho. I had them wait for me as I snuck inside the safe house, but there was no sign of him. Cursing myself for not killing him, I hoped to hell that he'd slunk off somewhere to die and that the Pack hadn't rescued him.

After I had arrived back at the cemetery, we cut across some empty fields and a wooded area to a creek bed hidden by dense trees and vegetation. In the past, the trees and bushes were likely more sparsely grown, but now nature had taken its course and provided us with ample cover along what I assumed to be our route north.

We silently entered the ravine, and Matthew gestured for everyone to crouch down and take cover. Then, he motioned me over to where he and Christopher squatted next to the small stream. Christopher grabbed a stick and drew in the sand. "We're here." He stabbed at the sand. "Here's the creek." He drew a squiggly line north. "And here's Kill Valley." He drew a line about twelve inches above our position that intersected the creek at a right angle. "And here's where the Corridor pack resides." He drew a rectangle about six inches further north of where the squiggly line ended.

"We can take you as far as here, but no further." He gestured to the end of the creek. "Honestly, we'd leave you here, but you're never going to get past Kill Valley before dusk. So, we're going to take you to an emergency safe house we've set up not far from there."

I held up a hand in protest. "Wait a minute—I thought this," I gestured around us, "was 'Kill Valley'?"

The boys looked at each other, and Matthew responded with a wry grin. "Surely you jest? This area is child's play compared to Kill Valley." He adjusted the quiver at his waist and fingered his bow nervously. Apparently, this would be no cake walk. "Now, from here on out, I must ask you all to be silent. We'll be killing the dead as we go with our longbows, hopefully without attracting attention from any of the rest of their kind who roam this area. You won't see many ghouls or revenants in this area, because there is a vampire who roams Kill Valley who keeps most of them at bay. However, the large numbers of dead are trouble enough. Because there are so many, this is the only safe route through this area."

I nodded. "Lead the way."

The boys exchanged a glance before standing, each nocking an arrow. As they took off at a careful pace, we silently followed after them.

———

As promised, it was slow going the whole way. We'd run into two or three deaders at a time, and often Gabby would have to pull duty taking them out with headshots in tandem with the boys. Once or twice, we drew the attention of shamblers up on the ridges above the creek, so we'd have to kill them and wait while the boys retrieved their arrows. It was well into the late afternoon before the boys signaled for us to pull up and gather round.

Matthew drew close enough to whisper in my ear. "We're almost at the safe house, but it's best if we wait until nightfall to head over. Too risky right now. We'd almost surely be seen by a herd, and with the number of dead around here we'd be surrounded within minutes."

I looked around to make sure that Gabby and Bobby had heard. "Understood. While we wait, I want to see what we're facing tomorrow," I whispered back. He nodded once and tilted his head to signal me to follow him.

He led me up the creek several hundred feet further. By this point, the water had dried up to barely a trickle. We crawled up a low rise next to a bridge that loomed overhead, then belly-crawled through some undergrowth and low-hanging juniper trees. Here he stopped and I paused next to him. I could feel the trembling in the ground long before I saw them, but when he parted a branch I still nearly shit my pants.

The street ahead was wall-to-wall with deaders. Thousands of them. It had to have been the largest herd I'd seen since the bombs had dropped. I shook my head in disbelief; Matthew slowly released the branch until it concealed us completely again. I took much greater care in moving back down into the creek bed than I had previously in crawling out of it and snuck back to rejoin the others.

After that, we hid under a rocky overhang until well after dusk, listening to the footsteps and little moans and growls of deaders that seemed to be all around us beyond the ledges above the creek. Once it was good and dark, Matthew gestured that we should follow, and slipped off into the night. How he and Christopher were moving so confidently in the dark was beyond me. I chalked it up to the moonlight and being intimately familiar with the area.

We followed them up the ravine, to a wooden fence that bordered what had once been someone's backyard. Matthew held up a hand and motioned for us to wait, then pulled up a section of the fence and slipped underneath. A few moments later, he returned and gestured for us to follow.

We went through the backyard, out a gate, and along the side of the house. There were deaders in the streets, small pockets of them here and there. I looked ahead and saw several cars blocking the street in a mini pile-up. We followed Matthew and Chris while moving rapidly in a crouch, tailing close behind them as they disappeared into a small, almost unnoticeable pathway that went between the cars. We followed them out the other side, then backed between the cars again at his silent command, pausing to wait as a lone shambler shuffled past.

Once it was gone, we moved silently and quickly to the other side of the street, ducking through another backyard and into a third, where we stopped and listened to determine if any deaders had spotted us. After being certain that we weren't followed or noticed, Matthew and Christopher led us along the side of the house to a small window that revealed a rarity among Austin homes: a basement. Matthew fiddled with the window for a moment, then held it open as he motioned for us to go inside.

I went through first, concerned that there might be something lurking in the dark. But my nifty new night-vision revealed nothing more than a standard suburban family room. The rest of the group followed me in, and Christopher paused to shut the window and lock it from the inside. They gestured for silence, which was unnecessary, and motioned once more for us to follow them.

Matthew led us into a bedroom, and then to what appeared

to be a closet door in the corner of the room. He opened it, revealing a wall of clothing hung neatly on hangers across a closet pole. Matthew turned and smiled, then slipped through the clothing and disappeared with Christopher on his heels. *Freaking Lion, Witch, and Wardrobe*, I thought to myself. I ducked through the hanging jackets and coats after them, only to find a false panel open at the back of the closet.

Behind the panel was a small space the size of another closet, and on the other side of that a metal door that opened outwards. The door was ajar, and Matthew and Christopher were already inside the room behind it. I entered after them to find a small, windowless safe room stocked with bunks, blankets, and shelves of canned goods. Matthew lit an oil lamp, then stood and shut the closet door, the false panel, and the metal door to the safe room once we were all inside.

Matthew unslung his bow and quiver, laying it on one of the bunks. "Now we can speak. So long as we do not raise our voices, no one can hear us outside this room—not even one of the wolves."

I looked around and shook my head enthusiastically. "Impressive. How'd you guys find this place?"

"Scavenging. One of the squires was searching the closet and just happened to lean on the false panel. We rarely come here since it's so close to the Valley, but it has served us well during times that we've come here to spy on the Pack." He gestured around. "Please, make yourselves at home."

Gabby and Bobby wasted no time in picking bunks and starting to stow their gear. The only downside to the room was that it was cramped and had little ventilation; soon we were smelling each other's funk. But otherwise, it was a perfect little hideaway, safe from the hordes of undead presumably roaming just a few feet from our heads.

Matthew caught my attention, and I knelt down near where

he sat. "We won't be able to get much sleep tonight," he said. "We'll need to leave before first light."

I nodded. "Got it. Who'll take first watch?"

He tilted his head. "I will, then Christopher. We're familiar with the house and the area. If something happens, we'll signal you by tapping on the floor or wall three times."

"Sounds good. I'm going to sack out. Wake me when you think it's time to go." I picked an unused bunk and crashed, wasting no time in making up for the sleep I'd missed the night previous.

A few hours later, Matthew woke me up with a hand clamped over my mouth. "Christopher is on watch, and he gave the warning signal several minutes ago. I haven't heard from him since, and he has not returned."

I removed his hand from my mouth. "Shit. Wake the others and have everyone ready to go ASAP."

He looked at me and frowned with confusion, so I elaborated. "That means double-time, pronto, fast as possible." He nodded and went about waking the others. I got my gear together, laced up my mocs, and loosened the sword in its scabbard. Something told me I was going to need it soon.

We stacked up and exited the safe room with me in the lead, sword drawn. Bobby was at my back with claws out, still in human form but looking less like a surfer and more like Wolverine's little brother at the moment. Gabby and Matthew backed us up, longbow and crossbow pistol at the ready. Matthew was a bit freaked at Bobby's claws, but he cowboyed up and took his position before I led us out and into the house.

We headed upstairs, and Bobby, Gabby, and I each scanned our sectors, looking for signs of trouble. The place was empty as a bird's nest in December, but I caught a whiff of a familiar smell when we hit the front of the house. It was a combination of clotted blood, graveyard dirt, and desiccated flesh.

I turned and whispered over my shoulder to Bobby. "You smell that?"

He nodded. "Nos', for sure."

I silently cursed myself for being so stupid. That nos' that I'd run into must've come back and picked up our trail. When it smelled multiple and distinct human scents, it probably thought that I was holding out, bringing through slaves and trying to sneak them by without paying tribute. Probably also figured it'd take one of us, just to teach me a lesson.

That meant Christopher could have been dead already. *Shit.*

It was still dark outside, so I knew that we might yet have a chance to save him. I signaled everybody to huddle up and leaned in close to whisper the plan. "Matthew, how much night do we have left?"

"Three hours, give or take."

"Good. Now, do you have any idea where this nos' holes up during the day?" I figured Bobby could track him and the kid by scent, but we'd be better off if we could take the direct route.

"Yes. He hides in an old movie theater by day. The building has few windows, and the dark is preferable to his kind. I believe he has two or three revenants in thrall that stay inside with him as well."

Matthew was talking about this thing like it was a person, but I didn't bother to correct him. I'd developed my opinion of the creatures long ago, and regardless of their apparent human characteristics, they were "its" and "things," all the way through. Ignoring his choice of words, I continued my line of questioning, staying focused on getting pertinent info from him that could help us rescue Chris. "How far is this place?"

"Less than a quarter-mile, as the crow flies. But, we'll need to avoid the horde of dead who stand between the theater and us. We'll take the creek north again, then cut over and come up behind the theater through the neighborhood that borders it on the northern side."

I corrected him. "Not you, just us. You'll have to mark it on my map. You're staying here until sunup, and waiting for us to come back with Christopher."

Matthew bristled, quietly seething with indignation. "I will not wait. Christopher is my brother in arms, and I'll not cower in craven fashion whilst you rescue him for me."

"Look, kid, I don't have time to argue; you'll only slow us down. I don't know if you've figured this out yet or not, but none of us are fully human. I wasn't supposed to reveal any of this to you, by order of Sir Reynard, but it's something you need to know now. So that's that. Believe me when I tell you, we three alone are best equipped to get your friend back."

He remained still and silent for several heartbeats. "Are you all lycanthropes?"

"No, just Bobby. Gabby and I have been genetically modified, so we have some of their characteristics and talents. We have faster reflexes, greater endurance, and heightened senses. All told, it gives us an edge against these things that you don't have."

He nodded. "Well, I don't know what sorcery 'genetically modified' is, but I've seen you fight, and I've felt Gabby's fist. And Bobby—his current state speaks for itself. I believe you." He paused. With my enhanced vision I could see by the look on his face that he weighed his options. "I will mark the place on your map, and wait here."

I sighed in relief. We might not bring Christopher back alive, and the last thing I needed was getting Colin's best boy killed, too. Matthew and I went back inside the safe room where he could have some light, and he marked the place on my map and explained how we should sneak up on it. My plan was for us to move through that residential area like famine, war, plague, and death, dropping anything that got in our way like a bad habit. Speed and surprise had to be on our side, because the odds were still stacked against us, no matter what skills we had between us.

"One last thing, kid—you got any extra lamp oil in here?" He rustled around on the shelves, and finally came up with a half-gallon of clear lamp oil. I grabbed a couple of empty mason jars, filled each with oil halfway, topped them off with some Sterno and hand soap that I found, and I capped them up tight. I wrapped them in a few articles of spare clothing and stuffed them in my bag.

Matthew and I clasped hands before I left the safe room. "I will do everything in my power to get your friend back."

"Please do. I'll never forgive myself for staying behind if he doesn't come back alive."

I clapped my hand on his shoulder. "Lock up behind us, son. If everything goes well, we'll be back just after sunup and your friend will be back safe and sound."

———

WE EXITED the house at a trot, me in the lead with the katana, Gabby running center with the crossbow, and Bobby watching our backs. Just past the front yard, I snuck up on a small group of deaders in the pitch black and cut them down with two quick sword strokes as I ran by. Their dismembered bodies dropped in a heap. The only sounds we made were the wet soft smacks of body parts hitting the ground as we passed.

I moved as quickly as stealth and common sense allowed when I heard a crossbow bolt whiz by me and a deader hit the pavement twenty feet ahead. As I leapt over the body, I glanced back over my shoulder to make sure I wasn't leaving anyone behind. Gabby barely slowed as she snagged the bolt from the thing's head with a slight sucking sound as she passed. Bobby was running in a crouch about ten feet behind her, nearly on all fours, scanning the night around us as we sliced through the neighborhood and deaders like Teflon death.

While we worked as a team, I felt a thrill rise within me. I knew the sensation wasn't human. It was the thrill of the hunt, the thrill of the pack. I barely suppressed an urge to howl with delight as we stalked the night. On this night, man was no longer prey, but predator once more. We were in our element.

Soon we reached the relative cover and safety of the stream bed, and I motioned for them to crouch down beside me, leaning closer to whisper almost inaudibly. "From here until we reach the residential area north of the bridge, we use pure stealth. We can't risk drawing even the slightest attention from the massive herd of deaders that'll be above us."

Both of them replied with a short nod and a look of eager determination. I could see it in their eyes; finally, we were striking back, and hard. I realized that this might as well have been a dress rehearsal for our coming attack on the Corridor pack, but stuffed any emotions I had about it down and out of sight. No sense in getting giddy now; that could come later, after we got Christopher back.

I took a deep breath, let it out slowly, and gave the command. "Alright, stay close and don't get separated." I moved out at a stealthy trot, my feet sure on the hard ground and rocks beside the stream. Once we reached the bridge, I happily noted that the sound of thousands of feet and half as many moans and groans mostly masked our approach. I led the wonder twins under the bridge, sticking to dry ground and making certain I didn't step on a single branch or leaf. We passed the bridge without incident and followed the creek further north until we saw the apartment complex Matthew had described to me.

I snuck up the ridge until I reached the remains of a fence that surrounded the apartment buildings. There was more cover on the far side of the parking lot, so I headed back into the gully and led us further north until we were just past the apartments. I climbed up again and vaulted a fence, landing in a backyard overgrown with weeds and littered with junk and debris. Bobby and Gabby followed and landed beside me, one each side.

The yard was full of deaders, and one of them had already seen us drop over the fence. She was moving quickly toward us and moaning loudly. Gabby shut her down with a crossbow bolt to the head, but that merely attracted more of them. Within seconds, the whole group was coming after us. Although they might ignore me due to the infection running through my blood, I knew they wouldn't hesitate to attack Bobby and Gabby.

From experience, I knew their moans would rise to a crescendo within moments of our discovery, which would draw the herd we'd just passed right to us. Despite the danger, a bloodlust rose in my veins and I wanted nothing more than to tear these things limb from limb. Without hesitation or even a plan, I strode calmly forward and wielded the sword like a scythe, chopping off heads and severing torsos with reckless abandon. I lost all sense of time and place; there was only me, my blade, and the dead who fell like stalks of grain before me.

One grabbed at me and I spun the blade, cutting its hands off at the wrists; in a smooth arc, I turned that cut into a backswing that split the deader under its right armpit and came out the other side of its neck, effectively decapitating it while keeping the shoulder and arm intact. I spun and swung the blade almost lazily, catching three more through their necks and dropping them instantly. On instinct, I ducked from another's grasp and came up with a diagonal upward forehand cut, cleanly slicing through its throat and half its jaw. As I flowed through my dance of death, my blade followed a pattern determined by the rhythm of the fight: step-step-pivot, slice-cut-spin, chop-sever-duck, roll-rise-stab...

What seemed like an eternity must have lasted only seconds. Before I realized it, the fight was over, and all the deaders were down. Bobby and Gabby hadn't even had time to enter the fray. I blinked, and everything sped up at once. I sucked in a breath as the kids took one final stride toward me, then blacked out and collapsed in a heap.

"Scratch! Scratch, can you hear me?" Bobby frantically whispered, lightly slapping my face. His claws left little scratches under the three-day beard growth that adorned my face, but due to his excitement, he barely noticed. I grabbed his wrist as his hand came toward my face, stopping him from striking me again.

"I'm awake—shit, stop slapping me!" I whispered angrily. I wiped at my face with my other hand, feeling the sticky wet residue of my blood between my fingers. "You know, you could retract those things before slapping a guy in the face. It's only common courtesy."

He scratched his head and frowned. "Hell Scratch, I thought you'd had a heart attack or something. I mean, your heart just stopped beating, and you collapsed! What the hell, man?"

Gabby was looking at me with a mixture of awe and shock on her face. I looked past her and realized we were inside a house. "How'd we get in here?" I asked.

Gabby spoke up. "When you passed out, we pulled you inside the house. You've been out for a good ten minutes."

Bobby put his hand on my chest. "Yeah, and I had to pump your chest for three of those minutes. First, you went all Agent Smith on us, and then you just dropped in a heap. I've never seen a human move that fast. One second you were there, and the next, bodies were flying all over the place. What the hell, Scratch?"

I rubbed my sternum in consternation. "Is that why my chest hurts so bad?"

Gabby started gesticulating wildly. "Um, hello? You were like, dead. Like, *dead* dead, as in not breathing dead, no heart-beat dead, *Jesu Christo ay Dios mio* dead. Scared the living crap out of us both."

I had no idea what had happened, but there was little time to discuss it. I stood up, slowly, feeling the job that Bobby had done on my ribcage with every move and breath. I braced my side with my hand. "I think you might have cracked my ribs, kid."

He looked at Gabby with mock disgust. "I save the guy's life one more time, and again he complains."

Gabby apparently didn't see the humor in the situation. "I think you're doing too much, too soon. La Araña said you needed time to let the serum do its work. You should have listened to her."

"Got no more time for rest, not until I get Kara back. Now, let's move out." I shook my head slowly, searching around for my katana. "Where's my sword?" I growled. Bobby retrieved it from the corner and handed it to me. Gabby chewed her cheek and gave me a look that was more concern than defiance or scorn, but even so, I knew we'd be having this conversation again. Unconcerned for my own safety, I focused my mind once more on the task at hand and half-staggered out the door and into the night.

The rest of the way to the theater, I took a path that allowed us to avoid deaders. We snuck around houses and cars, jumped fences, and hid behind overgrown shrubbery until we made it to our destination. Once there, we jumped another fence and hid behind some trash dumpsters behind the theater.

I took a peek over the garbage dumpsters and smiled. "Huh. I remember this place. I came here for a Kurosawa film marathon back in the day. They served beer and food during the movie. Damn, I miss civilized living."

Gabby rolled her eyes. "You can reminisce later, *viejo*— what's the plan?"

"The plan? It's simple. This thing knows that it can keep Christopher alive for a while if it rations its feedings. So, Chris'll be a few quarts low by now, but still breathing. The revs that Matthew spoke of are probably still out hunting, and chances are good they won't be back until right before sunrise. That nos' is probably all by its lonesome in there, so— "

Bobby broke in and spoke in a rush. "So we drop in, snag Tubby, kill the vamp, and leave before the revs get back. Brilliant!"

I wagged my finger at him. "Um, not quite. We're going to drop in, all right—but then we're going to burn the place to the ground."

———

WE GAINED access to the roof by way of a drain pipe that ran all the way up the side of the building. None of us had much difficulty climbing the building that way, although my ribs were screaming bloody murder at me the entire way up. Once topside, I walked them over to the side of the building furthest away from the front entrance. I brought their attention to the area where the roof and wall met.

"Bobby, put those claws to use and start peeling up this asphalt—quietly. I want to see what's under it."

"Sure thing, boss." He dug his claws in, and soon had a good-sized section peeled away. As I'd hoped, under several layers of asphalt the roof was plywood and not steel like some modern buildings. I directed him to keep pulling the asphalt and tar paper up until we found a seam.

"Alright, Bobby—dig those claws in and start peeling back that roof panel, just as quietly as you can manage." Within a minute or two, Bobby had removed an entire four by eight sheet of the roof decking. It made a considerable amount of noise, but I banked on the fact that these theaters were built to be sound-proof, so hopefully the noise wouldn't carry to the front of the building where I figured the nos' was laid up.

Under the roof decking and insulation there were ceiling tiles suspended in a frame, which we removed and set aside. I peered into the dark of the theater below, listening for any sound that might indicate something waiting for us down there. I heard nothing, so I dropped down into the space from the edge of the opening, swinging from the roof joists to the wall immediately adjacent. I grabbed the decorative curtain and used that to climb the thirty feet or so down to the floor.

At the bottom, I rolled left and landed on the balls of my feet in a crouch. I was still a little weak and dizzy from the episode I'd had earlier, and swayed slightly as I stood. Bobby and Gabby followed soon after. We each stood motionless, listening for movement from the building around us. Hearing nothing, I moved toward the theater's front exit.

As I walked down the exit ramp, I noted a number of corpses lying around the place in various states of decay. The smell had escaped me on the way in, likely being trapped near the floor by the cool, stagnant air of the theater's interior. But now it hit me full force. I gagged for a moment before my nose adjusted to the scent. I'd never been one for strong smells—and especially not of dead, rotting flesh. How I ever decided that killing zombies was a good career choice was beyond me.

I had to remind myself that we were here to rescue Christopher. We didn't have time to wait around and end the things that had killed these people. Stowing my anger, I led us to the exit door and listened for movement in the hall outside. Dead silence. Since the window in the door had been spray-painted over, I cracked the door to peek out into the hallway. No movement, either. It seemed that we were alone, after all.

As we exited the room, I waved Bobby over. "Can you pick up Christopher's scent at all?"

He grunted softly and took a long whiff around him. "Now I can. Too many competing scents back there. He's here, or he was not long ago. That way." He pointed down the hall.

I looked at Gabby. "Make sure you have that crossbow ready, and your nine as well. No need to worry about making noise inside this place—no matter how loud we get, not much sound will escape. But if we run into anything before we see the nos', take it out quietly. I want to extract Christopher without alerting that bloodsucker."

"Not a problem." She made sure the crossbow was cocked and loaded, and checked her Glock 9mm to make certain she had a round chambered. She also checked the little .22 she had holstered in cross-draw position on her left hip, pulling it out and screwing the silencer to the barrel. *Good girl*, I thought, with no small amount of pride.

All warm fuzzies aside, I still felt guilty about her acting like my personal Femme Nikita, even now that I knew she was older than she looked. Regardless of my guilt, I was going to have a serious discussion regarding transparency with Captain Perez later. I had begun to see why they called her The Spider, and how she'd used the kid to pull my strings. It really chapped my ass, thinking about it.

Turning my thoughts back to the task at hand, I motioned Bobby into lead position and drew the katana. We stalked down the hall toward the front of the theater, careful not to make a sound and to maintain our tactical awareness. Our vigilance was rewarded when a rev' came barreling out of a doorway as we passed. Gabby pivoted smoothly and placed a bolt right in its eye. We waited for her to retrieve the bolt and reload, then moved on.

When we reached the front of the theater, I split off a few yards to scan the front area. Someone had painted the windows, and it was just as pitch black up here as it was inside the theaters. As I was finishing my sweep of the area, Bobby tapped me on the shoulder, pointing at a side door that was marked "Staff Only."

"That's where Christopher is. I'm almost sure of it."

I took point again and tried the door. It was unlocked, so I pulled it open an inch or two, only to find that the hinges squealed loudly. I shut it again, then went behind the counter and found some cooking oil to grease the hinges. After a liberal application of hydrogenated soybean gunk, I tried the door again. The door didn't protest half as much, but it was still louder than I would have liked.

Beyond the door was a staircase that did a u-turn about ten steps up. The blind corner made me nervous, but there wasn't much we could do about it. I stalked forward quietly, catching the scent of fresh blood at about the third or fourth step up. When I hit the landing, I heard shallow breathing coming from above us. I switched the sword to my left hand and drew my Glock.

I moved around the corner, scanning the space above. There was still no sign of the nos', so I proceeded up the steps and into the area ahead. It was an employee lounge space, or it had been at one time. We found Christopher tied up, bloody and unconscious, on an old orange pleather couch. I assumed the nos' was hiding behind the door at the back of the space that said, "Manager," possibly semi-conscious in a blood-drunk state. I'd seen it happen before; still, I wasn't taking any chances.

I motioned to Bobby, and he picked the kid up and slung him over his shoulders. Christopher was stout, but his weight was nothing to Bobby's werewolf strength. I signaled for them both to head downstairs, and we let Gabby lead while I backed out, watching the door to the manager's office, worried that the nos' might burst out at any second.

As I edged out of the room, Gabby moved past the landing and around the corner. Just as she slipped out of view, I heard the *THWAP* of the crossbow and the report of the little .22 firing three times in rapid succession.

Ambush!

[18]
SOILED

I vaulted the waist-level pony wall that served as the safety banister for the stair, nearly landing on Gabby in the process. I wanted to get in front of Bobby to give him time to either retreat or to set his load down and fight. But what I saw when I hit the lower set of steps was heart-warming; Gabby had already dropped one rev' with a bolt through the throat, and another with three small holes punched in its face.

I admired her work for a moment. From the looks of things, we weren't necessarily ambushed, but instead had just been the victims of bad luck. The revenants who inhabited this place with the nos' had returned from their evening hunt, and they'd walked in at the exact moment that we'd decided to leave.

Unfortunately, Matthew had grossly underestimated their numbers. Instead of three or four revs, there were eight that I could see; this could put a serious cramp in my plans. Revs were much faster than deaders and even ghouls, and almost as deadly as vamps. The only saving grace we had was that they weren't as durable as a nos', so that was something in our favor. But we needed to take them out quickly, before that nos' came running up our asses. I holstered the Glock and took a two-handed grip on the katana, leaping off the stairs into the crowd of revs below.

I caught the first one across the face, slicing its head neatly into upper and lower halves. But there were a half-dozen more, and they responded quickly to my attack. Within seconds, I was fighting for my life. Three of them came at me all at once, but luckily they came from the same direction and at the same time, so I could deal with them as a single threat.

I held the sword low and across my body as I backed up, moving just enough to make them think I was scared, but not enough to pull completely out of their range. As they lunged at me, I brought the sword up diagonally in a vicious backhand slash, severing the first one's leg below the knee, the arm of the next at the elbow, and catching the last one across the face deeply enough to give it pause, but not enough to punch its ticket.

As the first one collapsed, I sidestepped and beheaded it, then kicked the falling corpse forward to trip up the handless one coming at me with prejudice. I waited until the last moment, then raised the sword and stabbed it through the neck and out the back of its head. I kicked it off my blade just in time to slash the last of the three from stem to sternum, splitting its torso almost in two and taking it out of the fight. It dropped to its side and began mouthing the air like a fish out of water. I didn't think these things needed to breathe, but they needed working lungs to scream. This one was shit out of luck in that department at the moment.

Peripherally, I saw that Bobby had set Christopher down on the stairs, leaving Gabby to guard him while Bobby entered the fray. Currently, he was kicking serious ass with those massive claws of his. He'd disemboweled one, leaving it tripping and slipping over its entrails, and practically beheaded another that lay on the floor with limbs akimbo. Its severed head hung on like the top of a broken Pez dispenser, at an odd angle and useless to boot.

Gabby, on the other hand, took precision shots from the stairs and kept the revs at bay. The suppressed .22 she was using was underpowered for fighting revs, but even so she'd killed another one and was working on ending her fourth momentarily. Christopher was still out cold, so she stayed close to him and used the higher ground to her advantage.

That left two revs to kill. I looked around frantically to see where they'd gone when one landed on my back and clamped its teeth right on my shoulder. I howled in fury and agony, stabbing it in the face over my shoulder with the sword. It jumped off me and skittered into the corner, cowering, whining and moaning like a thing possessed.

Which, I supposed it was. But now it was a thing possessed and in agony. Unfortunately for me it wasn't a complete win, since I was hurt too. It had bitten deep. My shoulder went numb and made my grip weak. I sheathed the sword and drew my Glock again, fumbling for the silencer that I'd stashed in my cargo pocket, and taking my sweet time getting it firmly tightened on the barrel.

Meanwhile, Gabby had reloaded her crossbow and casually walked around the room putting bolts in heads and making sure everything that still moved didn't. We had one rev' unaccounted for, and I checked high and low for it to no avail. Then, I remembered the nos' upstairs.

———

I TURNED toward the steps to head back up, but I was too late. The thing was already crouched over Christopher, hovering menacingly with one clawed hand on the boy's throat. I froze, as did Bobby and Gabby. Well, sort of. I heard one more crossbow bolt drive home in an undead creature's skull, then silence. That girl did not mess around.

It spoke. "I knew you weren't with the slavers. You thought you had us fooled, but I've been around too long—yes, too long to fall for human tricks."

It drew each 's' out like a snake, and I honestly couldn't decide if it was just trying to be creepy, or if it had a lisp. I decided to stall for time so I could save the kid. "Eight years isn't that long at all," I replied. "Although considering the rate I've been killing your kind, that would be ancient in these parts."

It chuckled in that dry, raspy voice they all seemed to have. "Eight years is a raindrop in the sea, compared to how long I have been alive. I watched pharaohs rise and fall, saw empires crumble. How insignificant your lives are to one such as me."

I looked it over, and to be honest, it did look extra crunchy for a nos'—a little gray around the gills, so to speak. "Well, then. Such a shame your life has to end here, in this dump."

It inclined its head toward me. "Indeed. I saw you fight my brood, and I am overmatched." It paused and raised one bony, clawed finger on its free hand. "However, I know you came here for the boy. I can kill him, or you can leave, and I will allow him to live."

I clucked my tongue. "Hmmm. I have a better plan. You slither on back to whatever Elvira-style lair you have going upstairs, and we take the boy and leave. Or, I kill you where you stand."

It stood still as marble for several long seconds, considering my offer. "It seems we are at a détente."

I gave a frisky shiver and smirked. "Oh, I just love it when you creepers speak French. It lets me know you have a sensitive side, to go with your homicidal killing streak." I composed myself and glared at the vamp with menace. "There's no standoff here. We hold all the cards. If you want to live another three thousand years, you'll back off and hide somewhere while we cart this boy back to where he came from."

It glared at me and blinked. "You have a spine. That's something I haven't seen in a human since the Middle Ages."

"Well, Skippy, get used to it, because a lot of shit is fixing to change around these parts, and soon."

It tilted its head, as if trying to puzzle me out, then it sniffed toward me and grinned in an evil rictus of a smile. "Ah, Mr. Sullivan, I presume. Come for the girl with the Titian hair. I should have known; you have her scent all over you."

That gave me pause. What the hell did this thing know about Kara, and how did it know my name? If Glocks had external hammers, I'd have cocked mine right about then. My voice took on a dangerous timbre. "What do you know about her, you dried up mummy-looking piece of shit? Tell me!"

The nos' looked me up and down. "Well, I believe I am starting to gain a certain fondness for you, Mr. Sullivan. You—amuse me." Then it drew itself up, coughed slightly, and if I didn't know any better, I'd have to describe the look it gave me as... pitying. "There's nothing you can do for the girl now, boy. Go home, lick your wounds, and leave the Pack alone. There will be other battles to fight, ones that you can win."

I glared and shook my head slightly. "Just what do you care about us, and whether we live or die here?"

The thing tilted its head and gestured flippantly. "I care a great deal. It is no small coincidence that I chose to locate here, so close to the Corridor pack and Piotr. They are upsetting a balance that has lasted for millennia. I would not see your kind destroyed by their machinations."

"Only because you feed on us, and fear what would happen if we become extinct."

"Touché, Mr. Sullivan, touché."

I never trusted much of what these things had to say before, and after what Colin had told me I wasn't about to start to now. I was losing my patience with this nos', and was also eager to get the hell out of Dodge. I realized that it was probably trying to stall us until dawn, so we'd be at the mercy of the horde outside. *Tricky, tricky.*

I shooed him away with the barrel of my Glock. "You just crawl back on up to your nest, and we'll be out of your way shortly." I held up two fingers. "Scout's honor."

The nos' smirked, acknowledging that I had figured out its plan. "Very well. Since I am curious to see what happens when you clash with the Corridor pack, I will acquiesce to your demands. But make no mistake, Mr. Sullivan—we will see each other again." And like that, the thing tilted its head in a slight bow and did what I'd suggested by rapidly slinking back up the stairs and out of sight. I reflected that I'd never be able to figure the damned things out, but I wasn't about to look a gift horse in the mouth. I shook my head and called for Bobby, who immediately zoomed over and checked on Christopher. After he made sure the kid still breathed, he hoisted him up on his shoulders and backed away from the stairs.

I pointed down the hall toward the theaters. "Go on ahead and exit through the way we entered—I'll just be a moment. And if I don't follow you right out, rendezvous with me back where we left Matthew."

Bobby answered, chipper as ever. "You got it, boss."

Gabby lingered after Bobby took off for the back rooms. "Go on Gabby. I'll only be a moment. Bobby needs you to watch his back while his hands are tied up with the kid." She stood her ground for another moment, concern etched on her face. "Go, I said. I'll be right behind you."

Her eyes narrowed. "You'd better be, or I swear I'll come back here and kill every last thing I find looking for you."

"Just go, kid, I'm one step behind you."

Finally, she did what I asked and vanished down the hall.

After she had gone, I opened my pack and pulled out the Molotovs I'd made at the LARPers' safe house. I used my Bowie to stab a jagged hole in each lid, then I stuffed some rags in both and lit the first one up. I backed up almost into the hall and tossed it underhand through the door and onto the landing between the upper and lower half of the stairway. It shattered, bursting into flames. The carpet ignited immediately, and the fire spread quickly up the stairwell. *Good.*

After I was sure that I'd trapped the nos' upstairs, I ran back to the theater where we'd come in only minutes before. I lit the second Molotov and smashed it on the carpeted floor a few yards down the hall. Same action, same effect; the carpet went up almost immediately, and I ducked into the theater to avoid the flames and smoke.

I watched the flames leap and spread for a moment, then shut the door and sprinted for the emergency exit. I was just a few feet from the door when a four-foot-nothing ball of teeth, claws, and fury tackled me. The last rev' had set a trap for me, and I'd walked right into it. Its momentum bowled me over on impact, and immediately I was in a fight for my life on the ground.

Folks who do jiu-jitsu think that their art can deal with just about anything and anyone on the ground. For the most part, they're right. But factor in more than one opponent, or throw a blade into the equation, and the dynamics of a ground fight change pretty quick. That's roughly the situation I was in, with a ninety-pound evil dynamo made up of claws, teeth, and gristle trying to rip my eyes and throat out while I attempted to fight it off.

I scrambled for space in order to keep it away from my eyes, trying to get into a position to kill it without getting my arms shredded all to hell. Finally, I got tired of its bullshit and grabbed it by the throat, holding it at arm's length while it savaged me with those claws. I drew my Glock with my other hand and blew its brains out at near point blank range. My left arm was a bloody mess now, but the look on its face when it realized I was about to end its miserable existence had been worth the price of admission.

I tossed its carcass away, resting for a second with my hands on knees, exhausted. Catching a whiff of smoke and the nasty chemical stew that it carried, I realized that I didn't have much time to spare. I cut some strips of the decorative curtain from the wall, quickly dressed my arm in makeshift bandages, and popped open the emergency exit just as the smoke started billowing into the theater from the hallway. Fleeing the smoke and fire, I ran out into the rapidly approaching dawn, hoping like hell I could make it back to the safe house before I the morning light revealed my sorry, rev'-bitten ass to the dead. They might very well ignore my presence—but among thousands of undead, I didn't care to risk it.

And I still had the wolves to deal with after this. *Ain't life grand?*

———

I LIMPED into the safe house just as the first rays of dawn peeked over the surrounding houses. Bobby and Gabby greeted me just inside the front door. On my way back, the deaders had mercifully left me alone, and I'd done my best to leave them alone as well. It was like I was almost one of Them; even when I stumbled and accidentally bumped into one, it acted as if I wasn't even there. I didn't find it to be amusing in the slightest, that I might be turning into the very thing I fought to kill. Of course, Gabby had retained her humanity and then some; but then again, she didn't have deader juice running through her veins, either.

Bobby grabbed me to keep me from falling as I stumbled through the door. They each took an arm, half-carrying me down to the basement and into the safe room. Inside, Matthew cared for Christopher, who was laid out on a bunk in the corner, sipping liquids and looking a little less peaked than he had at the theater. They guided me into a chair, and Gabby soon started pulling clothing away from my wounds and scrubbing them with a clean cloth and water.

Bobby glanced at my shoulder and arm and shook his head. "Boss, you look like you got into a fight with an angry blender and lost. You feel any different? Woozy, feverish, dizzy?"

"Nope, just bone-ass tired like I just got my ass handed to me on a platter. That last rev' caught me flat-footed leaving the theater." I turned my arm over and looked it up and down. "Nicked me up pretty good, I suppose. I splattered the thing's brains all over the screen. The place is a smoking heap by now, so that nos' is toast."

Bobby shook his head ruefully. "What a shame."

Gabby grabbed my arm back and sucked air between her

teeth, cursing silently in Spanish as she cleaned the cuts. She splashed something on my wounds that felt like liquid fire.

"Oh, good Lord. What the hell was that?"

Matthew looked over from the bed. "Hey, you found the moonshine. Great antiseptic, that stuff. Works like a charm, but burns like the devil." Then a confused look crossed his face. "Gabby, you did see the tincture of marigold in the med kit, did you not?"

She nodded with an evil grin as she wiped off my wounds with clean gauze. "Oh, I did—La Araña loves that stuff. But it doesn't sting nearly as much as grain alcohol." She scrubbed at my wounds furiously with gauze doused in moonshine, making me wince at her not-so-gentle ministrations until I tried to take over. She slapped my hands away in response and gave me a dirty look. "It's what you get for making us leave you behind, *viejo*."

I shrugged and took a slug from the bottle of moonshine. To say that it was harsh was an understatement. Although it burned all the way down, I kept taking small swigs until a feeling of warmth and numbness had worked its way all through my body. The buzz made it easier to tolerate Gabby's care, and after she had finished I collapsed on the bunk opposite from where Christopher rested.

He lifted a few fingers at me in acknowledgment. "Sir Scratch—I owe you my thanks," he whispered.

"Oh, don't thank me. Bobby's the one who hauled your ass out of there. And you can thank Gabby, too, for standing guard over you while we fought our way out."

He gave her a dreamy grin. "I would kiss your hand, milady, except that I am not fond of black eyes," he mumbled as he drifted off to sleep.

[20]
UPROAR

The next day, Christopher felt well enough to head back to the castle house, or at least that's what he said. I felt bad about sending him and Matthew back by themselves, but they'd both proven to be more than capable trackers and hunters. I was certain they would be able to make it home without a hitch. Or, so I kept telling myself.

Honestly, I was more than a bit upset by the hints that the nos' had dropped about Kara, and itching to get on with this rescue and get my people back to the Facility. Time seemed to be running out on us, and although I hadn't based my plans on a single, precipitous event, something told me that any delay was going to cost me something fierce when all was said and done.

I eventually found a compromise between my conscience and my eagerness to get on with the mission by talking the boys into staying behind at the safe house one more day. Another day wouldn't hurt them in the least; it'd allow Christopher to recover from his ordeal with the bloodsucker, and it'd make me feel a whole lot better knowing he was heading back in top form. Granted, we wouldn't be able to help them at all once we were out of contact, but it was better than letting them go back with Christopher still under the weather.

Happy to have that settled, it was time to move forward with rescuing Kara and the settlers. My plan was to observe the Corridor pack while remaining unseen, determine their movement patterns, and then set an ambush for them. I took out the maps we'd been given by Donnie the Wendigo and consulted with Matthew and Christopher regarding the area. They said they'd stayed away from the local stores and avoided scavenging them, simply due to the proximity to the wolves. I hoped that meant we'd find a few places that hadn't been picked clean. I knew of at least one warehouse store and an outdoor goods store I wanted to hit for supplies before I set my plan in motion.

I had an idea of what I wanted to do and how I wanted to do it, but without the right gear we'd be back to square one. I had Gabby and Bobby rest up until nightfall; then we said our good-byes, loaded up, and headed out. We traveled a few miles northeast until we found a place to hole up in, isolated by geography and terrain. We settled in an abandoned mega-church that sat up on a hill, bordered on two sides by freeways that kept the larger deader herds away. After a few hours of work clearing the upper floor of deaders, we got situated and set up a watch, just in case any of the wolves came sniffing around.

We spent the day hanging out and generally just resting up, taking naps and taking turns on watch. It was uneventful, at best. I didn't see any of the wolves during my time on watch, and the kids reported the same. I had a sneaking suspicion that either the wolves had gotten lazy over the years, overconfident and assured of their superiority in the local food chain, or that they had other creatures keeping watch for them. Considering what I'd heard about this Van character, I suspected that it was the former and not the latter. Big egos led to big mistakes.

Eventually I just couldn't sleep any longer. I got up and

started searching the rooms on the second floor. I found a small kitchenette that yielded some crackers, a few jars of baby food, and some bottled water. Bottled water always came in handy, despite being heavy and taking a lot of space. Boiling water to disinfect it was often difficult in the Badlands, since a fire could bring down baddies on your head if you weren't careful. The smell of smoke would carry for miles, and certain top-level supernatural predators had learned to follow the scent to its source for an easy meal.

Most folks just hauled as much water as they could when away from the settlements. Me, I liked to hedge my bets. I kept some iodine tabs with me in my pack. They kept indefinitely and were quite reliable for disinfecting water collected from natural sources. The tablets came from my stockpile of various survival items I'd hidden at my ranch back out west. Although those resources wouldn't last forever, I'd been judicious enough in their use to make them last until now. I also made a habit of scavenging for resources wherever I went; my miserly ways were much of what had kept me alive for so long.

A search of the other rooms revealed a nursery, more class-rooms, and a church library. Most of the books they had were nothing but Christian pop psychology garbage; pray this way and you'll be blessed with wealth and all that happy horseshit. However, I did find a copy of *The Lion, The Witch, and the Wardrobe* that was in good condition, so I read it while I waited for the kids to wake up.

After that, I busied myself with cleaning my weapons and counting ammo. I still had my Glocks, Bowie knife, tomahawk, and the MP7's, the Stoner, and the light .50 in the bag. We had plenty of ammo left, as well as the other party favors I'd packed back at Kara's place. All in all, I'd say we were ready as ever to make the shit hit the fan once the wolves showed up.

That was the problem: getting them to show when we were

ready, and choosing the field of battle so we'd have home court advantage. Both would be key to getting out of this alive. I also needed to ensure that I didn't place the kids in more danger than was necessary, that we took out as many wolves as possible as quickly as possible, and that we drew them away from their compound before we engaged the fight.

I just had to do the impossible. Business as usual.

I spent the remainder of the day mulling over my plan as I cleaned and oiled each weapon, taking particular time with the katana and the fully-automatic weapons; I'd be relying on them once we locked horns with the 'thropes. By the time Gabby and Bobby started to stir, I had a good idea of what we'd do and how we'd do it. I felt fairly confident we'd be able to pull it off.

I gave Gabby and Bobby a few minutes after they woke up to get ready. Then I rubbed my hands together and grinned. "Good news, kids. Tonight we're going shopping."

———

WE LEFT the building at a trot, heading across the access road and sneaking over to the other side of the expressway. I left most of the ordinance behind at the church; I'd send Bobby back for it once we were secure in our observation post later. But first, we needed some gear.

One of the reasons I'd selected the church for our temporary hideout was because it sat near a large outdoor sporting goods store. I hoped we'd find most of what we needed there; if not, I'd have to revise my already crazy plan considerably.

We got across the expressway without a hitch and moved at a steady pace while avoiding contact with deaders as much as possible. They were sparse here, but still a danger. Any bodies we left would let the local wolves know that someone was operating in their territory. My plan relied on absolute stealth until we sprung the trap, so we did our best to avoid attracting attention from the odd shambler we ran across.

The thing about Z's was they were attracted to differences in their local environment. In a sense, they were a lot like animals in how they functioned, naturally curious regarding anything that might result in a meal. My hope was that we'd be able to cross the half-mile or so to our destination without incident, and that the front of the store would already have some sort of breach, like a broken window or an open door. That way, we could enter and leave without any of the local deaders being the wiser.

As we edged past the supermarket across from the sporting goods store, my heart sank at the scene before us. Not only was the front of the store intact; someone had boarded it up tight. But that wasn't even the real kicker, not by a long shot. Nope. The real boot to the balls was the huge herd of deaders milling around in the parking area out front, moaning and banging on a minivan at the center of the lot.

I gave Gabby and Bobby the signal to move back and stay hidden. Meanwhile, I pulled out my monocular and snuck to a place where I could get a good look at what had these deaders riled. But unfortunately, I couldn't see inside the van; there were just too many deaders in the way. *Probably some punter who got separated from his crew*, I reflected. *Not even worth the trouble to save.*

I moved in a crouch back to where Bobby and Gabby hid and directed them to follow me around the back of the grocery. The good news was that all the deaders in the immediate area were in front of the sporting goods store, giving us a clear path to the back of the building, where I hoped we could find a way to get inside. That it had been buttoned up tight when the shit hit the fan was a bonus, but I wasn't going to get my hopes up. Anyone might have come along before us and cleaned the place out already. If the store had gone all this time entirely unmo-lested, I'd be shocked.

We snuck to the back of the place and found the loading dock; sure enough, the back door showed signs of forced entry, but there was little chance we'd be able to open it ourselves without drawing attention from the deader herd. The door had recently been jimmied. Whoever had gotten through before us had damaged the door mechanism so badly that there was no way to pick the lock. Bobby gave it a couple of good tugs, but even he couldn't budge it. Either it was latched from the inside, or they'd somehow managed to jam it shut to protect their find. Or, they'd broken in and locked the door behind them and never left.

Well, time to get inventive. I searched the back wall for a moment until I found a drain pipe that led up the side of the building, signaling Bobby and Gabby to scale the wall while I kept watch. I followed them up, and we began our search for a roof access point. Nothing. Time for plan B, then. We'd have to make some noise.

I pointed to one of the air vents on the roof and whispered to Bobby. "That's our way in. I need you to rip if off, as quiet as possible. And by 'quiet' I mean fast, just like ripping off a Bandaid. The faster you rip it off, the louder it'll be, but the sound won't last as long so it'll be less likely to attract the wolves. Got it?"

He nodded and whispered back. "Just let me know when you're ready."

I leaned against the wall at the front of the building and kept an eye on the deader herd. Then, I gave him the signal. Bobby grabbed the vent cover with one hand and tore it from the roof like a carnival strongman tearing a phonebook in two. The noise was loud, but not as bad as I thought it would be. I crossed my fingers that none of the pack was near enough to hear.

I peeked over the edge of the roof, just to see how many deaders we'd riled; roughly twenty were headed toward us. We weren't in much danger unless they rushed the front of the store, and even then they might not get through. Still, a hundred deaders banging on a plywood barricade would just draw in more deaders, so I was glad the noise hadn't been any louder. Satisfied that we were undiscovered, I was just about to go check out the hole in the roof when I noticed movement inside that minivan. Apparently whoever was trapped inside had heard the racket.

Out of curiosity, I pulled out the optic again and took a look at the van's occupant. From my higher vantage point, I could just see through the windshield into the space between the front seats, and was greeted by a face I'd never thought to see again.

Lo' and behold, it was Sam Tucker.

S am Tucker was a caravaneer and scavenger who worked all the abandoned cities south and west of Austin in the Corridor. He had based his operations out of the settlement where Kara and I had lived and frequented her bar before the 'thrope attack. He was also one of the few friends I had in this world, and on the even shorter list of people I trusted. No way I was going to leave him to die.

Through the monocular, I could see he was looking around to locate whoever or whatever had made all that racket. From what I could tell, he looked to be in pretty decent shape. The weather had turned cooler, so he couldn't be baking too much inside the van during the day. Still, I'd bet dimes to donuts he was running out of water and food, and that he wouldn't last two more days. Most folks couldn't carry more than three or four liters on them, and even if he'd rationed his water out, he was probably on his last dregs.

I put the monocular up and crawled over to Gabby and Bobby. "New plan. We're going to go inside this place and get what we need, then I'm going to draw off that herd while you two rescue the occupant of that vehicle down below."

Gabby arched an eyebrow and smirked. "I take it you know this person?"

"He's not a punter—he's a friend from the settlements. And not only that, but I figure he was tracking the wolves after they took everyone—there's no other reason why he'd be here. He might have some useful intel on the status of Kara and the settlers, and what we're facing."

Bobby raised his hand. "You should let me do it. I'm a lot faster, plus I'm not sick." I started to protest, but he held up a hand to shut me up. "Now, now, you know as well as Gabby and me that you're not exactly up to snuff. All it would take is for you to have another episode, and then those shamblers would have you for dinner. I'll draw them off, and you and Gabby get what you need from inside. I'll meet you back at the church before dawn."

I couldn't argue with his logic. "Alright, you win. Let's get what we came for, and then we'll deal with Sam."

I stuck my head into the hole we'd made, and saw nothing but a lot of HVAC vents and a drop ceiling about ten feet or so below. We'd lucked out and broken in over the upstairs offices. I pulled a rope out of my pack, tied it off on one of the HVAC units on the roof, and swung into the darkness below, sliding down until my feet hit a ceiling tile. I kicked it to the floor below, then I followed it down, sliding down the rope with care so I didn't tear more flesh from my already damaged hands.

At the bottom, I moved off to one side and drew the sword. The tomahawk might have been better for close spaces, but I had tied it to my pack, so the katana would have to do. Gabby and Bobby dropped down and fell in behind me, and we moved forward to explore the store.

We stopped at the exit to the room we'd dropped into, which was a storeroom for returned goods. I looked around and grinned; it was a mess, but if previous visitors had ransacked the showroom floor, this was where we'd find what we needed. I signaled Bobby to listen for deadheads outside the door, and he indicated that he heard nothing moving on the other side.

We entered the store's stock room, which looked similarly neglected by looters. Something was off with this place, and I wondered what the hell had kept people from ransacking it after the bombs fell and They came. Experience taught me that something bad had to have been keeping people away. Could've been the wolves, or maybe a seriously heavyweight supernatural baddie had decided to make this place their home. Regardless, it was definitely a proceed with caution situation. I gave the "eyes and ears" signal to the kids, and they acknowledged.

I paused at the storeroom door and peeked out the window. If anything was out there, it was quiet as a church mouse. I cracked the door and listened, sniffing the air on the odd chance that I'd catch a whiff of whatever was waiting for us outside. I picked up diddly squat, so I turned to the wonder twins to see if they had caught anything I missed. Both shook their heads with wide eyes and furrowed brows.

I slowly pushed the door open and tiptoed out into the short hall that led to the retail area, sneaking along the wall the whole way. Still, nothing.

I stepped out onto the sales floor and whispered, "Looks like the coast is clear, guys."

And that's when I got blindsided by the biggest, ugliest-looking thing I'd ever seen.

———

ONE SECOND I was whispering to the kids that the coast was clear, and the next I was flying through the air, sailing across the room into the outdoor clothing section. I landed on a rack of ski jackets, which partially cushioned my fall, but hitting the metal frame underneath was still no picnic. I picked myself up and shook the cobwebs off only to see Bobby in his full-on wolf-boy mode, battling it out with a seven-plus-foot-tall monstrosity. The thing had hands the size of dinner plates and wore a military trench coat over a hoodie, cargo pants, and the biggest pair of hiking boots I'd ever seen. It looked sort of human, but I couldn't see its face within its hood, so it was anyone's guess what we were dealing with here.

The first thing I thought when I got a good look at it was, *I didn't know they made hiking boots that big.* The second thought that came to mind was, *Bobby doesn't look like he's doing so hot against this thing.* And he wasn't. The kid would dive under a huge swing of the creature's arm, take a couple of swipes back at the thing's legs, torso, or back, and then the massive beast would snatch him and toss him across the room like a sack of potatoes. All the while, Gabby was filling it with crossbow bolts like a voodoo priestess taking revenge on her cheating ex-boyfriend, with little to no effect.

How did I know it wasn't human? Call it instinct or observation, but between the way it was moving—sort of like a herky-jerky puppet on crystal meth—and the fact that Bobby's attacks didn't slow it in the slightest, I had a strong suspicion that it wasn't of the species *homo sapiens.* Whatever this thing was, it was either impervious to werewolf claws, or it just didn't care. Either way, I needed to get over there and even the odds.

I reached over my shoulder for the katana, only to realize that it flew away from me when I'd sailed across the room. So, I went for the next best thing. I dropped my pack and grabbed my trusty old tomahawk in one hand, and drew my Bowie knife with the other. Weapons in hand, I sprinted back across the room and into the battle.

As I got close to being within striking range, the creature seemed to sense me and swung an arm in my direction. But the battle lust sung a war song deep inside my chest, high and pure and sweet, so I didn't even slow down. I just slid underneath that huge tree limb of an arm and hacked at the thing's right thigh above the knee as I slid past. Then I spun and slashed the back of its leg above the knee with the Bowie knife, ducked as it tried to grab me with its other arm, and slashed at its Achilles' tendon on the other leg.

I rolled away as the thing staggered and fell to one knee. Bobby jumped on its back and began ripping and tearing at it with his claws and teeth. Gabby, now out of crossbow bolts, threw cutlery at the thing with reckless abandon. Where she'd found the knives was anyone's guess, but she had buried about half-dozen folders and fillet knives into the thing already.

Then, the damnedest thing happened; it got back up. *What the hell was this thing?*

As it clambered to its feet, it grabbed Bobby off its back and threw him clean across the place into a climbing wall about thirty feet away. The kid bounced off it and landed on his feet, but I could tell he was loopy from the impact. Meanwhile, Gabby backed up some stairs, drawing down now with her little silenced .22 pistol, for all the good it would do. Neither she nor I wanted to start firing unsuppressed rounds in here, not with that huge deader herd outside. We were making enough noise as it was, and I was sure there were probably a couple dozen of them trying to find a way past that plywood already.

With the situation as grim as it was, I needed that katana. *Let's see you get back up with your legs chopped off, you son of a bitch*, I thought as I scanned the room. I searched left and right, high and low, until I saw it, still quivering slightly where it had pierced a mannequin in mid-flight, about twenty-five feet on the other side of the retail floor. I ran as fast as my legs could carry me to that sword, wrenching it free like Arthur pulling the sword from the stone, eager to rejoin the fight.

22

SUBSTANCE

B ut just as I headed back into action I saw something moving, hidden in the shadows of one dark corner of the room by the shoe section. It was a small figure, moving its hands in odd patterns in the dark. Intrigued, I stalked closer, using the shelves for cover so I could blindside whoever or whatever was back there. Sneaking up from behind, I came upon a small man dressed in an old-fashioned black suit, gesticulating and murmuring in some strange, vaguely-familiar foreign language that I couldn't place.

Odder still, he wore a WWII military web gear harness over his suit. An assortment of pistols, knives, metal spikes, grenades, and glass bottles filled with various liquids and powders were attached to it. He also wore a blue Yankees cap to top off the whole ensemble. In short, he was a very a strange sight indeed. The weirdest thing, however, was that his hand movements and murmuring corresponded directly with the creature's movements. *He's controlling it*, I thought. *Son of a bitch.*

I snuck up behind him and placed the sharp side of the sword against his neck. "Call that thing off, or I'll bleed you like a stuck pig."

The little man raised his hands in surrender, and the creature turned toward us and crouched as if ready to save him. The man gave a small gesture, and the thing sagged in place and froze, more puppet-like in stillness than the way it had moved and fought just moments before.

"*Ja*, no need to get ugly. If you were one of Them, I'd be dead already. I surrender, *gewiss*, as it seems I have no choice in the matter." He turned his head, slowly, then gingerly pulled the sword blade away from his neck, more to avoid getting cut as he looked me in the eye than out of fear, it seemed. "Now, if you will please allow me to explain, perhaps we can make further introductions and greet like civilized people, *ja*?"

I considered his request and went with my instincts. "Sure, my interest is piqued. Why not?" I lowered the sword.

He smiled. "*Gut!* Then we should eat while we make acquaintances."

————

I DROPPED the sword to my side, and the little man turned around and nodded. "Rabbi Manny Borovitz, at your service." He gestured to the creature that had attacked us earlier. "My associate, Josef, whom you have already met. He doesn't speak, much—that is to say, not at all, *ja*?" He pronounced 'Josef' as "yo-sef," which I assumed was either the proper German or Hebrew pronunciation.

Although I felt its gaze following me, the creature didn't move a hair as the rabbi spoke. I noted that although he seemed to have a habit of sprinkling German words in here and there, the rabbi had only the slightest accent. If he was from Germany, he'd been gone from his country for a long, long time.

I sheathed the sword and motioned for the kids to join me. Bobby had to pop his shoulder back in place, but he'd be back in fighting form within the hour. Gabby was none the worse for wear, although she kept looking over at Josef with suspicion.

I introduced us each in turn. "I'm Aidan, and that's Bobby, and this is Gabby. Now, can you tell me why your creature attacked us?"

"For the same reason you attacked it. You appeared to be a threat."

I rubbed my back where I'd landed on the clothing rack. "Well, I have to say that getting thrown clear across the store might have had something to do with our assessment of the situation."

The little rabbi shrugged and thrummed his fingers against his stomach. "*Ja*, well, now that's all settled, and no harm has been done. Come, I will feed you, and you will tell me what brings you so close to the wolves and their den." He motioned for us to follow, leading us to a previously hidden corner of the store where he'd set up camp. The space included a stove, sleeping pad and bag, and various camping implements. He lit a small camping lantern and blinked as his eyes adjusted to the light. I observed that his ability to move around the store in the dark indicated he'd been staying here for quite some time.

Rabbi Manny gestured around and grinned. "This store has everything, you know. Camping supplies, dehydrated food, cookstoves—I daresay I don't know why someone didn't clean it out already. But the wolves living in such close proximity are surely a strong deterrent." He began busying himself with various pots and food packages, heating water on a small camp stove and pouring the contents of those packages into different containers as he spoke.

"So, I have been fighting Them for a very long time, *ja*? And, now things are bad, very bad, so I come here to keep the evil ones from making it much, much worse. But there is only me, and Josef, so all I can do is watch, and wait for an opportunity to present itself." He poured hot water into the pots and bowls he'd prepared, then dropped aluminum sporks into each and began handing them out to us. I set mine aside, as did Gabby. Of course, Bobby threw caution to the wind and chowed down. The rabbi shrugged, then gave me a pointed look. "So, I have explained why I am here. Now, perhaps you tell me why you are putting the lives of these young ones in danger, and yourself as well?"

"Fair enough. I'm a hunter for the safe zone settlements out west. The wolves came through a few days ago, rounded all the people up, and brought them here. I aim to bring them back."

He nodded. "Ah yes, I saw the wolves leading some people through a few days back. Weeks ago there were more who came in a smaller group."

Gabby grabbed my arm and whispered in my ear. "He must be talking about the people from Canyon Lake."

I turned to her in time to see a giant meaty fist full of crossbow bolts extend over her shoulder. The hand opened and they fell into her lap. To Gabby's credit, she didn't flinch, although she did give the thing the stink eye. I looked back over my shoulder and watched Josef tromp back off toward the back of the store.

I tilted my chin at Rabbi Manny and jerked a thumb at Josef. "I thought the rabbinical order frowned upon golem creation."

The rabbi sipped from a mug of tea he'd prepared and raised his cup to me. "Ah, a student of history! What do you know about golems, Aidan?"

Since Bobby seemed to suffer no ill effects, I took a bite of whatever dish the rabbi had handed me, if only to give me a chance to think. It was macaroni, and not bad considering it had been dehydrated and sitting on a shelf for the last eight years. I chewed, swallowed, and replied. "Legend has it that golems were created to protect the Jewish people from the Romans. But, the stories go back centuries before that, perhaps to the time of King Solomon."

He tilted his head and smiled. "Indeed, they do at that. The knowledge was passed down from that time to us, perhaps as a means of protecting our people, or perhaps as a test for us, to see if we'd give in to our own hubris. Nonetheless, he is not a golem, per se—at least not in the truest sense."

"Wait a minute. That thing is a deader?"

He pursed his lips and took a sip of tea. "Yes and no. When a Primary—that is, an evil spirit from beyond the Veil—takes over a body, generally speaking they kill the human while taking over their body. 'Kicking out' the person's soul, as it were.

"So, I found this man, who was inhabited by a Primary, and I kicked out the Primary spirit and replaced it with—something else."

I nodded. "You exorcised the spirit, and now you control that thing?"

He sipped his tea. "*Ja*, that is what I am saying."

Bobby raised his hand, and Rabbi Manny nodded to acknowledge him. "So Josef is sort of like Frankenstein's monster?"

The old man wagged a finger in protest. "No, nothing so crude. Where Frankenstein's monster was a misshapen and cruel scientific distortion of the will and intent of Yahweh, Josef is a more pure imitation of His will. Frankenstein's monster was a rebellion against God, an effort to prove that man can become God—Josef is no such thing."

Bobby looked genuinely shocked. "You mean Frankenstein was real?"

I set down my bowl and took a deep breath, deciding Bobby's question led to a deep well with depths I didn't care to explore at the moment. However, I did take umbrage with what the rabbi suggested.

"You're referring to the act of creation in Genesis. No offense, rabbi, but it all seems like the same pretension and vanity at play here. And, if you don't mind me saying so, what you are suggesting seems just as unnatural as anything Shelley wrote about."

The rabbi smiled and cocked an eyebrow. "You are traveling with a lycanthrope—does that not seem unnatural? And both you and the girl are much more than you appear. Yet, you accuse me of unnatural acts?" I tried to keep my face neutral, but I was curious how he might have determined that Gabby and I were... well, altered. He gestured offhandedly. "Do not act as if you do not know what I am talking about. I see things through Josef's eyes that others cannot."

I decided to change the subject. "So, you're telepathically linked to Josef?"

He shook his head slightly. "Not all the time. Just when he is in battle, and I am communicating with him. I wasn't quite sure if you were completely hostile, so I was guiding him earlier to make certain he didn't injure you too badly, at least not until your intentions became known."

Bobby worked a kink out of his shoulder and whispered under his breath. "Gee, thanks."

He raised his hand again, and the rabbi answered. "Yes, *dummkopf*?"

Bobby smiled. "Hogan's Heroes—great show." He scratched his head as if reminiscing for a moment, then he continued. "Um, that thing is huge. Where'd you find him?"

The rabbi nodded. "I found him wandering the streets of Austin, terrorizing survivors. I put a stop to it and put his body to good use. As for his size—if I am not mistaken, he was a professional wrestler when he was alive."

Bobby's eyes lit up. "Cool! Which one? The Undertaker, Kane, The Big Show—oh, The Great Khali?"

The rabbi scowled and ignored Bobby. I glanced around to locate the creature and finally found him staring at us from a distant corner of the store. I realized then that I'd never heard the thing move—not once since we entered the store—which was spooky, considering its bulk. "So, getting back to what you were saying—Josef does have some autonomy, then?"

"Yes, more than I intended. Most golems do not, and those that do nearly always have to be destroyed. However, Josef is unique."

Gabby looked over at it with a puzzled expression on her face. "Does he eat?"

Rabbi Manny's eyes twinkled. "No, *meine liebe kleine*, he does not."

Gabby looked down at her bowl. "Oh. I just thought he might be hungry is all."

The kid must be missing her dog, I thought. I got the feeling she hadn't had many friends growing up, and although I'm sure Bobby and I were swell company, she'd gotten attached to that pup in a hurry. Hopefully we'd be back with the LARPers and on our way to the facility soon so she could reunite with Ghost.

But this was no time to be maudlin; I focused back in on the conversation. "So tell me, Rabbi, what were your plans for stopping the wolves from—how did you put it—making things much worse?"

"I had no plans, really. You see, before all this happened, I was retired. I have lived a very long life—unnaturally long, you might say. There are always side effects to using the Kabbalah, and I have lived well past my years. All the people who I once worked with against the dark are long dead. And things were quiet, for a time. I thought my work was done."

He looked out into the dark corners of the room. "But,

perhaps we can help each other, *ja*? You help me stop the wolves, and I help you rescue your friends. Well, Josef and I, of course."

Bobby sat up and raised a finger in the air. "Scratch, this is interesting and all, but aren't we forgetting something?" I looked at him like a dunce, confused. He pointed to the front of the store. "Or someone?"

I slapped my palm against my head and jumped up. "Crap, I forgot about Sam!"

23

FLY

"Who is this Sam?" the rabbi asked.

"He's a friend of mine from the settlements, and he's stuck in a minivan out in front of this store."

The rabbi nodded. "Oh, yes—he's been there a few days. I've been waiting for the dead to disperse so I could send Josef out to help him, but they seem to have fixated on his presence for some reason. Unfortunately, their numbers are too great a challenge at the moment, even for Josef."

I rubbed my chin and puzzled the matter over once more. "Well, we need to get him out of there, or else he'll die from thirst or starvation. Bobby can safely lead the bulk of the dead away, but I may need your friend to clear a path through the stragglers for me. And, it'd be nice if Sam could rest up in here after we rescue him."

"He is welcome to stay here if he is a friend of yours. Although, I cannot guarantee his safety if the wolves should find us."

I nodded. "Understood. Can you open the back door for us?"

Manny scratched his nose and rocked back on his heels.

"Certainly. Josef and I rigged the door, so it only opens from the inside. Just Josef has gone out since we arrived here. Come, I will let you outside, and see to it that you can escape back to the safety of the store once you have rescued your friend."

We followed Manny to the back of the building, and he unlocked the door so we could leave. Watching Josef squeeze out the doorway was an amusing—and somewhat disconcerting —sight. I followed after him, then paused mid-stride. "Manny, do I need to give Josef any commands while we're out here?"

He laughed. "Oh, *nein*. I assure you, he would not listen. I will guide him from here, *ja*?"

"Sounds good. Be back in a jiffy." I gave a mock salute and exited with Bobby and Gabby on my heels. Once outside I huddled up with the kids. Josef stood several feet away, gazing off at nothing. "Bobby, you know what to do. Raise a fuss, and don't run faster than they can follow. Gabby, follow my lead and help me drop the stragglers who don't take the bait."

Bobby nodded. "You got it, chief." He sped off around the corner and we snuck after him, watching to see how many of the dead would follow. The kid ran straight through the herd, all while singing *Bohemian Rhapsody* at the top of his lungs. When one of the dead got too close, he'd push them over. Within seconds, he was through the herd, with probably ninety percent of them following after him.

That only left twenty-five or so of them to kill. *Peachy, just peachy.* I was about to run forward to start chopping off heads when Josef came barreling out from behind us like a freight train in a tail wind. He began picking up deaders and tossing them onto the roof of the building next door, one after another. It was probably one of the funniest and scariest things I'd ever seen.

Gabby whistled softly. "Damn, remind me not to piss off the old guy. Or his pet monster."

"Ditto that, kid. Let's hope he stays on our side."

Gabby squinted at me. "You think he won't?"

"First rule of the apocalypse: trust no one." I looked back to check Josef's progress, noting that he'd cleared a nice, broad swath out to the van. He turned and looked over his shoulder at us as he tossed two deaders at once about forty feet, in a high arc that landed them on the adjacent roof. "Looks like that's our cue. Let's get Sam before more show up."

We ran out to the van, but Sam was nowhere in sight. I looked through the passenger window and behind the front seats, where I found him cowering in hiding, likely scared shitless after watching the golem toss those dead around. I tapped on the window, just to see him jump.

Once he recognized me, he sat up faster than I'd ever seen a middle-aged guy move, unlocking the side door and sliding it open with alacrity. The smell that wafted out of the van was a combination of old piss, sweat, and fear. His face was ashen, and his eyes were practically bugging out of his head. "Scratch, holy shit! You're the last person I thought to see here." He paused and looked around, finally locating Josef behind the van, still tossing deadheads like frisbees. "Is the big guy with you?"

I screwed my face up to the side and gave half a shrug. "Sort of, but it's a long story. I'll explain once we're inside." I grabbed him by the collar and attempted to haul him out of the van. "Now, let's get moving, old-timer, before any more company shows up."

"Wait, wait, wait—hang on just a minute! I didn't get stuck in a minivan for three days just to lose what I risked my skin for." He snagged a messenger bag and tossed it out the door to me. "Carry that for me. My legs are asleep."

Gabby and I pulled him out of the van and started helping him limp back to the rear door of the building. But before we could take three strides, Josef had snatched Sam up, cradling him as he sprinted ahead of us. It was frightening how fast, and how quiet that thing was. I wasn't sure if I wanted to kill it or become a rabbi so I could make one of my own.

Sam slapped and struggled against the thing to little, if any, effect. He finally gave up, apparently resigned to the indignity of being hauled around like a sleepy child. "I'm too old for this nonsense, being carried by Grape Ape here like a sack of damn potatoes," Sam mumbled under his breath, likely thinking no one could hear him.

I chuckled and looked at Gabby, who looked amused by his antics as well. Giving me a puzzled look, she leaned over as we jogged after the golem. "What's a Grape Ape?"

"I'll explain it later. Let's get back inside before more of the dead show up."

———

SAFELY BACK INSIDE, introductions were made all around, and we got caught up on what had happened since I'd last seen Sam. I gave him the Reader's Digest version of our story, and he gave me a shit-eating grin as I finished up.

"Well, Scratch, you always were one to end up knee deep in manure with no boots on."

"Yeah, I'm a regular Barney Fife. That's our story. Now, tell me how you ended up locked inside a minivan in Austin with two hundred shamblers for company."

He rubbed the back of his neck and took a deep breath. "Well, when those wolves showed up I knew it was going to be suicide to fight back. I ain't no hunter—never have been and never will be. But, I couldn't just leave all those folks to get caught and be taken away without a trace, either.

"I hid until they were gone, and I followed 'em. Tracked 'em all the way out here to where they have all the settlers held captive. Hardest part was staying close enough to them to keep the deaders clear. Damnedest thing, you know. Those deaders would just scramble as soon as the wolves got within a few hundred yards of 'em."

The rabbi chimed in. "Did they have the vampire with them?"

Sam nodded. "Yeah, that pretty one? Every step of the way."

"Hmph. Piotr must be feeding very well, to have such control over the dead."

That caught my attention. "Second time I've heard that name in as many days. You know this creature?"

The old man nodded. "*Ja,* he is a vampire from the old times, many centuries old. He has been moving behind the scenes in world politics for some time, I believe. And he is very dangerous. I might not even pit Josef against him if he's as well-fed as I think he must be."

I filed that info away under "intel that might save your life someday" and nodded at Sam to continue.

He cleared his throat and sipped the tea that the rabbi had made for him. "I followed them to that compound of theirs and hid close by, hoping I might get a chance to communicate with some of the people they took. Then about a week ago, who do I see but your girl Kara, wandering around the place with that creepy vamp.

"I watched them for a while, observing where they went. Wolves couldn't keep that whole place on lockdown all the time —they don't have the bodies, you see. I waited until that blood-sucker left her alone in the building they were working at, and I snuck inside."

I leaned forward and stared at him intensely. "Sam, please tell me you spoke with her—"

He held a hand up and cut me off. "Now, now—I'm getting to that—hang on a minute. So I creep into this place, and it's a lab or something. I walk down a hall and turn a corner, and through this window I see Kara working on some machinery. Part of it is submerged in water, and there's this blue glow coming from it. She's wearing a lab coat of all things and seems to be fiddling with the gear, then checking some computer and doing calculations. Scratch, I think she's working with Them."

I shook my head, not willing to believe what the wendigo had told me, even with the corroboration of Sam's account. "No way, she would never—" I paused mid-sentence, realizing why the Pack took the whole town. "Unless they threatened the other settlers. Especially the kids. It would make sense if that's why they took them, to use as leverage to get her to cooperate."

Sam scratched his chin. "If you don't mind me asking, what's she to Them?"

I looked around the room at each face in turn and sighed. "Well, I didn't believe it, mostly because my source was unreliable at best. But, apparently Kara was an expert on nuclear energy, back before the War."

Rabbi Manny slapped his knee and sat up straighter. "This all makes sense if they have a nuclear reactor where they are working." He gave me a grave look. "You know something about what this means, I take it?"

"Yes, now that I have some confirmation about what my 'source' told me. From what I understand, they're trying to create a permanent door through the Veil, from our world straight into Hell."

[24]
PALE

J aws dropped all the way around the room. Sam spoke up first. "You're shitting me, right? A doorway to hell—not downtown Austin during South by Southwest week—but the real thing?" He threw his hands up in the air. "Oh, now I've heard it all."

Rabbi Manny leaned back with his thumbs in his suspenders and clucked his tongue. "Do not be so quick to discount what Aidan," he inclined his head toward me, "who you call Scratch, has said. You have seen the results of these evil ones crossing over with your own eyes. And this would only be the beginning, should Piotr find a way to open a gateway through the Veil."

Sam crossed his arms and pursed his lips. "Well, I'm no theologian, nor am I a scientist. I was just a pissant history professor working at a pissant community college teaching pissant kids revisionist history before all this shit started. But, I can tell you this; they're looking for something, and they haven't found it yet. And they need it to do whatever they're trying to do with that machine Kara was working on. Take a look."

He reached into the duffel he'd asked me to carry earlier

and pulled out a satchel, tossing it over to me. It was light, so I assumed it held papers of some sort. I opened it, and sure enough, it was full of maps—maps that someone had scrawled on with notes, written in a flowing, Victorian script. I studied them for a few minutes, then handed them to the rabbi. "Looks like they're trying to find more fuel for the reactor."

Sam nodded slowly. "Hmmm. I figured they were just trying to create a source of electricity, but I suppose your explanation makes more sense." He shook his head. "I can't believe I just said that, but it does."

The rabbi's brow furrowed and his eyes narrowed as he shuffled through the maps. "This, this is bad. If they get what they are looking for, they will possibly be able to create enough energy to make a breach between worlds. And based on these notes, I believe you are correct. Piotr wants to make it permanent."

I sucked air through my teeth as I considered the implications. "Rabbi, what would that mean if they were able to do what they intend?"

He tapped his chin with a finger. "Well, the creatures that we have dealt with so far, they are powerful and dangerous, certainly. But we have long suspected that they are merely foot soldiers, low-level creatures doing the bidding of some greater entity, or entities. I do not think we wish to see what would step through such a portal, should these wolves and the vampire be able to accomplish their task."

"And your girlfriend," Sam added.

I scowled at him. "It's not her fault."

"Yeah, Scratch, it kinda is. I did speak with her, right after I snagged those maps. She didn't seem to be at all nervous about what was going on, and she also refused to leave with me."

I had to take a deep breath before I spoke, to keep from

losing my cool. "They're holding the other settlers hostage to make her work for them, Sam. Isn't that obvious?"

"Maybe." He rubbed a hand across his bearded face, and I realized how haggard he looked. He'd been through hell, trying to do whatever he could to save Kara and the settlers. He had balls the size of boulders, to sneak into that compound and back out again.

But also, I recognized the indecision in his eyes as he struggled over what he would say next. "I wasn't going to say anything about this, but you deserve to know. Kara and that vampire—they've gotten very cozy. Like knowing each other in the Biblical sense, cozy."

I stared daggers at him, unwilling to believe it. Even so, the soldier and pessimist in me tended to look at things from all angles. That part of me constantly expected betrayal and subterfuge. I took a few deep breaths and allowed my analytical side to take over.

The room was deathly quiet as I spoke in a low, calm voice that was in direct opposition to my emotions. "You saw this with your own eyes?"

He hesitated. "Er, not exactly, but the way they—" he stopped himself, unsure of whether to go on. "You sure you want to hear this?"

I nodded and maintained eye contact. "I need to know."

He sighed. "Shit. Alright then." He scratched his head and looked down at his hands as he fumbled around with a loose thread on his trousers. "They were kissing and holding each other like lovers, Scratch. All intimate-like. And she looked like she was enjoying it."

I was a bit numb at the news, to be honest, but not shocked. I knew that the women, and even the children, might be abused by the punters who worked with the wolves. I even considered that the 'thropes might rape the women; although from what

Bobby had suggested, it seemed that they preferred the company of their own kind over humans.

But never did I imagine that Kara would take up with a bloodsucker. The thought hadn't once crossed my mind because I'd never seen a nos' show any sexual interest in a human at all. We were all just cattle to them, blood sacks, waiting to be drained. Apparently, this Piotr character, he was different. I exhaled forcefully, and it came out as a growl.

Rabbi Manny took a deep breath and sighed. "This means nothing. Piotr and his kind, they are fond of using their powers to control humans, to bend them to their will." He tried to catch my gaze, but I continued to listen while staring a hole in the wall. "I assure you, she is not doing any of this of her own free will."

Gabby was seated next to me, and I could feel her staring, although she knew when to leave me alone. She was like that—sharp enough to know when to talk, when to listen, and when to let things lie. But, I could tell this had her on edge. The kid took her lead too much from me these days. I worried that it'd get her killed before this mission was over.

I erased those thoughts from my mind and let the icy calm of professional detachment settle over me, up from that place way down deep that I'd discovered back in the 'Stan. No one else had anything to say, so I let the quiet wash over me, counting my breaths. And when I'd slowed my heart to below sixty beats a minute, I spoke.

"I'm going to kill that evil bloodsucking sack of shit, and send it straight back to hell. And there ain't nothing that's gonna stop me from doing it, not in this world or the next. I swear it."

BREAD

We gathered up what we needed from the store, and Gabby and I headed back to the church within the hour, eager to get back to Bobby and see that he'd made it there safely. Sam stayed with the rabbi and the golem, although he clearly had his reservations about the creature. "That thing ain't natural—that's for sure," he'd mumbled under his breath with a sideways glance.

Me, I wasn't so sure it was as dumb as it looked, nor as the rabbi let on. I reflected on the fact that humans had been transformed into monsters due to being inhabited by Them, and I wondered what sort of supernatural entity could kick one of Them out to take over one of us. The thought did not fill me with confidence in Josef's reliability as an ally.

Despite my misgivings, I asked if the rabbi would be up for helping us when the time came. He said he'd help us, *quid pro quo, Clarice*, but like everything else, I'd believe it when I saw it happening.

We made it back to the church by morning, and Bobby was waiting for us. "Man, that was a blast! I had those deaders behind me for a couple of miles. Left them behind about three miles north of here. Hopefully they're still heading that way."

"Did you see any of the wolves?" I asked, with a tinge of frustration in my voice. My impatience wasn't aimed at Bobby, but at the shitty circumstances that had brought us to this point. I was upset about Kara, and I was letting it affect me. I realized that I needed to tighten my shit up until it was time to let the Kraken loose, or else yours truly might blow this whole freaking thing before I could put my plan into action.

Bobby cocked his head and frowned. "No, I didn't see any of them. In fact, I haven't smelled a fresh trail since we got here. I wonder what they're up to. Are they holed up inside that compound, or out doing long range patrols?"

I just grunted and walked away. I knew it wasn't fair to Bobby to be short with him, but I wasn't in the mood to entertain an infectiously chipper werewolf.

As I walked out of the room, I heard Bobby whispering to Gabby. "Geez, what'd I say?"

"I'll tell you about it later, wolf boy," Gabby replied. The walls were thin in this place, and I could hear her smoothing things over for me as I walked off. "Go rest up, because I got a sneaking suspicion that we're going to be busy tonight. Tell you what—I'll take first watch so you can rest before you have to go out again."

Bobby agreed, but continued mumbling and bitching to himself as he walked off. "Whatever you say, Gabs. Sheesh. Scratch sure has his panties rolled in a wad today. Does he have the decency to say, 'Good job, Bobby, on leading off the herd of two hundred zombies?' Or, 'You're a valued member of the team, and we wouldn't be able to pull off this rescue mission without your exceptional and unique lycan skills?' No, we couldn't have that, because a little pat on the back and team member recognition would just be too much to ask, no siree Bob—"

I tuned him out and decided to break out the old deep breathing exercises, the ones I used when I first got back from Afghanistan. I'd been a wreck of a man back then and had hated taking the drugs they gave me. So I'd got into deep breathing, prayer, and I spent a buttload of time by myself in the woods. It's what saved me when the shit hit the fan, because I happened to be out in the sticks when the bombs dropped. Hopefully, I could use some of that Zen mind juju today to get my head right.

But my thoughts kept returning to Kara. All I could think about was that I'd failed her, because I hadn't been there to protect her when she needed me. I remembered what she'd said to me during the last conversation we'd had, right before I left to investigate the threat the wolves presented to the settlements.

"You're always so busy saving other people, Scratch, that you don't consider the people closest to you."

Her accusation was a bitter pill, a lump in my throat that kept coming back up to remind me of my failure. I sat down close to the wall, legs crossed, and recited Psalm 23, my prayer of protection. But the passages that kept coming to mind were from Exodus 21, verses 24 and 25:

"Eye for eye, tooth for tooth, hand for hand, foot for foot, burning for burning, wound for wound, stripe for stripe."

And I was prepared to burn the whole place down if that's what it took to get back my Kara. I nodded off and dreamed of killing Them.

———

WHEN I WOKE, it was already getting dark, and Gabby was sitting at the window keeping watch.

"I decided to let you sleep. You looked like you needed it."

I rubbed the back of my head and shook out the cobwebs. "You didn't have to do that, kid."

"Yeah, well—I did. Alright?" She said it like a challenge, rather than a question. I knew better than to make a big deal out of it. That was one thing I'd learned from four years of dating a fiery redhead. Instead, I did the polite and smart thing to do.

"Thanks, kid." I tightened up the laces on my mocs. "Did you talk to Bobby?"

"You mean, did I explain why you were all grumpy and pissy with him, for no apparent reason?"

"Uh-huh. That's what I meant."

She smirked. "Well, I did—but that doesn't get you off the hook. He's sensitive for a werewolf, if you hadn't noticed."

I grunted. "I've noticed. I'll talk to him."

She nodded, and that was that. That was another thing I liked about the kid; unlike some people I'd known, she knew how to let things go. You talked about it, you settled it, it was done. That's how the kid rolled. I admired that quality in her.

I grabbed some food from my pack and went off to find Bobby. Gabby called after me as I walked out of the room. "He's in the kitchenette. Something about making pudding. I don't know what pudding is, so I just left him to his—um, I have no idea what to call it."

I raised a finger over my shoulder in acknowledgment and wandered down the hall to the little kitchenette, where Bobby was elbow deep in a mixing bowl, whisking something that smelled like chocolate, and looked like baby poop.

He looked up at me and grinned. "Big night, so I figured we'd celebrate. Gabby said she'd never had chocolate pudding before, so I decided to see if I could salvage what I found in the cabinets."

I nodded. "What'd you use for milk?"

"Dry baby formula." He dipped a finger in the concoction and licked it. "It tastes okay, once you get over the consistency."

He offered me a spoonful. "Um, I'll pass." I ran a hand through my hair. "Look, kid, about earlier—"

Bobby kept whisking away. "Don't sweat it. Gabby told me about Kara." He stopped whisking and looked up at me. "Look, no wolf expects their alpha to be perfect. All we expect is that we can rely on our pack leader when they have to lead. And I know I can follow the calls you make. So, no worries—we're good." He went back to whisking.

I didn't know what to say, so in typical guy fashion, I said nothing. Then, I had a real brainstorm. "Thanks, Bobby. I appreciate it."

He didn't look up, but he smiled a little. "Yeah, well, you saved my life. Those punters would've taken me to Van, and there's no telling what would've happened. He might've killed me, or more likely he would have held me hostage."

"Hostage? For what?"

"Oh, didn't I mention this? My dad's the Coastal pack alpha."

Now that was a revelation. "Um, nope."

He nodded and stirred the bowl for a few more seconds, then pulled out the whisk and checked the bowl. "It's almost starting to peak." He whisked furiously now. "And like I said—" *whisk whisk whisk,* "I owe you—" *whisk whisk,* "but also—" *whisk whisk,* "so does my dad."

"Huh." I considered what he was saying and shook my head. "You know what, kid, you don't owe me a thing. I helped you because it was the right thing to do, not because I wanted something. As far as I'm concerned, we're friends. So, I have your back, you have mine. End of discussion."

He stopped whisking and admired his work like Michelangelo admiring the Sistine Chapel. "Perfect." He wagged the whisk at me and cocked his head to the side. "I know why you did it. Because you're a good guy. Why do you think I'm still hanging around? You may not realize it, Scratch, but people like you are few and far between these days."

I was flattered, but also a little embarrassed by his frank statements. He grinned. "Don't bother saying anything. I know you're no good at talking about your feelings. But do me a favor and let Gabby know my mousse is ready."

I was glad he'd let me off the hook. "Will do, kid. And, uh, good talk."

Bobby just shook his head and chuckled.

———

THE "MOUSSE" was a hit with Gabby, but I skipped it since I didn't want to risk getting a case of the runs before our mission. Gabby decided to go for it, but she had a tougher stomach than me, having grown up eating bugs and bark with her uncle and Captain Perez. And Bobby, well—that kid could eat anything.

"Hey, I thought chocolate was bad for dogs," I quipped as I watched them wolf down the contents of the mixing bowl.

"That's only true for house dogs, I think," Bobby replied, with chocolate baby formula pudding all over his face and hands.

Gabby licked her fingertips and grinned. "I don't care what it does to dogs or wolves—all I know is that chocolate pudding is now my all-time favorite food."

I laughed. "Yeah, you're not going to be saying that when you're sitting on the toilet for the next two days."

Bobby frowned. "Uh-uh! I sniffed every ingredient. You think don't know what salmonella smells like?"

I held up my hands in mock surrender. "Alright, Chef Boyardee, I believe you."

Gabby wiped her hands daintily with a slightly damp rag and patted her stomach. "Oh, that was good." She looked over at me and arched an eyebrow. "So, fearless leader, what's the plan?"

I pulled out the map Sam had drawn of the local area, including the wolf compound and all the buildings adjacent to it. I plopped it down on the table and stabbed a finger at an X I'd drawn. "We're packing up and going here, to this high-rise across from their base. It's about ten or eleven stories tall—plenty high to set up an observation post and get a handle on their movements."

I pointed at our target on the map. "Once we have an idea of how many are here, how many are in the field looking for more uranium or whatever else they are trying to use to blow a hole in reality, and what their patrol schedules are like, then we spring the trap on them." I clapped my hands shut and interlaced my fingers tightly. "And squeeze."

Bobby gave me a thumbs up. "Oh, I liked that last part. That line is going in my book, for sure."

Gabby looked at him with derision. "What book?"

"My memoirs, of course."

She put her hands on her hips and lifted her chin. "Bobby, I've never seen you writing anything, not even a to-do list."

He pulled his shoulders back and gave her "the hand." "Oh, I'm writing, believe it. But just because you don't see me writing, it doesn't mean I'm not writing." He tapped a finger on his skull. "It's all up here. I've got eight chapters in my head already."

Gabby rolled her eyes and I coughed to get their attention. "Anyway, back to the plan. We're taking that building tonight—it's probably infested with the dead, but we only need to take the stairwells and the top three floors. The plan is for us to work our way through the bottom floor to the emergency stairs, then secure the doors to each floor as we work our way up, taking out any deaders we come across with as much stealth as possible. When we get to the top three floors, we'll clear them out one at a time. Then we'll set up observation posts on the top floor and the roof."

Gabby sat back in her chair and crossed her arms. "I still don't see how we're going to take out those wolves. You nearly died fighting just one of them. Granted, you hadn't yet taken the serum at the time, but you're not exactly one hundred percent right now, either."

I pulled up my sleeve and showed them the bite mark. There were still some gangrenous black lines emanating from the site, but it was clear that they were receding. "I'm not one hundred percent, and that's a fact. But, that will work to our advantage tonight. Now, here's how things are going to go down—"

We got to the building a little after midnight, and I had Gabby and Bobby stay hidden while I scoped the place out. There were a couple of shamblers around, but not in serious numbers. I looked up at the building and counted floors, noting the broken windows on the south side. I assumed that was from when the bombs had fallen, but I didn't think the pressure wave had been powerful enough to reach this far away from the blast area.

On closer inspection, it appeared that the someone or something had broken the windows in random patterns; it could have been due to random violence or just plain old entropy. At any rate, we weren't going to be staying long. I jogged up to the doors and snuck in while moving as carefully as possible. I wasn't concerned about the deaders, as they'd likely ignore me. But, if there were any revenants in here, they'd come running for a meal just as soon as they spotted me.

The first floor was mostly clear of the dead; I pushed the few stragglers I found into offices and locked them inside. I located a stairwell and did a quick visual and auditory on it. It sounded like it might be busy, but not very. I searched around for a second set of stairs and found a door, but someone had barricaded it from the inside. *Weird.* Intrigued, but with no time to solve any mysteries, I returned to the entryway and signaled Gabby and Bobby to come inside.

"Probably a few dozen deaders in the stairwell. I'll lead, Gabby follows, and Bobby takes up rear position. No firearms. We don't want to draw attention to ourselves yet—not until we're ready to spring the trap. Now, let's go." I had my tomahawk in hand, knowing the katana would be too big to do much good on the stairs. I opened the exit door, and we began our eleven flight battle.

The first few levels were easy, since the dead were only coming at us two or three at a time. I'd take the first one head on, Gabby would pop the second, and that would give me time to handle the third if there was one. No big deal. But, the more noise we made, the more deaders we alerted to our presence. Soon, we heard lots of slow, ponderous footsteps coming our way.

"I think we're about to get overrun. We're going to have to lead them onto one of these floors and lock them in while we take the other staircase. Then, we can go up a flight and doubleback to this set of stairs. Bobby, you take point and lead Gabby to the other fire exit, which is on the opposite side of this floor. Just be aware that someone barricaded the first-floor exit door from the inside. So, if things go south, you'll have to head up and not down. Got it?"

He nodded. "No problemo, boss."

Gabby cocked her crossbow, loaded another bolt, and followed him through the door. And with little time to spare; in seconds, I was ass deep in the dead and swinging for the fences. I took out a few to trip the others up and to serve double-duty in keeping the door open for the rest. Then I followed Gabby and Bobby inside the building.

Once, these floors had housed tech firms, attorneys, accountants, and publishing companies. Now, they housed only the dead. The general layout of the building was pretty standard, consisting of a square hallway that went all the way around the floor. Office entrances were every thirty feet or so, with the odd storage or mechanical closet thrown in for variety. Other than that, it was a straight shot to the other stairs, with little opportunity for slowing the dead down or evading them, should something go wrong.

My strategy was simple. It consisted of moving slowly enough so the bulk of the deaders in the stairwell would follow me in, but fast enough to stay ahead of them so I didn't get swamped. The problem was, I'd forgotten that these things mostly ignored me these days. So, I had to get ugly. Once I started splitting heads, they perked up quite a bit and took an interest. After that, it was just a matter of leading them down the hall, and then circling back to the stairs and shutting the door behind me.

After I had moved the bodies out of the way and locked them in, I listened for Bobby and Gabby to return to the stairwell from the floor above. I waited for a good two minutes, then realized that something had gone wrong. *Shit. I should never have allowed us to get separated*, I thought. But there was no sense crying over spilled milk. I headed up and see what was keeping them.

———

I SPRINTED up the stairs to the floor above, slowing only enough to open the door without announcing my presence to every shambler that might be present. I listened for sounds of violence coming from the halls, but only heard faint echoes of conversation coming from the left-hand hallway. One of the voices was

Bobby's, but I didn't recognize the other. I tiptoed my way down there to see what the hell was going on.

As I got closer to them, I began to catch pieces of the conversation. "Tell me, why are you here? Did Van send you to spy on me?" The voice was deep and gruff, and somewhat pained, as if the speaker was ill or perhaps injured.

I heard Bobby reply. "Look, we didn't mean to bother you. Just let her go and we'll leave."

"Maybe I will, or maybe I'll just have a meal at your girlfriend's expense. Or is she your sister?" I heard whatever it was sniff loudly. "No, she's not a wolf. Van didn't send you, then. He'd never let valuable merchandise get away, that's for sure. So why is a whelp like you traveling with a human?"

Bobby muttered a meaningless reply, but I could tell that he was out of excuses. I drew the Glock and screwed the silencer on the barrel, stepping into view and putting a bead on the thing's head as I did. It was a 'thrope, that was for certain, but it didn't look right at all. It appeared as though it had started to shift and gotten stuck between its human and werewolf forms. It also looked scraggly and sick, sort of like a stray dog with the mange. It had one long, clawed hand clapped over Gabby's mouth, holding her firmly in place by pressing her head against its chest. He'd disarmed her as well; her crossbow lay in one corner, and her kukri and Kabar had been tossed into another. Gabby was fighting—scratching and kicking with everything she had—to no avail. She may as well have been fighting a brick wall.

"Oh goodie, another visitor," the wolf said, smiling in a grotesque manner that pulled the features of its half-human, half-werewolf face into a mockery of amusement.

"I'm packing silver-tipped rounds, and I'll put one right in your eye if you even think about hurting the girl."

The wolf chuckled. "I doubt you're that fast. Or that good."

Years before, when the bombs dropped and the chaos started, I'd found that I wasn't that handy with a pistol. Since then, I'd spent years training myself, doing hours upon hours of fast draw and dry fire drills, and using pellet guns to work on my accuracy without wasting ammo. These days, I rarely missed what I was aiming at with my sidearm.

In the blink of an eye, I dropped the barrel of the pistol a few centimeters and put a round in the thing's shoulder, just inches from Gabby's head. It staggered visibly and gasped as the round hit—not from the impact, but from the pain. Based on my experience with killing the 'thrope at Kara's place, I knew that one round in the shoulder would just be a nuisance to it. But one to the head? That might ruin its day, for good.

It got the message. "Aw, gosh—shit!" The thing clutched at its shoulder and gave me an evil look, releasing Gabby. It stomped around some and jumped up and down in frustration. "I mean, really—who shoots someone to make a point? Doesn't anyone ever talk things out these days?"

Gabby glared at the wolf as she gathered up her weapons, replacing them one by one, except for the crossbow, which she kept in hand. She quipped, to no one in particular, "Yeah, it's like we're living in a post-apocalyptic world or something."

The wolf turned and pointed a long, ugly finger at her. "Exactly! That's what I tried to tell Van. Just because we were living in a savage world, we don't have to act like savages."

I looked over at Bobby, and it was apparent the kid was puzzling something out. He kept his eyes on the wolf while he explained what I was looking at. "Sometimes the weaker wolves can't shift fully, so what you get is a sort of half-werewolf, like this guy. They're seen as being weak, and a liability—omegas. No one wants them in their pack."

The wolf in question was digging a long claw into the hole that the round had made in its shoulder, cursing all the while.

Finally, it pried the bullet out, dropped it on the floor, and sighed. "Ah, that's much better. Much, much better." It looked over at me with a furrowed brow. "That hurt, you know. And it was totally, completely unnecessary."

I ignored the protest. "Okay, so you say you were once a part of the Corridor pack. But if you're an omega, then why'd they let you stick around?"

The wolf chuckled sarcastically. "Well, good question. As it turns out, I was the only one left who knew how to work the reactor." He pulled over the lapel of the dirty white lab coat he wore, pointing to an I.D. badge clipped to his jacket. "Joseph Conway, first-year master's student in nuclear and mechanical engineering, at your service. You can call me Joe."

I tsked and scratched my chin. "So you were their best boy. At least, until someone replaced you recently, you mean."

He nodded sagely. "But such is life. Besides, I didn't know enough about the reactor to get it to do what they wanted. You know how hard it is to cause a controlled meltdown? I mean, seriously, that's way above my pay grade. Anyway, that reactor was never built for that—it's just a test reactor, designed to keep half-stoned grad students from causing another Chernobyl."

His jaw was doing funny things when he spoke. It reminded me of a snake eating a rat. I realized his appearance was weirding me out, and waved my pistol around, gesturing at him randomly. "Do you think you could—you know—change back or something? Your appearance is a little off-putting."

He looked at me with a hurt expression. "That's just racist, man, that's what that is—and plain hurtful besides. I can't help what I am. I mean, I didn't ask to be like this, you know."

I looked up at the ceiling and sighed. "Just change, please. Okay?"

"Fine, whatever." He shifted back into human form, and before us sat a dumpy, nerdy-looking man in his late twenties.

He was going prematurely bald, with a slight potbelly, pock-marked skin, and poor posture. "Happy now?" His voice had gone up three octaves at least and went from gruff to nasally to boot. He pulled a pair of what we in the Army affectionately called "birth-control glasses" from his pocket, and put them on to complete the effect. The guy was like a cross between Booger and Lewis from *Revenge of the Nerds*.

Gabby muttered under her breath. "I think he looked better the other way."

Joe plopped down on the ground and sneered at Gabby. "Oh, sit on a stick, Selena Gomez. And by the way, Pat Benatar called and said that she wants her look back." He huffed and glanced sullenly around the room. "Comes in looking like an extra from *Les Miserables*, and tells me I'm the one who looks bad. The nerve."

Of course, the insults went right over her head, but it got a rise out of Bobby. He looked at Gabby and snickered. "Oh, don't worry Gabs—he may as well have complimented you."

She rolled her eyes. "Whatever."

I glanced at Joe. "Thanks for the info. Now, do you know anything about what they're trying to do with that reactor?"

"Sure, absolutely, but from a scientific standpoint, I don't see how it can work. Then again, I'm a werewolf who gains fifty pounds when he shifts, so I don't know if the laws of physics apply anymore."

Bobby nodded sagely. "Pocket dimensions, dude. That's my theory."

Joe cocked his head and pursed his lips at an angle. "You know, that's entirely possible. Quantum manipulation of compactification manifolds using dark energy to shift matter could create such an effect—"

I interrupted his nerdgasm. "Back to the topic at hand, guys. Can they do it with this reactor? Do they have enough juice?"

He shook his head. "Nope. Based on the calculations I saw from Piotr's notes, they can't do it."

I sighed, and my shoulders sagged with relief. Then Joe raised a finger and continued.

"That is, not until they get the highly enriched uranium they've been looking for."

I did a double-take, then closed my eyes and squeezed the bridge of my nose between my fingers. "Say that one more time?"

Joe looked rather pleased with himself as he explained the situation. "Okay, so the TRIGA reactor that we have at the school was just designed for research and for training future nuclear engineers. Nothing fancy, you see. It runs on UZrH—uranium zirconium hydride—perfectly safe stuff. With UZrH, as the core temperature of the reactor increases, the reactivity of the fuel decreases. Like I said, it was designed to keep stoner grad students from causing a Three-Mile Island incident. But if you replace the fuel rods with enriched uranium, you end up with a reactor that can put out some serious energy."

"By how much?"

He chewed his cheek and squinted. "Oh, I don't know—I mean, I'm just a first-year student, or I was—but I'd say by more than enough to create a sustained meltdown. At least, that's what Dr. Delicious seemed to think."

I bristled at his last comment. "Excuse me?"

"Dr. Delicious? She's the redhead they brought in to replace me. Man, she is so hot—I mean, like smokin' hot. Legs that go on for miles, and those eyes—"

Bobby cut him off mid-sentence. "Let me just stop you right there, dude, before you get hurt."

"Huh?" He looked at me, then at Bobby, and then at Gabby, and put two and two together. "Do you guys know this chick?"

Gabby grimaced and pointed at me. "Um, he does."

Joe's face got beet red, and he started fiddling with his lab coat. "Wow. Oh, I am so sorry. What, is she your sister? Girl-friend? Um, like I said, sorry—and, congratulations?"

I massaged the bridge of my nose again and took a deep breath. "Okay, let me get this straight. Right now, the reactor doesn't have the juice to punch a hole through to this other dimension where they come from. But, if they push enough juice through it, there's a good chance they'll get the desired result?"

Joe cleared his throat. "Yeah, that pretty much sums it up."

"So where are they getting the uranium?"

His face lit up, and he grinned from ear to ear. "See, that's the best part. There's always been this rumor in the depart-ment that there's an old reactor buried under the library at the main campus. Apparently, the government was doing some top secret shit there during World War II and the Cold War—"

"And when are they not?" Bobby mumbled under his breath.

Joe pushed his glasses up on his nose and plowed right on through without missing a beat. "I've always wondered if it was true, you know? Like, a top secret lab, right under campus! Wouldn't that be crazy?"

Gabby yawned. "Thrilling."

"I know, right? So, I mentioned it to Van, and he passed it on to Piotr, and they sent some of the Pack over to check it out."

I rolled the barrel of my gun in a gesture of impatience. "How long ago did they send them?"

Joe shrugged. "I dunno, two, three days? I mean, they kicked me out as soon as Dr. Deli—I mean, your girlfriend—started getting results. I only know about it because sometimes I sneak over there for supplies and stuff, and I overheard Van and Piotr talking about it."

"What else did they say?"

"Well, they said they were having a hard time locating it since that area of Austin was practically ground zero when the bombs fell. But, just a few days ago I heard them say their scouts had found the library, and they were confident they were making progress. They just needed some more help to do an excavation to get under the rubble."

Finally, some good news. "Joe, how many wolves are left here?"

"Maybe half the pack—eight wolves, tops, plus Van." He looked back and forth at all three of us, and especially at our gear. "Wait a minute, are you guys thinking about taking them on? You're freaking crazy. They'll murder you. Even with only half the pack around."

I shrugged. "We'll take our chances."

Joe stood up and wrung his hands. "You don't understand, man. Van isn't like other werewolves; he's an original alpha. Do you know what that means? I mean, think about his name. Van? Ring any bells?"

We looked at each other. "Nope."

Joe rolled his eyes. "C'mon, you don't remember your Scandinavian mythology? Van? Vanagandr? The monster of the river Van? He's freaking Fenrir, the wolf that bit off Tyr's hand."

I drew a blank. "Seriously, you have me at a loss. Who's Tyr?"

He threw his hands up in the air. "Ugh! You guys are hopeless. Tyr was the Norse god of war, and probably a really tough dude in his time. So if Van bit off his hand, think about what that says about him."

I arched an eyebrow. "Yeah, but those are all just myths."

"Just myths? Just myths?" He pounded his hands on his chest. "There's a myth standing right here in front of you. Werewolves are just myths. As are vampires, zombies, and all the other crazy stuff running around out there. I'd say the chances that Van is the Vangandr of the myths are pretty darned good. Not to mention his two right-hand guys are named Skull and Hate. You know, Sköll and Hati, the sons of Fenrir?" He exhaled loudly. "Of course, you don't—why did I even ask?"

I turned to look at the kids. "Bobby, you have anything to add about this?"

He shook his head. "I don't know. I mean, my dad is second gen, one of Van's get. He just told me to stay away from him. I think Dad respects him, but I also suspect that he's more than a little scared of him. And I never really knew my dad to be scared of anything."

Joe raised his hand. "Hey, I'm lost here—who's your dad?"

I decided to keep that info under wraps. "Not important. What is important is that we take out the remaining wolves before the rest of the pack gets back with that uranium. Then, we trash the reactor and get the hell out of here with the settlers. And Kara."

I turned around and headed out the door, gesturing for the kids to follow. "We have work to do. Let's go."

Joe hollered after me. "Hey, what about me?"

I turned around to face him. "What about you? From what I can tell, you've been helping them all along, complicit in everything they've done, from killing and kidnapping settlers, to whoring the women out to punters, to helping them build this doomsday doorway. I'm doing you a favor by letting you live." I paused for effect. "Come to think of it, why don't you tell me why I shouldn't just kill you outright?"

Joe turned a paler shade of pink at the threat. "Look, I'm not much of a fighter, but I hate the Pack. I've been their whipping boy for years. The only reason they turned me was to keep me around to help them with their crazy-ass project." He paused and cleaned his glasses on his shirt tail. "I may not be much of a fighter, but I am smarter than any of you..." Bobby growled next to me, "Just saying, don't get all huffy, because it's probably true. And I know that place like the back of my hand. Hell, I've practically lived there for the past nine years. I know things that can help you out."

"You know things, huh? Well, what do you know about killing deaders? Because we need to clean out the top three floors of this place before dawn. You up for getting your hands dirty?"

"It's not really my thing, but I'm willing to help if it means getting back at Van and his goons."

I looked him in the eye. "Alright, but if you screw us, I'm going to tie you to a cross and disembowel you, and let the vultures eat your entrails. It'll take you months to die. I guarantee it."

Joe gulped loudly. "Okay then, so long as we understand each other."

PERCEIVE

We cleared out the rest of the place without a hitch, then headed to the identical building next door, where we repeated the process. Despite his nerdiness and my distrust of him, Joe turned out to be fairly handy at killing deaders. In fact, he had been responsible for many of the broken windows in the buildings, as he'd found that tossing deaders through the plate glass windows was an easy way to be rid of them. He wasn't nearly as deadly as Bobby, but it so happens that even a runt werewolf is still a force to be reckoned with. I made a mental note to keep an eye on him. He'd be dangerous, if he ever decided to turn on us.

Once we'd gotten the top floors cleaned up, we settled into our new digs. A high-tech conglomerate had occupied the place in the pre-War era, so the area was actually pretty cozy—despite being a bit breezy in places. The tenth floor had a large employee lounge area that came complete with several couches, a foosball table, Nerf basketball, dart boards, and a snack bar that was more or less untouched. It was full of graham crackers, peanut butter packets, trail mix, candy, and microwave popcorn that was useless to us. The place was big, and there was plenty of space even without those offices, so we just shut the doors to keep the wind out and enjoyed the relative comfort of the lounge area.

The other floors and rooms were a bit creepy, though; it was as if the place had been frozen in time. The bombs fell in the middle of the night, which meant almost nobody had gone to work the next day. From what I understand, people panicked, they fought, and they died, and that's when it got interesting— because that's when the dead started walking, and they woke up hungry. After that, it was all chaos. I saw it with my own eyes, albeit a few weeks after it all began. Maybe I missed the worst of it; I really don't know. All I do know is, what I did see was a good indication that things went to shit, and fast.

But, the timing of it all meant that they'd left this place pretty much intact. Not many people thought to hide out in high-rise office buildings once the shit hit the fan. Too bad we weren't going to be staying. Also, too bad we didn't have much time to enjoy it. We had a lot of setting up to do before the big reveal I had planned. I sent Bobby off to run some errands for me, including getting a message to the rabbi and Sam that we were in the building and would be springing the trap come next nightfall. Gabby and I got to work on booby trapping the build- ing. I had grenades, claymores, and other party favors I'd collected over the years, mostly from Army Reserve and Guard units that had either been overrun by the dead or abandoned. They would all be put to good use when the Pack showed up.

We spent a considerable amount of time setting the traps. I placed IEDs and grenade traps at about every third floor on the way up the stairs, and then I began rigging the rooftop with clay- more mines. The trick would be funneling them into key areas so I could hit them with a direct blast. From what we knew, werewolves were durable and they healed fast, but they weren't indestructible. My plan assumed that high explosives in close quarters and eleven-story falls would be fatal to the average werewolf. Hopefully I wasn't placing a sucker's bet.

I made sure we had everything in place, and waited for Bobby to get back with Sam and the stuff I'd sent him to retrieve so I could finish setting the booby traps on the stairwells. After they showed up, I kept Bobby and Joe with me, and sent Sam and Gabby to the adjacent building. They'd be on overwatch duty, and they'd also be instrumental in springing the trap. The only problem was that we'd be separated. If they got into trouble, I couldn't help them. I felt pretty sure I had a reliable means of egress for them if things got too hot, but they still worried me.

But the plan beat having Gabby and Sam in the middle of an all-out rooftop rumble with the wolves. We'd be funneling them into the unobstructed stairwell, and then I hoped they'd trigger the IEDs I'd set up and blow themselves back to hell. I assumed they'd head for the other stairs at some point, so I made sure to trap the doors to the other stairwell on each floor, knowing the first wolves would trigger the traps, then the ones behind them would probably try the other stairway. If we were lucky, I'd cripple or kill half the wolves before they got to the roof of the building. That's where I planned to have my special surprise in store.

My primary concern, beyond keeping everyone alive, was getting all the wolves onto the roof without getting myself killed in the process. Somebody had to spring the final trap, and I'd volunteered to do that myself. But if I got dogpiled by even two of those 'thropes, it could turn into a bloodbath. I felt stronger than I had even a few days before, and from what I could tell the serum was finally getting an edge over the deader venom in my veins, but I still wasn't sure I wouldn't have another episode. I knew it did no good to worry, so I simply rehearsed the plan, over and over again in my head, and tried to get some shut-eye before night came again.

One way or another, this thing was going to be over by tomorrow morning. And whether I lived or died, one thing was for sure; if I was going to have my ticket punched, I'd take as many of those 'thropes with me as possible on my way out.

————

THAT AFTERNOON, I got Bobby and Joe up and prepped, and signaled over to Sam and Gabby to see how they were doing. Sam indicated that things were five by five, so I sat Joe down with the sketch I'd gotten from Sam and started going over the layout of the compound.

He stared at the hand-drawn map for a bit, then started jotting things down. "Let's see... The reactor lab is here, which is where you'll probably find Piotr and your girl. Van and his goons stay in these buildings, and they usually have one or two wolves over here guarding the hostages." He made more notes and circles on the map. "I think that about covers it."

"Alright then." I looked at Bobby and smiled. "You ready for this, champ?"

He nodded. "About as ready as I'll ever be. Besides, I wouldn't miss this for the world. And something tells me you're going to need someone watching your back before this is all over with." He looked pointedly at Joe. I guess the kid didn't trust him either.

Joe looked at us both, and spread his hands apart as he spoke. "Look, if you guys don't believe I'm with you, I can just leave. But, I'd rather stay and have a chance to prove myself. Basically, I'm screwed out here living on my own with no pack. Lone wolves typically don't last long, and especially not runts. I'd be dead anyway within the year on my own, so I see this as my best chance."

I looked him over and tried to determine if he was legit. It was impossible to tell if he was playing us, but I couldn't deny him the chance to prove himself. It just wasn't my style. "Tell you what, Joe. You stay and help us kill these 'thropes, rescue the settlers, and get my Kara back, and I'll take you with us when we leave. But if you cross us—"

"I know, I know—a long, slow, painful death awaits." He leaned back in his chair with resignation. "What choice do I have? I'm going to help."

I glanced at Bobby, and it was apparent that he wasn't buying it. I considered that it was entirely possible that Joe was going to betray us to get back into Van's good graces. But, it was worth the risk. We were short on bodies, and if Joe was sincere, he might help tip the scales in our favor. Even if he turned on us —one more runt wolf wouldn't make much difference.

I stood up and brushed my hands on my pants. "Well, I guess it's settled then. I'm going to check all the traps, then I have to head next door to talk with Sam and Gabby. When I get back, it's going to be go time. Be ready."

Bobby got up as well and followed me out of the room. Once we were well out of werewolf earshot, he spoke up. "I don't trust him, Scratch. His story doesn't add up, and he smells like fear and nervousness."

"Could be anticipation. He doesn't seem like much of a fighter, and he's probably scared of most of the Pack."

Bobby scowled and looked off to the side. "He makes one wrong move, and I'm ripping his throat out."

"You'll get no argument from me there. Now, go fuel up, or lick your nuts, or whatever it is that werewolves do before a big fight. When I get back up here, it's on—"

Bobby interrupted me as he went for a high-five. "—like Donkey Kong! Man, you set me up for that one. Do you know how long I've been waiting to say that in the context of prepping for a fight?"

He didn't pull his hand back, and instead looked at me expectantly. So I figured what the hell and gave him his high-five. He beamed. I chalked it up to nerves and youthful enthusiasm and headed off to finish preparing our little surprise attack.

I walked both stairwells and checked all the traps, starting by setting the tripwires in the blocked off side. Then I went down the other side, checking placement and angles just in case. I figured I'd place the rest of the tripwires on my way back up, but I was being anal on purpose, just to make sure I didn't miss anything. I headed down to the bottom floor, sneaking like a kid skipping school, just to make sure that I didn't tip the wolves off to our presence before we were ready to go.

"So, am I early to the party?" someone said as I exited the stairwell.

I turned and drew my pistol, only to find Colin and not some 'thrope or punter. He wore bike leathers instead of the chainmail he'd worn the last time I'd seen him—kevlar-reinforced leather, not a bad choice. He also had a humongous two-handed sword slung over his back, and various knives and stabbing implements strapped all over his chest and waist. All-in-all, the guy looked pretty freaking dangerous. I was pleased as hell to see him because of it.

"Shit, Colin, I could've shot you." I holstered my weapon

and stuck out my hand. "Damned happy to see you. We're going to need all the help we can get."

Colin shook my hand firmly and grinned. "You kidding? I wouldn't miss this for anything."

"Yeah, I keep hearing that, but somehow I think that once the shit hits the proverbial fan, things are going to go sideways, fast."

He popped some gum and smirked. "Again, not my first rodeo. Besides, these 'thropes have been a thorn in my side for years. I'll be glad to see them go."

I cocked my head and grimaced. "Hopefully, everything will go to plan. If not, nice knowing you."

He shook his head. "Trust me, things are going to turn out alright. I have a feeling about it."

"Well, if you say so. C'mon, I have to brief Gabby and Sam on some last-minute details. I'll fill you in on the way." Colin moved as silently as smoke behind me as I ghosted to the building next door. The few shamblers that were out ignored me, and strangely they ignored Colin as well. I gave him a funny look as a deader shuffled right past us, and he just grinned. Once we got inside the other building, I asked him how he did it.

"It's Celtic magic, believe it or not."

I thought about it for a moment and scratched my chin. "Huh. Can you teach anyone else to do it?"

"Yeah, but you have to be celibate to make it work."

"Oh, bullshit."

He laughed. "Yeah, I'm just messing with you. I killed a deader and rolled around on it just a few minutes ago. Works like a charm until it wears off."

"Thought you smelled a little ripe."

"Eau de zombie. Keeps away women and the dead. Like I said, you have to be celibate to make it work."

"I didn't think you needed any help in that department, the way Anna keeps turning you and Mickey down."

He trudged up the stairs next to me and faked getting stabbed in the chest. "Oh, you really went there, didn't you? That's low, man."

"Hell, man, I'm not laughing at you, I promise. Truth be told, I was never too slick with the ladies myself. Partially because of this," I pointed at the nasty scars on my face, "and partially because I've never been good with most people. If it wasn't for the apocalypse, I'd probably still be single."

He leaned on the railing and popped his gum again. "Well, I wasn't exactly experienced before things fell apart, either. I had a sort of girlfriend, but that didn't go the way I expected."

"What—she turn you down, too?"

He frowned. "Now who's jacking with whom?"

"Pfft. I see how you are, making me feel stupid with your grammar and crap." I knelt to check another trip wire, then stood and brushed myself off. "C'mon, stinky, let's get moving. I want to start killing 'thropes before the sun goes down."

Colin frowned as he pushed off the wall. "Hey, Scratch, before the killing starts, I have one more thing to ask you."

"Sure man, what is it? You want me to convey your undying platonic love to Anna if you don't make it?"

"If you croak, can I have dibs on your girl?"

"Piss off, Colin."

———

I FILLED Colin in on the plan as we headed up the last few flights of stairs. After I'd explained it in full, the big man grinned with delight at the crazy idea I'd cooked up for taking out the pack. He asked me a few questions, and once satisfied with the answers he nodded his approval and slapped me on the back with enthusiasm. It flipping stung like hell, but I wasn't going to tell him that.

We got to the top floor, and I gave a low whistle as I cracked the door so Sam and Gabby wouldn't put a bullet in me. We walked in to find Gabby hiding in a blind spot behind the door, her crossbow in hand and kukri at the ready. Sam was nowhere to be seen, but I knew he was around somewhere.

Colin tilted his head at Gabby while looking at me. "You train her?"

I wiggled my hand. "Some, but mostly she came to me in condition one. She's been pretty much high speed and low drag since I've known her."

Gabby sheathed her kukri and set her crossbow down before waving her hands in front of us. "Hello? I'm right here—you don't get to talk about me like I'm not in the room."

Colin ignored her, covering his hand with his mouth as he leaned over. "Is she always this sensitive?"

I played along and feigned ignoring her as well. "Not always. Sometimes she's worse." Acting as if I was surprised, I looked up and acknowledged the kid. "Gabby! Oh, fancy seeing you here. How's things?"

She picked up a glass paper weight and launched it at me, narrowly missing my head. Then, she narrowed her eyes in mock anger, with just the slightest hint of a smile playing on her lips. "Would've been better if I'd hit you upside the head. Next time, I'll just shoot you to be sure." She turned and beckoned for us to follow. "C'mon, Sam's in here setting up."

We followed her past a reception desk and down a short hall, to a door at the end that was marked, "Lisa Johnson, V.P. of Marketing." All the other doors were closed, presumably to avoid backlighting Sam and Gabby in the sniper's nest they'd set up. While Sam hadn't been a military man, he'd assured me that he'd spent time with a long gun on the range before the War, volunteering with Project Appleseed. Project Appleseed had been a program to teach long gun skills to civilians, with the intention of passing said skills down to a civilian populace that could serve as an apolitical militia in time of need. I wondered how many Project Appleseed attendees were still alive, in part due to the skills they'd picked up at the two-day course.

As we walked into the room, Sam was stretched out on the floor with the .50 caliber sniper rifle set up on a bipod before him, sighting through the scope and practicing picking up targets and estimating ranges. We watched without interrupting him for a good minute or so. He had a notebook next to him, and would jot something down every so often, likely estimating the range to different landmarks around the wolf compound.

It was pretty much guesswork without a rangefinder, and if I had my way, it'd be me up here manning the sniper rifle. But we only had one long gun that was capable of taking out a 'thrope with a single round, and I needed these two watching my back while I drew the wolves to the other tower. They had explicit instructions to take out one wolf, if possible, and then to immediately retreat and head to the north side of the roof in order to provide support to Bobby, Joe and me as we tried to lure the wolves into a trap that would hopefully thin the pack out enough to make it an even fight. Bobby had come through on the goodies I'd asked him to procure, so if we could lure them up, it'd be one hell of a surprise. With Colin here, I thought we just might have a chance.

Sam finally took his eye off the scope and spoke over his shoulder to us. "Two guarding the hostages, one roaming the main compound. I think I can take out the roaming guard, but the other two are too far off. The rifle can make that shot, but I don't think I can."

I knelt down and got on my stomach next to him, elevated on a makeshift platform formed by two desks, a good six to eight feet away from the broken glass pane in front of us. I pulled out my monocular and had a look. He was right; it was a good thirteen hundred yards to where the wolves stood guard. I swung the rifle right and scanned the compound instead, most of which was within a thousand yards of us. If he waited for the guard to do his rounds, he could pop him from within six hundred yards. Not an easy shot on a moving target, but not impossible for a decent marksman, either.

I looked again at the targets and nodded. "Just get the roamer and head to the roof before you're spotted. I need you to trigger the alarm and then get out of sight, so I can finish the job by drawing them to me in the other tower." I sat up and turned to Gabby. "You know what to do if the wolves start heading up here, right?"

She frowned and tilted her head. "We get out, and fast."

Sam groaned softly. "Let's hope it doesn't come to that. I'm too old for all that military operator bullshit."

I nudged him with my elbow. "Yeah, but you're not too tough and chewy for a 'thrope to gnaw on."

He rubbed his eyes and sighed. "The images your words paint just fill me with confidence."

I chuckled. "Wait for the signal, then take that 'thrope out. If you just wound him, don't take another shot. Drop back and head for the roof, no matter what."

"Roger that. I'll keep Gabby safe."

Colin spoke up from the rear. "Chances are, she's going to be doing you the same favor, I think."

I nodded. "He's right, you know. Gabby's here to guard your back, just like you need to watch hers. And her senses are a lot keener than yours are, old man, so if she says trouble is on the way, listen to her." I looked at Gabby as I stood up. "I know I can trust you, kid, but don't get cocky. If the wolves try to crash your party, you crash theirs first."

She crossed her arms and leaned against the wall with one foot propped behind her. "I got this. Don't sweat it."

"Alright then." I looked around, trying to find something else to say and failing. I cleared my throat and stated the obvious. "Well, I guess we'd better get this show on the road."

As we walked out the door, I clapped her awkwardly on the shoulder in farewell. Before I knew it, she had me wrapped in a fierce, breath-stealing bear hug. I froze for a moment, unsure of what to do, then I hugged her back, briefly. She let me go after a few seconds and slugged me on the shoulder. Her eyes were damp, but I knew she wouldn't cry in front of me, at least not before a mission.

Then she smirked and looked me in the eye. "Don't get killed, or I'll kick your ass."

"Right back 'atcha." Colin was eyeing us both with amusement. I tilted my chin up at him. "You ready?"

"Hell yes, I'm ready. If you two are through having your Oprah moment, then I'd like to get on with kicking some lycanthrope ass."

We left without another word, with Gabby mumbling behind us. "I still don't know what an Oprah moment is, damn it."

C olin and I set the trip lines on all the booby traps as we headed back upstairs, then everybody got in position on the rooftop while I geared up. For some added protection I donned a ballistic helmet and vest, on which I had my .45's and the MP7's strapped where I could get to them immediately. I kept the katana strapped to my back, and I had my Bowie and tomahawk on my belt. Finally, I placed the Stoner light machine gun on its bipod on top of one of the HVAC units, where it provided me with a clear field of fire. I had the LMG set up with a belt-feed system that was attached to eight hundred rounds of silver-tipped 5.56, and it was pointed at the roof access door.

The Stoner would only be good for the rounds on the belt; then I'd fall back to the MP7's, and finally, the katana. I doubted that there'd be time to lock another belt in place, once the wolves started coming out that door. That was if the Stoner didn't jam; I'd done plenty of preventive maintenance on it, but it was fussy, especially with reloads. At least I knew I'd have Colin up here with that big-ass sword backing me up if it failed.

I did one last check on our routes of egress, also double-checking the "surprise" I'd set up earlier with Bobby's help.

That little dandy consisted of about forty pounds of Tannerite packed inside an HVAC unit, along with all the scrap metal we could find. Tannerite was an explosive that you could have bought over the counter before the War. A lot of gun guys used it for fun back then, because it would detonate when struck with a high-velocity round. So you haul an old junk car out to your cow pasture, put some Tannerite in it, shoot it, and watch the damn thing get blown to bits. Like I said, fun. It was relatively safe in small amounts, but in larger amounts it could be deadly.

Bobby had lucked out and found a bunch of it at a sporting goods store, and I'd asked him to bring every last bit of it. I had it rigged to blow outward in a near 360-degree radius, and if everything went according to plan, Colin and I would be safely off the roof when Sam hit it with a round from the .50 caliber rifle. If not, we'd both likely be dead and dismembered, right along with any of the wolves still on the roof when it blew. I saw a video once of a guy who'd had his leg completely severed with a piece of shrapnel after packing a lawnmower with just three pounds of Tannerite and detonating it from fifty feet away. So, I figured with forty pounds of it going off, the wolves were going to have a bad day.

With everything set and everyone in place, I gave Sam the signal and waited at the edge of the roof with my M4 and a few grenades. They were mostly just to get the wolves to come in this tower and not the one next door, where Sam and Gabby were set up. I watched the compound with the monocular and waited as their roving guard walked closer and closer to Sam's range. Earlier, Sam had mentioned that these 'thropes stayed in their werewolf form all the time, and right now I was definitely looking at a fully-shifted werewolf. This one was covered in brownish-grey fur from head to toe, longer and thicker on the back, shoulders, and hindquarters, and lighter and sparser on the arms, legs, torso, and stomach. Its face was elongated into a very wolf-like muzzle, with sharp, wicked-looking teeth poking out from a mouth that displayed a permanent leer. Sharp, pointed ears stood out at odd angles from its head, swiveling here and there at every little sound. The whole thing rippled with muscle, from its broad, banded shoulders, to its lean, cut torso, to its bizarre, triple-jointed canine legs. It was obviously a beast designed for killing, and there were at least seven more just like it waiting inside the compound.

It moved without a care in the world, secure in the knowledge that it was an apex predator with nothing to fear from its immediate environment. At least, not until six hundred and fifty grains of lead and copper hit it right at the shoulder joint at three thousand feet per second. I heard the sharp report of the rifle just a split-second after I saw the thing's arm viciously severed from its body. It looked around in confusion for a moment, and upon seeing its arm on the ground and the blood spurting from its severed shoulder, it roared in a way that was both animal and childlike. It reminded me a bit of the sound a wounded coyote makes when it's calling the rest of the pack; except that it began with a roar of anger, and then faded off into a high, lonesome tone that chilled me to my bones.

The thing clamped a hand over its shoulder and fell to its knees, continuing to howl and whine like a scared puppy. I almost felt sad for it; then I thought about Kara. I glanced at Bobby, who was shifting into his own compact, deadly form. Bobby's eyes held no remorse for this creature, only a thirst for blood that demanded to be fed. I got the feeling that his pack and the Corridor pack weren't on the best of terms, and he seemed to be carrying a grudge toward these wolves. Why? I hadn't a clue. But I'd never seen him in battle with one of his kind before, and I was both excited to see what that would look like, and also frightened for his safety. The last thing I needed was to get the son of the alpha of the Coastal pack killed. I'd damned sure be keeping an eye on him during the battle.

I shifted my gaze back to see what was happening inside the compound and saw werewolves swarming out of buildings left and right. But not just six or eight; the whole pack of fifteen or sixteen wolves came running out. I hollered over my shoulder to Colin. "We got complications! They must've found what they were looking for already, because I count sixteen wolves down there!"

I looked back through the optic and saw that several of them looked right at me. Guess I didn't need to do much to get their attention at this point, but I picked up my rifle just the same and started taking potshots at them. Within moments the entire pack was headed our way, running like a flood toward our position—some on all fours, some on two. In less than sixty seconds, they'd be inside the building. I continued shooting at them as they approached, figuring that any edge we could get would help. I dropped one with a lucky head shot in the parking lot as they approached the building, but decided to save the remaining grenades in case I needed to go out with a bang.

Two down, fourteen to go. I walked over to the Stoner, flipped the safety off, and waited.

———

WE HEARD the booby traps going off shortly after the wolves started entering the tower. There several seconds of silence before another one went off. They were moving fast. We'd left the door to the roof access open so we could hear them coming, which meant we heard every cry of anger and pain from the wolves who got hit by frag grenades as they headed up to our position. I had hoped they'd be in a frenzy, and I was right. Dumb sons of bitches kept running into the trip wires, one after another. I counted five detonations in all before somebody got smart and the explosions stopped.

Soon, the whines of the wolves who'd gotten hit by the IEDs became background noise to a cacophony of footsteps, barks, and growls that grew louder and louder. Moments later, three 'thropes came bounding out of the roof access door, mad as hell and looking for a fight. Joe performed his assigned task flawlessly, hitting the clicker on a claymore mine pointing at the door. The impact of seven hundred one-eighth inch steel balls flying at knee level at four thousand feet per second made our point; three wolves lay dead or bleeding to death just outside the doorway, their legs a bloody mess of shattered bone, flayed skin and muscle, and shredded sinews. I now counted five wolves who were down for certain, not including the wounded in the stairwell.

Eleven to go.

Colin bounced on the balls of his feet in anticipation to my right, swinging the big sword in slow, sinuous arcs. Every once in a while he let one hand leave the handle to thump his chest with the rhythm of his movements. It was almost hypnotic, the way he moved that big sword, all the while mumbling something in what must've been Gaelic under his breath. Seeing him and Bobby chomping at the bit to get at these wolves almost made me think we had a chance.

Seconds after the first wolves had been cut down by the claymore, the roof of the access shelter exploded in a shower of tar paper and wood fragments. An enormous 'thrope flew out of it, landing past our remaining claymores and damned close to our skirmish line. It tilted its head back and roared at us, leaving lines of spittle hanging from its mouth as it raged in challenge.

"That's one of Van's sons, Skull. He's mine," Bobby growled. I had other plans than to let Bobby take that huge wolf on, and swiveled the machine gun at it. But before I could get it in my sights, Bobby had jumped forward, slashing across its chest in a strike that he'd obviously meant for its throat. He followed up by going low with a slash to Skull's quadriceps, then another to his gut. Only the shot to the leg connected deeply enough to do any damage, and the beast staggered as it counterattacked.

I looked on in awe as Bobby took it apart, one swipe at a time. It was like watching a skilled butcher taking apart a side of meat. Even though Skull was twice his size, the big lug just couldn't touch him. Bobby slashed arteries and debilitated limbs in swipe after swipe after bloody swipe. Then, Skull got smart and began to back away so that he could use his reach against Bobby's speed. I wanted to see how the fight would end, but I got distracted by three more wolves who leaped out of the access shelter the same way, each one landing in a different direction.

That totally screwed up my plans to funnel them through our kill zone, so I lit up the closest one with the Stoner, cutting him down with a five-second burst of the gun. At nine hundred rounds a minute, seventy-five rounds of 5.56 made quick work of it. I swiveled to the second one, only to find that it was almost right on top of me. It leapt and I lit it up, picking the Stoner up and following the damn thing over me as I landed on my back to let it pass overhead. That jacked up the belt feed on the damn thing, and it jammed up on me. I didn't have time to screw with it, because even though Bobby had ganked Skull and was engaged with the third wolf, two more of them were already headed our way. I tossed the Stoner aside and ripped the little MP7 machine guns off my vest, sighting in on our latest party guests.

I was squeezing the triggers when Colin dove into my field of fire. "Shit!" I yelled, firing a few rounds that barely missed him, just as he started using that big sword like a scalpel. He took one wolf out at the knees, then parried a swipe from the second and split that wolf nearly in two down the torso. *Not getting up from that shit, that's for sure*, I thought as I watched him lever the blade out of the body. He yanked it free and beheaded the other wolf without a glance, scanning for more of the pack.

Seven left.

I knew that now they'd either wait or come at us in a rush. Either way, I wanted off this roof before they got us trapped up here. I hollered at my crew. "Guys, time to go!"

MISTAKE

B obby was painted in blood from head to toe and scanning the roof for someone else to rip apart. Colin, on the other hand, was backing away from the door, the professional warrior in him fighting against his baser, less rational instincts that said stay and fight. Unsurprisingly, Joe was nowhere in sight.

I yelled again, louder. "Bobby, let's go!" He turned to look me in the eye, savagery and civilization obviously warring inside him. I saw the challenge in his eyes and knew that with him in this state, it'd be a deadly mistake for me to drop my gaze from his. I spoke in a lower voice, clear and commanding, and held his stare. "I said, let's go. That's an order."

He stared a moment longer, then broke eye contact with me. I mentally sighed in relief. I didn't want to think about what would've happened if he hadn't. I wasn't normally one to play dominance games, but I knew with 'thropes, dominance was anything but a game. I spoke to Colin, keeping Bobby in my peripheral vision. "We need to get off this roof before they rush us. Snap into your harness and head over the side—I'll cover you and Bobby."

He nodded and rappelled down the side of the building within seconds. I watched him go, then turned back to see every last wolf pouring onto the roof like ants swarming out of their nest. I opened fire with the little MP7's, emptying both magazines and spraying the wolves at random. The rounds had little effect on them since I wasn't focusing my firepower on a single wolf. I turned back to Bobby and yelled at him.

"For Christ's sakes, Bobby, you can't take them all on! Over the side, now! I'll cover you and follow right after."

In truth, I knew I wouldn't have time, but I hoped he wouldn't realize it. I still had three grenades on me, and I planned to pull the pins at the last minute to take as many wolves with me as possible. With any luck, Sam would hit the Tannerite and take out the rest.

Bobby looked at the wolves and looked back at me, then shook his head.

"No," he growled.

He rushed at me and slung me over his shoulder, knocking the wind out of me, and then he ran like hell to the side of the building. I was still trying to catch my breath when I realized we were airborne. One moment we were flying toward the ground at bone-crushing speed; the next, our momentum was stopped with jarring force, and I saw that Bobby had grabbed one of the rappelling ropes.

The top of the roof exploded above us, right before we crashed through a window four floors down and I was knocked unconscious.

———

I CAME to with a two hundred and fifty-pound werewolf slapping my face. Again.

"Scratch, wake up, man! Scratch, you with me, buddy?"

The kid was practically screaming in my ear, and his gruff were-wolf voice and harder than human slaps were making my ears ring. Or maybe it was the forty pounds of Tannerite that I'd loaded that HVAC unit with, or impacting a plate glass window at what felt like terminal velocity just a few moments before. Regardless of the cause, my head felt like someone had been playing soccer with it all day long.

I reached up and snatched a large, furry, clawed hand from the air. "If you slap me one more time, I'm taking you to the vet to get fixed." I shoved his head away from me. "Now, quit screaming in my ear and help me up."

He pulled me off the floor and I assessed the damage. I had multiple cuts to my arms and legs, but thankfully none were serious. Bobby, on the other hand, was shredded but healing rapidly. I'd correctly assumed that werewolves could heal most wounds and injuries fairly quickly. However, based on what I'd seen, coming back from dismemberment seemed to be beyond their capabilities. Earlier, the kid had been more or less mum on the topic when I'd asked him how fast wolves could heal, calling it "werewolf stuff" and changing the topic. However, he was also enthusiastic about the prospects of using high explosives to ruin the Pack's day, which I'd taken as a sign that I was on the right track. Thankfully, my gamble had paid off.

At least, I hoped it had. "Bobby, what's the situation?"

"You were only out for a few seconds. So far, I haven't heard anything from the roof and I haven't heard anything coming down the stairwells, either."

"We need to go check it out." I picked some glass off my clothes and out of my hair, discarding it as I walked. Bobby followed me down the hall from the conference room we'd landed in, and I checked my equipment as we headed for the closest stairwell. Glocks? Check. Katana? Check. Rifle? No idea. Machine pistols? MIA. Stoner LMG? Probably scrap metal at the moment. What a damned shame.

I drew the sword, noting a distinct twinge in my shoulder that definitely hadn't been there earlier. I also still felt woozy, but I was operational. We approached the stairwell cautiously, listening for any sound or indication that some of the Pack had made it. I looked through the door glass. The stairs were full of debris and dust. No movement, though. We headed through the door and up two flights of stairs, until the way became barred by structural beams and cinder block fragments; it appeared the roof had collapsed.

Bobby grunted. "I doubt any of them made it."

"Agreed. What happened to Joe?"

He growled softly. "He went over the side of the building when we were about to get overrun."

"Can't say I blame him. I didn't think he'd stick around even that long. Bet he's ten miles from here by now." I rubbed my face and sighed. "Alright, let's go see how Sam and Gabby are doing."

We bolted down the stairs, forgetting momentarily that there might be undetonated booby traps and some not quite dead werewolves waiting for us. It was a mistake which nearly cost us our lives. As I hit the seventh floor landing at speed, a huge, wounded 'thrope came up from below, leaping stairs three at a time. It bled in several places, and was missing an ear and possibly a few digits, but it was also pissed as hell and ready to rumble. It knocked the sword from my hand, and I barely avoided getting my head taken off by a powerful swipe of its claws, only just ducking under it and diving awkwardly to the stairwell below.

I rolled as I hit the next landing, coming up on one hand. I looked up and saw Bobby fighting with the wolf at close range. His speed and agility advantage was negated by the close quarters, which meant that he was forced to grapple with the larger and more mature 'thrope. And he was losing. He had one of the 'thrope's wrists locked in his left hand, and the other was around its throat, barely keeping its slavering, snapping jaws away from his face. The 'thrope's other hand was savaging Bobby's torso and head with heavy blows.

I looked around and located the katana, reaching out for it and nearly grabbing it, just before I noticed that the blade was suspended in mid-air by an almost invisible strand of fishing microfilament line. I stopped myself with a sharp intake of breath, and slowed my roll considerably. I picked the sword up carefully to avoid placing any additional pressure on the blade. As I snatched it from the tripwire, I paused in anticipation of the distinct *plink* of a grenade spoon releasing.

Hearing nothing but the sound of my balls dropping out of my abdomen in relief, I rolled across the landing and came up with a right-to-left upward slash of the blade that severed the wolf's Achilles tendon on its right ankle, causing it to stumble and lose leverage. As it dropped down closer to my level, I reversed the cut and neatly beheaded it, narrowly missing Bobby's hand. The head fell and bounced down the stairwell to the landing below, where I skewered it to keep it from hitting the trip line.

Bobby collapsed on the steps behind him and checked his hand to make sure all his fingers and claws were still attached. Assured that he was still in one piece, he shook his massive canine head and let out a sound that was closer to a whine than a sigh. "When this is done, I'm going surfing."

I extended a hand to him. "The sooner we get out of here, the sooner we can get someplace safe and relax." After he was back on his feet, I pointed past the severed 'thrope head below. "Just please be sure to mind the tripwires on your way out of the building. I nearly blew us to kingdom come a second ago."

He laughed. "Now wouldn't that be ironic, if it was your klutziness and not mine that got us blown to bits?"

"Yeah, let's don't and say we didn't." I grabbed my sword, tiptoed over the wire, and headed down to the ground floor, with Bobby screaming, "Don't step there!" at random intervals and giggling, the whole way down.

[32]

DISMAY

Somehow, Bobby and I managed to avoid any more run-ins with booby traps and not-yet-dead werewolves on the way down to ground level. We did find a lot of 'thrope parts, though; apparently, they were the idiots who'd triggered the traps. The kill radius on an M67 fragmentation grenade was five meters, and in the confined spaces of the stairwell, the concussive force and shrapnel had made short and bloody work of them.

Even so, the day wasn't over yet. We still had to go through Van, or Fenrir, or whoever the hell he was, and then we'd face Piotr—a being who, by all counts, was some sort of super-vampire. By any measure, we still had a long night ahead of us. So when Bobby and I hit the ground floor and none of the others were there yet, I began to worry.

"Bobby, do you have eyes or ears on anyone?"

He shook his shaggy head. "Nope. Think they're still on their way down?"

I shook my head. "Colin should at least be here. I saw him heading over the side, right before you grabbed me and did that Jason Bourne maneuver."

"Yeah, that was pretty Matt Damon-esque, was it not?" He

brushed imaginary dust from his shoulders, then looked around. "Well, the good news is that I don't see any Colin bits lying around."

Not really in the mood for jokes, I grimaced and started to panic. The last thing I had wanted to do was get people killed. I headed to the other tower, calling out for the others. "Sam! Gabby! Colin!" No one answered. I yelled across the common area to Bobby. "Check around the perimeter of the buildings—see if you can find anything. I'll check inside."

"You got it, boss."

I bolted through the front door of the other building, intent on making a beeline for the stairs. But as soon as I entered, I was clotheslined by a massive hairy arm. I landed hard, bouncing off the ground as I hit. My brain must've got rattled pretty good, because I was seeing stars as a large 'thrope picked me up by the throat and held me at arm's length.

He backed away from the door as I dangled from his grip, leaving the tips of my toes dragging along the tiles. I tried kicking free, but he had his claws dug into my neck close to my spine, and his grip was a vice. No dice on that plan. I tried to draw my guns, but when I did, he shook me like a rag doll and scrambled my brains even more. That's when I realized that if he'd wanted to kill me, he'd have just snapped my neck already. With no alternatives left to me, I decided to make nice and see what he wanted.

I looked him in the eye and attempted a smile, a difficult task considering the grip the thing had on me. "I don't think we've been properly introduced," I choked out.

"My given name is Hati, but most call me Hate."

"Ah," I squeaked. "The other half of the hair band duo formerly known as Skull and Hate." Of course, the last thing I wanted was to tell him his brother was dead, being as he was just a twist and a crunch away from crushing my spine. I changed the subject. "Just curious, where's your dad at the moment? I have a bone to pick with that guy."

The 'thrope chuckled. "As he does with you." He pulled me in close and huffed hot, fetid dog breath in my face. It smelled slightly of dead, rotted meat—and toothpaste, of all things. "What big teeth you have," I quipped. "Must be hell on dental bills, though."

He growled in reply. "I should kill you right now, but Father would be very displeased with me if I did, as he longs to see whether you live up to your reputation. Granted, he might provide me with some leeway, considering that you helped kill my brother." I must have registered some surprise on my face, and he sneered. "Oh, yes, I'm aware of his death. Pack knows when pack bleeds. However, unlike the others you slaughtered, my brother will be back with us as soon as Piotr opens the gateway. You see, my kind can't die—we just get sent back to the other side—then we simply come back and kill more of your kind."

"Yeah? Well, I'm not really big on recycling," I said as I pulled my Bowie and attempted to stick it in his eye. He quickly blocked my attack, grabbing my arm with his free hand and breaking my wrist with a loud *snap*. I dropped the blade and screamed in rage and pain.

"Tsk, tsk, Mr. Sullivan. Although Father wants you alive, he won't mind if I break you a little. Behave." He tossed me across the entryway of the building, and I landed on the hard tiles and slid several feet to collide with the other wall. I cradled my arm as I sat up; from what I could tell, it was cracked, but not displaced. No telling if I'd be able to use it anytime soon, and it already hurt like a son of a bitch. *What I wouldn't do for some Vicodin right now*, I thought.

Hate cocked an ear and gave a small nod of his head. "Ah, the whelp is coming. When he arrives, tell the pup that Hati is waiting for him at the compound." He pointed one long, clawed finger at me. "And you, Mr. Sullivan. Father is waiting for you there as well." Then the thing beat feet for the back entrance. I sat there cradling my arm as Bobby walked in the door.

"No sign of them—" he said, pausing as he saw me sitting in a heap against the wall. "Holy crap, what the hell happened to you?"

"Hate happened to me. He just left." Bobby started to run off after him, but I held a hand up to stop him. "No, don't bother going after him. He's not going far. Based on what he just told me, he and Van will be waiting for us in the compound. Right now, I need you to stick tight and help me splint my arm. The fracking cur broke it."

He grinned a canine grin at me. "'Fracking cur'—gee, boss, your vocabulary has really improved since we first met."

"Yeah, every day's a new day. Now help me splint this thing so we can figure out where Colin, Gabby, and Sam went."

———

Bobby wrapped my arm in some carpet padding we pulled up from one of the offices, then he rolled a couple of old magazines around it and we duct taped it up tight. Since it wasn't displaced, it'd probably heal rapidly due to my quasi-werewolf powers. But as far as it healing before we ran into Van and Hate; well, I had my doubts about that. Thankfully, it was my left arm, so my dominant hand still worked just fine. But using a katana one-handed was going to be a chore. If worse came to worst, I'd just try to barrel through the pain and use my left hand; it might suck for a while, but it sure beat getting your head bitten off.

While he was fixing up my arm, I questioned Bobby on what he'd found outside.

"Nothing, and I mean nothing," he said. "Their scent ends

in the parking lot. No signs of a struggle, either. It's like they just vanished."

I pursed my lips and shook my head. "It just doesn't make sense. How could they disappear without leaving a trace of where they went or how they left?" I thought on it for a moment and had an idea. "Let's check upstairs and see if they left any clues up there."

Within minutes, we were in the sniper's nest where Colin and I had left Gabby and Sam earlier. All was as we'd left it, except that the smell of gunpowder still hung in the air, and there was a spent .50 caliber round on the ground. I saw no signs of a struggle. I looked at Bobby to see if he sensed anything, and he shook his head. "Let's move to the roof."

We exited cautiously. I noted that a hole had been made in the steel exit door by shrapnel. The blast the Tannerite made had turned out to be a lot bigger than I'd planned, and I worried for a moment that some shrapnel might have hit Sam and Gabby. When we got to the rooftop sniper's nest, however, there was no sign of blood or struggle. Ditto for the rappelling gear. It was in place on the opposite side of the building, and no lines had been cut. Their harnesses were nowhere to be found, which reinforced the theory that they'd at least made it off the top of the building.

"This has me worried, Bobby. Gabby and Sam both are skilled trackers and hunters. No way anything was going to sneak up on them, and so far we've found no signs of a fight. So, they either flew away, or they were spirited away by magic."

"Or something worse," he said.

I didn't want to think about the implications of that statement. "Let's just keep looking, and if we don't find them, we'll go free the hostages and hope they show up along the way."

I still had my harness on, so I opted to clip in and rappel down the building. Bobby took the stairs, saying one trip down

200 / M.D. MASSEY

the side of a building hanging onto a rope was enough. When I got to the bottom, Colin strolled up out of the brush that bordered the parking lot with a grim look on his face.

"Have you seen the others?" I asked.

His expression told me all I needed to know. "Bad news, Scratch. The vamp took Gabby and Sam."

"How? It's broad daylight out here. Ain't no way a vamp is going to be traipsing around in the sunlight—at least, none of the ones I've seen."

He shook his head slowly. "I don't know, Scratch. This thing is old, and sometimes older supernatural creatures grow much stronger, the longer they're allowed to remain on this side of the Veil. All I know is, I saw them get into a car and split across the bridge about fifteen minutes ago. I tracked them to see where they were headed, then came straight back to tell you."

"There aren't any cars still running, Colin. All the fuel went bad ages ago."

He smirked. "Believe it or not, he was driving a Tesla."

"Shit," I whispered under my breath.

He nodded. "The good news is, they didn't go far—just to some big white building on the compound."

I considered our options until Bobby came jogging around the corner. We filled him in and got him up to speed on the situation, then I began laying out how I wanted to do things.

"First, we check on the settlers and get them prepped to get the hell out of here. Then, we raid that compound, kill Van and Piotr, or Peter, or whatever the hell his name is." I paused and glared off in the distance at the compound. "And then, we steal his car."

———

On our way to the small hotel where the wolves had housed

the hostages, Josef and Rabbi Manny came running up the road toward us. Well, at least, Josef did. The good rabbi sat on Josef's shoulders, hitching a ride while all those knives and bottles strapped to his chest and waist bounced around like Christmas tree ornaments in an earthquake. They reminded me a lot of a scene from a George Lucas movie, and I wasn't the only one who picked up on it.

Bobby noticed him and scowled. "Great, Rabbi Sunshine is here."

"I take it you're referring to Yoda and the frost giant he's riding?" Colin asked.

"I'll explain it later," I told him quietly, as Josef jogged up and came to a halt in front of us with a few final, earth-rattling steps. I made introductions between them, and filled Manny in on the situation.

The rabbi rubbed his chin. "So then, how do you propose we deal with the wolf and the vampire?"

I rubbed the grip of my holstered Glock. "Well, first I plan to free the settlers. Then, I'm going to find Gabby and Sam. After that, I'm going to kill Van and the bloodsucker."

The rabbi stuck his lower lip out and squinted. "A simple plan—I suppose it will do." He looked down at my arm and then gave me a visual once over. "You look like *scheisse*. How badly are you injured?"

"I ran into Hate inside the building. He left me with this, and told me Van would be waiting for me in the compound." I held up my splinted arm and then pointed across the bridge.

In response, the old man pulled out a clear glass bottle with some foul-looking, brownish-grey liquid inside. "Here, drink this." He tossed it to me, so I snatched it out of the air and examined it carefully.

"Cool, power-ups!" Bobby exclaimed. "Got any for werewolves?"

"Bah! This is not a video game, you dimwit. It only dulls the pain, without dulling the mind." The old man spat off to the side and glowered at him. "Besides, your werewolf metabolism would eliminate it before it did you any good."

Bobby turned to Colin and whispered loudly behind his hand. "See why I call him Rabbi Sunshine? He's buckets of fun."

Colin spoke back sotto voce. "I'm starting to get that impression."

Tired of the banter and ready to kick some werewolf and vampire ass, I pulled the stopper off the bottle and slugged it back. It tasted like a cross between a well digger's ass sweat and mint tea, and it burned my throat all the way down. "Ugh. You should serve that with a whiskey chaser." I placed my hands on my knees and let the drink settle.

He waved me off. "Ach! You are all ingrates and jokers, the lot of you." He prodded Josef with his heels. "Come, Josef, before I have to put up with any more of this infantile humor." Josef quietly complied, heading in the direction of the hotel at a trot.

I looked at the others. "You guys ready for this?"

Colin nodded. "Lead the way."

Bobby rubbed his hands together and grinned. "I'm about to go spread some Hate all over this place." Colin gave him a fist bump to acknowledge the pun.

I just ignored him. I didn't want to encourage that sort of behavior.

"Alrighty then," I replied. "Let's end this."

33

WOMEN

The hotel was only a short jog away, and already settlers milled around in front arguing as we arrived. I was happy and a bit relieved to see Janie, who'd run the commissary for the settlement, at the center of one very heated discussion.

Janie raised her voice in anger as she spoke, and she waved her fists in the air. She had a black eye, a split lip, and there were bruises up and down her arms in various states of healing. On seeing her current condition, the thought of what had happened to these folks while I was convalescing made my heart sink. However, at the moment she appeared none the worse for the wear. She argued with an older woman who I recognized as Nadine, one of the old biddies who had always caused trouble around the settlement. As I looked around, I saw several faces missing from the crowd—more than I cared to think about, in fact. I was surprised that Nadine had made the forced march into Austin, and briefly felt guilty for thinking that it should have been someone else.

"This may be our only chance, Nadine. I say we get the hell out of here, *now*, before they come back!" Janie's voice hit a crescendo as she yelled, and spittle escaped from her mouth in her fury.

Nadine saw us coming before Janie did, and pointed over her shoulder with a snide remark; it was something to do with my tardiness and poor timing. Janie turned around in surprise, which turned to anger and fear when she saw Bobby. I realized that I should have had him transform back before approaching the settlers, but it was too late; the damage had been done.

She crossed her arms and squared her stance, tilting her head in Bobby's direction. "Scratch, I can't say I'm not glad to see you, but I also can't say I approve of your companion here."

I noticed several of the settlers beginning to back away in fear and waved Bobby back. "He's a friend, Janie, from the Gulf Coast pack. And he came to help."

She looked Bobby up and down while he made an effort to look harmless, a tall order considering that he was covered in dried blood. She then turned her gaze to Colin, and finally the rabbi who still sat atop the golem's shoulders. To be honest, Josef was a hell of a lot more intimidating than Bobby, but he kept his face hidden within his hood, so I supposed Bobby looked like the more immediate threat.

Finally, her expression softened, and she smiled a crooked grin. "Well, if this is our rescue party, I'm not going to look a gift horse in the mouth." She closed the distance to hug me, whispering in my ear as she held me tight. "Thanks for coming, Scratch. I knew we could count on you."

I hugged her back then released her, allowing her to take a step back. "Sorry I didn't come sooner. I was—delayed, you might say."

She looked at the makeshift splint and the other various scrapes and bruises that had marked me and smiled slightly. "At least you made it. That's more than I can say for some."

"Well, Sam followed you all the way out here, and he helped us take on the 'thropes. And Donnie—he's no longer with us." If she reacted to the news, I didn't notice. I was too busy looking around at the faces before me—mostly women, kids, and some teens. It looked like the wolves had either killed all the men or sold them off to the punters. I realized that some of the corpses back in the theater had probably been people I knew. My blood boiled at the thought.

"Look, Janie, I'd love to catch up, and I have my fair share of questions, but I need to know where Kara is right now."

Janie's face soured noticeably, and her brow furrowed. "No offense, Scratch, but I wouldn't have much to do with that traitor if I was you."

I sighed. "Well, I'm sure there's a lot I don't know, but there's a lot you don't know as well. Can you please just point me in the right direction?"

She hesitated, then shrugged. "Not much point in me trying to tell you she's a lost cause, is there?" I said nothing, waiting for her reply. "Well, no one ever could tell you anything you didn't want to hear. But don't say I didn't warn you." She pointed past some stores, across the road to the college. "Look for her in that big white building. That's where you'll find her."

I nodded. "Thanks, Janie. Now, do me a favor and get these people ready to leave. I have a safe place prepared for you, away from the settlements. Someplace no one will find us, where you can start over."

"That sounds great, but you're going to have a hard time making some of these people go." The confusion must've been evident on my face. "That vamp put the *ojo* on them, you see. They won't budge an inch unless he tells them to now."

"So why aren't you brainwashed too?" I asked, with just a hint of suspicion in my voice.

"What you're asking is, did he do the same thing to Kara?" She scowled. "You'll see."

I didn't know what to say, so I changed the subject. "I meant what I said, Janie. Be ready."

She spoke over her shoulder as she walked back to others. "We'll be ready, if you make it back."

————

WE FIVE LEFT the settlers to prepare for their departure, the sun setting as we strode across the road to the gates of the compound. We knew for a fact that Van, Hate, and Piotr waited for us, and we also knew they were using Gabby and Sam as bait to draw us in. I was determined get my friends back, and I didn't need to know anything else. I checked my pistols to make sure they were ready to go, and loosened the katana in the scabbard over my shoulder. I fingered the handles of the tomahawk and Bowie as I strolled forward, while Colin marched next to me with his massive sword resting over his shoulder.

Josef walked like an automaton, which I supposed he was, although to what extent it still wasn't clear. The rabbi fiddled with his bottles and blades for a few moments as he rode on the great monster's shoulders. He began muttering to himself in Yiddish, making strange motions with his hands and twisting his fingers in oddly contorted positions. Whether he was actually working magic, or just doing some Jewish *kuji-in* ninja mind-focusing shit, I had no idea. At this point, I didn't care, so long as the golem was fighting on our side.

Bobby, on the other hand, looked like a dog who'd just rolled in a dead animal and taken a massive dump. In other words, he was exuberant. Under his happy puppy demeanor, I knew that he was worried about Gabby, but something about this impending face-off with Van and Hate had him stoked. It made me wonder whether this was an event he'd been working toward all along.

Once we entered the compound, it wasn't long before we ran into the father and son. Now, I'd thought that Hate was a big 'thrope, and he certainly was; a good six foot six, if an inch. But he was dwarfed by the figure who stood next to him. That individual, who I assumed was this Van I'd heard so much about, was easily of the same height as Josef. At that moment, I felt like David facing down Goliath. Fighting him, I'd indeed be fighting a giant; what sucked was that he hadn't even taken his werewolf form yet.

Nevertheless, he certainly cut an imposing figure just as he was. His long Viking hair was pulled back in a ponytail, and his rugged Scandinavian face was clean and neatly shaved. He wore the typical tacti-cool outfit worn by modern mercenaries everywhere: loose khaki cargo pants and a black compression t-shirt that showed every last bulging muscle. Combat boots completed the ensemble. He made eye contact as I sized him up, and smiled. It was not a friendly smile.

Hate stood a step to his left and behind him, holding Sam off the ground by the scruff of his jacket. Someone had beaten Sam bloody; bruises and cuts made a mess of his face, and he struggled to breathe. Little flecks of blood shot from his nose and mouth each time he exhaled, his suffering evident as his chest rose and fell.

It made me angry to see one of my friends—one of my pack —injured and helpless like this. That anger stirred the bloodlust within me, and although it filled me, my mind was clear as a bell. I pictured their blood spilling at my hands and reveled at the thought. Van spoke and broke me out of my reverie. His voice was surprisingly pleasant, almost melodious, as he greeted us from across the parking lot.

"Scratch Sullivan, itinerant hunter and protector of the

Texas Hill Country. The rabbi Emmanuel Borovitz, and his pet abomination. Coileáin MacCumhaill, bearer of the wisdom of the Salmon of Knowledge and the curse of Cú Chulainn. And Robert Thomas Randolfson, adopted son of Samson Randolph, alpha of the Gulf Coast pack." He spread his arms wide and smiled with an amused grin that did not reach his deep-set gray eyes. "Welcome."

"You should let my friend go," I replied.

Van chuckled. "I should do many things, but I only do that which pleases me. That one was instrumental in destroying what remained of my pack after you so brutally slaughtered the rest. Blood cries for blood, Scratch—you know that, intrinsically now. The call of the pack, it sings within you, just as it drives you to protect this useless sack of meat.

"You thought that when they gave you our power, it would merely change your body? Of course not. No power comes without its price. Your very soul is marked by what science has done to you; for where does the soul rest, but within the very molecules and atoms of our cells?"

The rabbi spoke up, in a calm and commanding voice. "You have no soul, monster. Only a spirit that has been made corrupt. And now, you use what gifts that Yahweh granted you to desecrate that which you were meant to protect."

Van didn't even acknowledge the rabbi's words. He only had eyes for me. "So tell me, 'alpha': will you run to save your life, or die to save your people? Because after my son and I cut through you and your friends here like a scythe through stalks of grain, who will be left to save your people then?" He laughed. "Don't you see? You lose either way."

I looked at Sam, who was probably dying while we spoke, and realized that I was tired of this prick's jabbering, and most of all just plain tired. I'd already made this decision, weeks ago when I left the settlements to see what was going on here in the Corridor.

"Then I'll lose fighting," I said, pulling both .45's and firing them simultaneously at both Hati and Vanagandr.

34

FEAR

I was firing left-handed and with an injured arm at Hati, so I hit him in the arm instead of the head. That kind of pissed me off, because I seriously wanted to kill that son of a bitch. The good news was that Bobby wasn't far behind my draw, bounding toward the bastard by the time I'd snapped off the third round. Ol' Hate wasn't missing a beat, and had already discarded Sam like a broken toy to turn and catch Bobby coming by the fourth or fifth round.

Now Van, on the other hand... that was a totally different matter. I hit him four or five times in succession, all aiming at the head and neck. By all appearances, he didn't even flinch. I mean, not a muscle. Then, he sort of shimmered and began to change; well, if you could call it that. I'd classify it more in the "transmogrification" category, because he didn't turn into the same half-human, half-wolf form that all the other 'thropes had taken.

Nope. The freak shifted into a giant, horse-sized wolf. I mean, this thing was huge, easily a thousand pounds or better. And to be honest, he was beautiful and terrible all at once. His coat was a charcoal color, with shades of lighter gray and blonde mixed in, and flecks of black. His shape and muzzle were longer and slimmer than the North American wolves I'd seen at zoos before the War, and he looked like he was built for speed more than power. Not like a half-ton wolf would have a problem in that department; I figured if he got hold of me, I'd be done for in a heartbeat just the same.

I glanced over to check on Bobby, who was already violently engaged with Hate, and they looked like two cats fighting inside a burlap sack. Hate was almost as fast as Bobby and had a good hundred pounds on him. But Bobby moved like a greased weasel; every time Hate would swipe at him or try to snap those great jaws around an arm or leg, Bobby would slip just outside and swipe him or nip him. Never great big bites or deep cuts, but still attacks that were just enough to hurt.

I had no time to watch the show. Van/Fenrir had finished transforming and came straight at me—and man, could he move. I dove out of the way as he closed the forty-foot gap between us in seconds, and rolled up firing the .45's at him and backpedaling, jumping out of the way again over an old work truck's hood to avoid his rush. He collided with the truck and it shook with the impact, then he turned and coiled himself up for another leap at me just as I emptied my last rounds into his side and haunches. One bullet must've hit something important, because he stumbled a bit as he turned. But I had no time to reload, and I doubted I'd get the katana out before he could pounce over the truck and snap those massive jaws around me.

Thankfully, Colin chose that moment to charge in and distract him, swinging that hand-and-a-half sword of his, shouting *"MacCumhaill, MacCumhaill, MacCumhaill!"* and attracting the wolf's attention with his attack. That gave me time to draw my blade and leap over the truck into the fray, coming at him from the other side and landing several cuts on Van's flank in the process.

Van had twisted around and snagged Colin around the torso, snapping his head quickly and tossing the kid twenty feet through the air. I thought for sure he'd be dead on impact, but he rolled as he hit and sprang lightly to his feet, still hanging onto that great sword of his. Before suffering the same fate, I took a step back to give the wolf some space. I wasn't a coward; I just wasn't a fool, either. I looked around to see what had happened to the rabbi and Josef and saw the little man on the roof of a nearby building, making those strange signs with his hands and muttering in Yiddish, or Hebrew, or something. The old man paused and gestured for us to bring the wolf closer to his position. His golem was nowhere in sight.

Deciding that I'd have time to ask questions later, I rushed at Van, swinging at his face and then angling off to attack his flank. Colin followed my lead, and soon we had him backing up toward the rooftop where the rabbi was safely ensconced. We only seemed to be doing superficial damage, but at least we were moving him back.

Suddenly we heard the rabbi yell. "Move, you fools!" We dove left and right to make room for whatever surprise Rabbi Manny had in store. And a good thing, too; at that moment, Josef appeared right behind the wolf, smashing a glass receptacle squarely on Van's back. The bottle shattered, splashing a clear liquid over Van's fur and soaking him to the skin. Then the rabbi tossed something from his hands, a bright blue spark that caused the wolf to burst into flames. Josef backed away from the fire calmly, nonplussed about the flames that danced up and down his arm, and looked on as the wolf became engulfed in fire.

Vanagandr, it seemed, was not immune to fire as the golem was. He roared in pain and fury, turning about and trying to snap at the flames that had spread all over his neck and back. The rabbi's voice called out to us from the roof. "Now, attack while he is still burning! He cannot heal from both fire and steel at once!"

Taking the little man's advice, I ran forward and struck at Van's right forepaw, biting deeply into fur and flesh. Colin moved around the creature's backside and repeatedly stabbed at his haunches. We both continued to attack as the flames burned out, and Van stumbled off in retreat as we followed him, cutting and hacking with fierce, rapid blows in pursuit.

Without warning, Van rallied and kicked out with one rear leg at Colin, tossing him against a truck and stunning him; how badly, I couldn't tell. As Colin sagged against the truck, Van turned to lunge at him and finish him off. Sensing an opening and knowing that any hesitation would mean the end of Colin, I dove forward and drove my sword through Van's neck, in under one side of his jaw and out his shoulder on the opposite side.

———

As THE SWORD pierced his neck, Van/Fenrir staggered and then arched his back and coughed, like a dog with a bone stuck in its throat that it can't dislodge. He stumbled and fell, and I, still hanging onto the sword for dear life, got dragged with him. As I fell on him, Van turned his head and snapped at me, catching my shoulder and piercing it with two of those mighty, dagger-like fangs. I screamed with pain and wrenched the sword back and forth with my good arm while he crunched down on my shoulder blade.

No matter how each of us fought, both with flagging strength, neither one of us would let go.

Bobby appeared then, his face bloodied and horribly maimed, one side mangled and his jaw hanging at an odd angle. He landed on Van's head and drove both of his great clawed hands into an eye socket on either side of the wolf's skull, savaging each eye murderously. Van released me immediately, howling in agony and tossing me off to the side.

Once I was released, Bobby jumped off Van's back and landed, wobbly but still functional, a few paces away. Now blinded and skewered by my blade, Van dragged himself forward, still howling his fury—first five feet, then ten—then he fell to his side, panting, and began changing back into his human form. I pulled myself to my feet and stumbled after him.

Despite his injuries, Van pulled himself forward a few more feet to sit against a car. His eyes were a wreck, but he still turned his head toward me as he spoke. "Tell me, Sullivan: do you really think it's my destiny to be slain by a bard, a washed up rabbi, an orphan, and you, a broken shell of a man?"

I shrugged. "I'm sure there's a good bar joke in there, but you're missing a punchline. Please, continue."

"Yes, joke if you like, but for centuries I've walked this earth, and no man has bested me. You think I cannot heal these wounds?" He pulled my sword from his neck and tossed it to the side, and I noticed that indeed, the burn marks and slashes on his body were healing rapidly as he continued. "I am the monster of the River Van! I am Fenrir! I have defeated gods! I am eternal! I—"

Figuring I'd better end it before he fully recovered, I snatched my sword from the ground. Stepping forward, I separated his head from his shoulders with a quick flash of Japanese folded steel.

"You're dead meat, that's what you are." I watched as his head rolled away to rest at the base of a fire hydrant. It was a fitting resting place for it.

As I searched around for Sam, Colin staggered up to me, clapping a hand on my shoulder and pointing off to the side. The old man had landed in some shrubs, his arms and legs twisted and his breathing shallow. I ran over and gently pulled him from the bushes, laying him down and checking him over. He was conscious but struggling to breathe, and my once-over revealed massive trauma to his torso. It might have happened when Hate tossed him, but chances were good that the wolf beat him bloody before we even showed up.

I tried to make him comfortable and held his hand. The rabbi came over and gave him a few drops of some liquid under his tongue, saying it would ease the pain. Sam looked up at me and blinked, and I thought I saw some recognition in those eyes. He was trying to speak, so I leaned in to hear what he had to say.

"Too... strong. Couldn't fight them. Sorry... Scratch."

I squeezed his hand lightly and shook my head. "It's okay, Sam. You did more than any person should ever be expected to. Gabby will be fine. The wolves are dead, and we're about to end that vamp's miserable existence."

He started coughing and wheezing and got all worked up. "Not... the wolves... dangerous. Vampire... is real... danger. Careful..." Then he stopped breathing, and his eyes went dull.

I sat there for a moment holding his hand, and finally attempted to close his eyelids, but they wouldn't cooperate. I covered his face instead with my shemagh to give him some dignity. I stood up and wiped my eyes, taking a moment to collect myself. Sam was one of the few friends I'd had, and I had damned few of those. Seeing him go like this wasn't easy.

I said the Lord's Prayer over Sam's body, ending it with something to the effect of "commit this soul to your place of final rest," or some such. It was the best I could do at the moment; I'd give him a proper burial once we'd finished our business with Piotr.

Colin stood there silently for a few moments after I finished, then he spoke up. "You alright?"

"Nope. But there'll be time to mourn later. Now, we finish taking revenge."

A fter I'd taken care of Sam, I looked around to see how the rest of the crew fared. Bobby was sitting on the hood of a car not far away, getting patched up by the rabbi. He looked like a mess. The kid would recover, but he still needed to be put back together to heal properly. A further search turned up Hate's body several feet beyond, a nearly unrecognizable, bloody lump of flesh and bone. Josef stood statue-still on the other side of the parking lot, facing outward while standing watch.

The rabbi must have sensed how impotent I felt, despite our victory, and glanced at me momentarily over his bifocals as he sewed Bobby's face back together. "You acquitted yourselves well. I am sorry about your friend, but he was already dying by the time we arrived."

I just shook my head and decided to let it drop. "Bobby, how are you feeling?"

"Right as rain." Only his words came out like, "wight ath wane." His jaw was seriously screwed up. I looked at the rabbi. "Think you can fix that?"

"His jaw? Needs to be reset. It is dislocated, and I am not

going near a werewolf's mouth when he is in pain. You must do it."

"Alright, alright." I had Bobby sit facing me. "This is going to hurt, kid. So whatever you do, don't bite down." I stuck my thumbs inside his mouth, placing them on his back lower molars, and pressed down while pulling up on his chin until his jaw produced an audible "pop." The kid pulled away and moved his jaw around.

"Mush beh er," he exclaimed.

The rabbi looked at him and nodded his approval, then he looked at me and scowled. "Bah! You are worse off than he is! Sit down, sit down, before you pass out."

I waved him off. "Leave me alone, I feel fine."

"You only feel fine because you are high as a kite on that elixir I gave you. When it wears off, you will know it."

"Well, I feel fine now."

Bobby gave me the thumbs up. "Ane guh ty to beed."

Colin looked at him with an eyebrow cocked. "Huh?"

"I think he's saying, 'Ain't got time to bleed.' You know, Jesse Ventura from Predator?"

Colin made a sour face. "Ah, Jesse the Body Ventura. He was much cooler before he got into politics."

I smirked. "Isn't everyone?"

He cocked his head. "Mmm, except Reagan. His cool factor went up a few notches after he became president. *Bedtime For Bonzo* pretty much killed any swagger he might've had before then."

I tilted my head in acquiescence to his point, and waved the rabbi over. "Alright, patch me up. Last thing I need is to fall over while I'm kicking this vamp's ass." I sat on the ground, and the rabbi knelt as he proceeded to bandage my shoulder and various other minor cuts and scrapes. There was some sewing involved, but he was quick and efficient, and I was too busy reloading my

Glocks and spare mags and worrying about Kara and Gabby to pay attention to what he did.

While the rabbi wrapped things up, he spoke quietly to me as he tied off a bandage. "Are you sure you do not want to wait for morning to chase this vampire down? He will be weaker then, and we may be able to catch him unaware."

I shook my head. "No. No way. For one, if they have the uranium that the wolves were searching for, then waiting might be a mistake. Second, since the wolves took everyone, I've been trying to get Kara back and I've been delayed every step of the way. There's nothing and no one that's going to keep me from her right now. And third, he has Gabby." I clapped him on the shoulder and looked him in the eye. "Rabbi, there's no way in hell I'll leave that kid alone with that monster one second longer than I have to."

He sighed as he packed up his medical supplies. "It is hard to lose people you care for, and I have lost many over the years." He patted my leg in a very grandfatherly manner before he stood up. "This work is unforgiving in that way. Pray that you do not live a life as long as I."

I pushed myself off the ground with a groan. "I have a feeling that won't be an issue—not the way I'm going. But if I had my way right now, I'd retire somewhere quiet with no deaders around, and raise a nice little family with Kara."

He smiled a sad little smile at me. "I suppose there is always hope."

"I suppose there is at that. Now, let's go see about killing a vamp."

————

I LOOKED over at the old man as we gathered up our gear and prepped for the final showdown with Piotr. "What's the deal with all the blades? I saw you messing with them earlier, but you never used them during the fight with the wolves."

He patted his bandolier and touched his nose with one short, gnarled finger. "These are for the vampire. I coated them with a poison that will hopefully slow him down." He pulled a long, slender silver knife from a sheath and handed it to me, handle first. "Here. If you get close enough, stab him with this. Otherwise, you likely will not survive your encounter with him."

I took the knife and shoved it in my belt at the small of my back. I figured that it might come in handy, although I was growing awfully fond of the katana for this sort of work. Kind of hard for a vamp or a 'thrope to fight back when they're missing limbs. As I tucked the knife away, I double-checked my gear and took out a grenade that I'd saved just for this occasion. If I had to, I'd pull the pin and hang onto that son of a bitch, and take him out with me. Hopefully it wouldn't come to that, but these people deserved a chance to find freedom and safety at the Facility, and I knew that the Doc could give it to them.

I strapped the grenade to my vest and took a deep breath. "Alright, let's do this."

It was a short walk to the building that Joe and Sam had pointed out as the place that housed the reactor. The building itself was nondescript, and it looked like it could have been any building on any college campus anywhere. There was a sign that said "Nuclear Engineering Lab, PRC 159" in white letters on blue attached to the brick next to the front door. There was also a nuclear radiation warning sign below the placard, again faded by many long years in the hot Texas sun.

We listened to the sounds around us, trying to determine if there was a trap of some sort waiting for us on the other side of those doors. But we heard nothing but cicadas and the lonesome call of a nightjar from off in the distance. I tried the door to find it unlocked and pulled it open slowly, searching for traps and tripwires. There was nothing to fear; apparently, the front door had been left open for us and we were invited guests for the evening's festivities.

The rabbi grabbed my arm and stopped me before we entered. "Do not be alarmed if Josef disappears before we confront the vampire. He will be around, yet unseen. But I will stand with you this night, to give you what small assistance as I am able."

I nodded once to him, and moved on into the building. The place was lit with the occasional fluorescent bulb, but they'd been long neglected, and most flickered and gave off little if any reliable light. We didn't need it, at least not Bobby and I, but it still managed to add a definite sense of creepiness to the place. Besides the ballasts humming in the light fixtures, there were no other sounds.

We proceeded down the hall and followed the signs that pointed us to the nuclear engineering lab and reactor. The building itself wasn't particularly large, and we reached the entrance to the lab in little time and with no surprises. Nothing and no one was waiting to prevent us from making it to our destination; apparently, if the wolves didn't stop us, either Piotr had nothing else to throw at us, or he just didn't care. Either way, it spoke to his confidence in his abilities, or his lack of confidence in our own.

As we approached the door, I motioned them back against the cinder block wall and snuck up to the door to take a peek inside. There was a faint blue glow pulsating from a wall of glass on the far side of the room. Against those windows sat a row of ancient-looking computer cabinets like one might expect to see in an old sci-fi film from the fifties, as well as several modern computers and a line of monitors mounted to the ceiling. Kara was seated at one of the computer stations, her back half-turned to me with her face obscured. I'd nevertheless recognize that red hair and silhouette anywhere. She wore a white lab coat, and of all things, a pencil skirt and heels.

My heart raced at the sight of her.

Gabby was duct-taped to a chair just a few feet away, her mouth taped shut while her eyes bore holes in the figure standing next to Kara. It could only have been Piotr, and none other. He cut a startling figure, I'd give him that. Six-one, or maybe a little taller. A dark, full head of hair, of the kind that movie stars once spent a lot of money maintaining and replacing. Slim hips, broad shoulders. Expensive black slacks, Italian shoes, and a white dress shirt unbuttoned at the collar and most certainly Brooks Brothers, if I had to take a guess. He was half turned toward Kara, posing with one hand stroking his chin, the other arm draped across his chest to give him someplace to prop his elbow. He said something to her, but I couldn't make it out. Whatever he said, Kara started typing commands into the computer in response, and the glow behind the glass grew a little brighter.

I leaned back from the window and whispered to Colin, Bobby, and the rabbi, filling them in on the situation.

Bobby looked at me seriously, his brow furrowing. "How do you want to play this, boss?"

I turned to look at Rabbi Manny, who shrugged. "He is waiting for us, and unconcerned, which means he is well-fed and dangerous. I do not recommend giving him a chance to fight back."

I nodded. "Then I go in guns blazing, and we blitz the son of a bitch."

DIE

I switched the sword to my left hand and drew a Glock in my right, and instructed Bobby to pop the door open on my command. I nodded and he threw the door open. I sighted down the barrel through the doorway...

...and Piotr wasn't there. A white blur flashed before me, and the gun was gone. Then, Piotr was back in the room but behind Gabby, with one pale, white, manicured hand resting on her shoulder. Behind me, I sensed Bobby coiling himself up to spring into action, so I motioned for him to stand down with one hand without breaking eye contact with the vamp. Out of habit I stared at the center of his body, because my training taught me that staring someone in the eyes in a violent confrontation was an invitation to disaster.

For one, you couldn't watch their hands and feet well with your eyes that high, and second, skilled and experienced killers knew how to feint with their eyes. Based on what I'd heard about this bloodsucker, I decided to keep my eyes right where they were, although I could feel... *something* compelling me to— *look up look up look up*—but I resisted the urge, and then it passed. The thing let out a short humph, and then it turned to Kara and spoke.

"Kara, my love, look—our guests have arrived." I ignored the obvious jibe and focused on finding a way to beat this thing while he jabbered on. He spread his arms wide, as if challenging me to draw with my other hand; I didn't fall for that either. "Welcome, welcome, welcome. I'm so glad you could make it to this *momentous* occasion, and witness the coming of the next age. How honored you all are to witness the dawn of this bright future we're bringing to your world."

Like Van, his voice was melodious and almost soothing, but in his case it sounded more like the voice of a game show host or politician than an opera singer. He had an annoying habit of placing emphasis on certain words, and I wasn't really sure whether it was part of an act, or if he really was selling some sort of undead New Age Kool-Aid.

"Oh, but it's not *your* world anymore, is it? No, of course not, although I'm sure you'll find us to be more than generous to those of your kind who get with the program, as they say." He gestured toward Kara. "As the lovely Kara here can readily attest. Isn't that right, love?" Kara continued typing at the keys; whether she was ignoring him or oblivious to his nattering, I couldn't say.

I took a step closer to him, opening up some space behind me for Bobby and the rabbi to move. If I wasn't mistaken, the rabbi was still hiding just outside the door, and I wanted to give him room to toss one of his potions or elixirs or bombs or whatever the hell he had, if it came down to that.

The vamp gestured magnanimously. "Oh yes, do come in, one and all. You simply mustn't miss this event. It is a—well, a once in a lifetime occasion."

I sighed, not just for effect, but because I was really tired of these undead jokers. Like, really freaking tired. I just wanted to kill this damnable thing, take Kara, and head back to the Facility and make babies for the foreseeable future. And to hell with the planet, to hell with the United States, to hell with the undead, and to hell with everyone but the two of us. I was done stepping up because no one else would. We could recruit some of Colin's boys to take the serum, and let them do the stepping up. I'd be perfectly happy to train them and cheer from the sidelines from here on out. But, there was just one thing standing in my way.

Piotr.

"Look here, *Peter*," I said, emphasizing Peter as a juvenile jab at his name. I mean, come on; nobody named their kids Peter anymore. At least, not if they didn't want them to get beaten up. Heck, even the kid in *The Hunger Games* dropped the "r" off his name, because you know that punk didn't need any more beatdowns than life was already going to hand to him. "Let's cut the shit. I don't see any bright new future, and certainly not for my kind. In fact, all I've seen since your kind arrived is death for my people."

He tilted his head at me slightly, and placed a hand on Gabby's shoulder once more. Both terror and disgust were plainly written on her face, and her eyes begged me to do some-thing, but I shook my head. *Not yet.* I wanted to make a move so badly, though; this whole ordeal had been a lot for a teenager to take, and although she was highly resilient, she looked like she was about to crack.

"Well, Scratch—I can call you that, can't I? I mean, really—I've heard *so* much about you."

He glanced over at Kara, and the look he gave her inferred a level of creep that I'd only ever seen in pedophiles and serial killers in the past. I made a mental note to mar that Hollywood face, if given the chance. His gaze returned to me, and I fought the natural urge to make eye contact.

"As I was saying, I'll concede that point to you. If there's one

thing on which we can agree, it's that your race has been deci-
mated over the past eight years, has it not? However, I can
assure you that the last thing we want is for your kind to go
extinct. Think about it: what would we do for amusement, were
that to happen?"

I took another step closer to Gabby and the bloodsucker,
because I knew that the rabbi was up to something; I just didn't
know what. But when it happened, I wanted to be in range and
close enough to punch this asshole's ticket. I risked a look over at
Kara, hoping to get some sign that she'd noticed my presence,
but she was still typing away at the terminal in front of her.

Why wouldn't Kara look at me?

I ran through a million scenarios in my head, and finally
figured she was probably under Piotr's control. But even if she
was under some sort of vampire hypnosis, letting her know I
wasn't angry couldn't hurt. So, I gathered up my courage and
did my best to tell her everything was going to be okay.

"Kara, baby, I'm here for you. Please don't worry about
anything that's happened since this thing took you. There's
nothing to be ashamed of, and nothing I wouldn't do for you.
I'm going to get you out of here, and then we're going to go
somewhere safe. I promise."

Her head might have sagged a bit at the sound of my voice,
but maybe it was just my imagination playing tricks on me.
More than anything, I wanted to kill this thing and get her out
of here, but I still wasn't close enough to Piotr to act quickly
enough to hit him. He was just too damned fast, no matter how
much the serum had sped my reflexes up. I took another step
forward, closing more than half the distance across the room.

By this point my blood was on fire, and the instinctual rage
that I felt for this thing who'd hurt my pack was overwhelming.
It was taking every bit of self-control I had to resist the urge to
attack. Yet I knew based on how the serum had worked up to

this point that I might only get one shot, just one flash of super-human alacrity before my body and the sickness betrayed me. I needed to make it count.

As I stepped forward, Piotr twitched a finger and nicked the side of Gabby's neck with one of his perfectly manicured nails. "Drop the sword, please, or I'll spill her blood all over the console." He patted Gabby's shoulder. "And what a waste that would be, to end this *succulent* young lady's life before I've even had a taste." He tsked. "So *wasteful*."

I relaxed my fingers and let the katana tumble to the hard tile floor. Kara continued clicking away at the keyboard, and the glow from the room beyond the glass became brighter still. Piotr's eyes nearly closed in apparent ecstasy as a beatific smile split his face.

"Ah, I can feel Them coming. My brethren! How they course and champ at the bit; how eager they are to cross over and experience all the carnal thrills offered in this wonderful playground that you unfortunate monkeys have called home for millennia. How its *pleasures* have been squandered by your kind." His eyes opened and he tsked again at nothing in particular. "But no longer. Your kind will now serve my kind, and you will revel in your servitude." He lifted one hand and beckoned me forward, toward the glass. "Come, Scratch. Come and see what your *beloved* has wrought on your kind."

———

I MOVED FORWARD SLOWLY, wary of any trick or ruse that might be in play, but Piotr had all but forgotten my presence, as well as that of Gabby at his side. He was staring out the glass at the scene beyond. I looked over at Kara as I approached the glass, but before I could get a glimpse of her face, the madness happening down below drew my gaze away.

As I looked out into the reactor room, I saw that we were about fifteen feet above the reactor room floor. Roughly twenty feet away at the center of the room was a pool approximately ten feet in diameter, filled with water and containing a strange apparatus that I assumed consisted of the reactor rods and mechanical controls. The blue glow was emanating from the pool, but within that glow were faint outlines and wraith-like figures that were nightmares come to life. Ghastly faces and figures bubbled up from the glowing pool, fighting and scratching and clawing at each other, each one jockeying for a position at the forefront of that mass of spirits.

They were in some cases only vaguely human, and in others, so alien as to make me nauseous to look upon them. Yet I couldn't turn my gaze away. As I looked, I could see beyond that slowly opening doorway, past the boundaries of this reality and through the gates of Hell. There were thousands; no, tens of thousands, literally legions of those evil, twisted creatures waiting to cross over and finish the job they'd started.

With extreme effort, I tore my eyes away and looked at Piotr. "No. I won't allow it."

He chuckled and turned to face me. "Oh, but my good man, there's really *nothing* you can do about it. If you try to stop us in here, I'll simply kill the girl. And if you went in *there*," he gestured beyond the glass, "you'd fry like an egg on a hot skillet."

I glanced back to the scene below, just in time to finally realize what Rabbi Manny had been up to all this time. I grinned maniacally and pointed. "You're right, I can't do a damned thing. But he can."

Piotr's head turned faster than my eyes could follow as he tore his gaze from me and back to the reactor floor. Down below, Josef was wreaking havoc on the reactor equipment, ripping the machinery to shreds and forcing the control rods one by one back into the reactor's containment structure. As he did so, the glow slowly faded, and those horrible faces and figures became less distinct with every passing second. Piotr's palms landed on the glass partition, leaving spider-web cracks in the glass as he screamed loudly, "No, you fool!"

It was time to act. I reached behind my back and whipped forth the blade the rabbi had given me, a twelve-inch stainless steel and silver Damascus rondel. In a single burst of inhuman speed, I stabbed it under the left side of his ribcage from behind and up toward his heart. Piotr sagged slightly, then he back-handed me quicker than I could block, even when running on bullet time. I caught it on my helmet and my cranium snapped back as I rolled with it, coming up with the katana in a crouch, head swimming and vision barely focusing on the vamp just a few feet away. He was trying to reach around to pull the dagger out, but he was weakening. With each flailing movement of his arms, he dropped lower and lower toward the floor. Whatever the rabbi had put on that knife, it must have been some powerful stuff.

I began to move forward to finish him off, but Kara moved faster than me, grasping the vampire's head between her hands and twisting in a rapid, counter-clockwise motion. His neck snapped and his body sagged; she released his head and he collapsed in a heap. Then, hiding her face from me with her lab coat she ran from the room in a blur. I wasn't sure if my eyes were playing tricks on me or if it was some kind of sick joke. I turned to follow her, but staggered as the infection in my blood-stream betrayed me yet again. I stumbled against the glass, and barely held myself up as I watched the scene below.

Down below, Josef's hands blackened and smoked as he forced the control rods deep down into the containment housing by hand. As each rod was lowered, the glow from the reactor faded, slowly but surely receding to a faint blue glow. The demonic faces howled in frustration with each moment he worked, receding back into their imprisonment in that place beyond the Veil. Soon, only darkness remained. As he was done, the great monster collapsed at the side of the pool, sitting child-like while his clothing still smoldered and steamed from the heat of the reactor.

I stumbled around and slid down the wall of glass and cinder block to the floor. As I did, Bobby rushed over with Colin on his heels. I waved them away and pointed to the vampire's body. "Colin, put that big ginsu knife of yours to good use and make sure that thing doesn't get back up." Then I gestured at Gabby, who was crying silent tears with pity in her eyes. "And Bobby, please untie Gabby and see to it that she's okay."

Then I slowly tilted my head back, and the world grayed out as I slipped into unconscious oblivion.

W hen I regained consciousness, I was lying on a couch inside a break room of some sort. I hurt like hell all over. I had a headache to end all headaches, and felt like I wanted to puke. My head was fuzzy, and everything had a sort of grayish cast to it. *Concussion*, I thought. *It figures. That vamp packed a wallop.* After the room stopped spinning, I sat up and glanced around. Gabby sat at the foot of the couch, and Bobby leaned against the wall across the room, munching on a stash of potato chips and peanut butter crackers he'd liberated from somewhere.

"Where's Kara?" I asked to no one in particular.

"We don't know. No one's seen her since she took off," Gabby replied sullenly.

I nodded, even though it made my head pound to do so. "And the rabbi and Colin?"

"They decided to bring the settlers over here, for safety's sake. They should be back any minute."

"What about the golem?"

Bobby spoke up from across the room. "Hasn't moved since that stunt he pulled. The rabbi says he'll be radioactive for a while. Not safe to be around anyone living. So, he's keeping him in the reactor room for now." He munched on some chips and sprayed crumbs as he continued. "Plus, he said he wanted Josef to keep an eye on the area, to make sure nothing got through."

I grunted something unintelligible in reply, and sat there collecting what little thoughts I could gather while suffering the aftereffects of a grade 3 concussion. I took a deep breath and whispered as I held my head in my hands. "Gabby."

"Yeah Scratch."

"Is Kara—one of Them?"

Her voice was so soft I could barely hear it, despite the deathly silence of the building. "Yes."

She wrapped her small arms around my shoulders, and I wept until I had nothing left.

————

I SLEPT until the next day, when I awoke to the sound of Janie and Nadine bitching and griping at each other from outside the break room where I'd crashed the night before. Apparently, Nadine was of the opinion that I hadn't roused my happy ass early enough to satisfy her expectations. My head still pounded from the stunning blow that Piotr had given me, and if the way my face throbbed was any indication, I probably looked as bad as I felt.

The good news was that the general feeling of fuzziness had passed. Concussions were like that; your brain would go on autopilot for a time, while it tried to fix whatever had short circuited the connections that normally allowed you to walk, speak and think coherently. Then, hours later you'd get what boxers called "your wake-up call," and suddenly the world was brighter and you could do simple math and think rationally again.

Of course, I knew that you weren't supposed to go to sleep after suffering a head injury; I just didn't care much after the revelations of the previous evening. We'd found out that there were perhaps tens of thousands of Them trying to come across the Veil; that there was a race of super-vampires that could move like Speedy Gonzales and who hit like the Hulk; and, oh yeah, my girlfriend had been turned into a vampire. No biggie.

As I reflected on the events of the past day, and Nadine's shrill voice bounced around the room and drove nails in my skull, I felt every single ache, pain, bump, and bruise from every fight and scrape I'd been in over the past few weeks. Something inside me just snapped. I jumped up and stormed out of the room, slamming the door against the wall with a crash and rudely interrupting whatever conversation they'd been having before I busted in.

Nadine turned and looked at me, only momentarily shocked by my sudden appearance. And just as she cracked those nasty, puckered, smoker's mouth lips to complain, I shouted with menace in my voice.

"Just one more word, Nadine—one more ever-loving word from that disgusting open sore you call a mouth, and I will personally hogtie you and leave you here to get eaten by the shamblers when we head for freedom!"

She took a step back with one hand on her chest, stunned. Then she gathered herself and glared at me as she took in a short breath.

"Not one more word!" I said with menace in my voice.

She tucked tail and ran from the room.

Janie just stood there with a hand over her mouth, trying to avoid laughing and doing a piss-poor job of it. "Well Scratch, I—"

I cut her off, knuckling my forehead as I spoke at a whisper. "You too, Janie. I'm just not in the mood today." She looked as though she might say something, then she turned up her nose and walked off, head held high and in no particular hurry. She reminded me of my mother; nothing could rattle that woman, and she'd been nigh on unflappable, just like Janie.

Gabby walked into the hall from an adjacent room, shaking her head. "Well, I think that straightened them out." She grabbed my arm and gently pulled me down the hall. "C'mon, *viejo*. I have something that should cheer you up a bit."

She led the way and I followed without resistance, fully worn down and spent from all that we'd been through over the previous days and nights. Gabby walked me into another room, where the smell of coffee—real, honest to God coffee—quickly perked me up and gave me a reason to live, if only for a few more minutes.

"Good Lord, kid—you struck black gold?"

She shrugged. "I didn't. Bobby turned up a bunch of it while he was rummaging around for snacks. When I saw what he'd found, I snagged it all before anyone else could grab it. Figured you'd need a cup this morning." She poured, I sipped, and although it didn't fix my broken heart, it did make my pounding head feel a little better.

After downing half a cup, I took a seat at the break room table and looked around. "Any chance that furry little bastard came across any sugar?" In reply, she dug around in her pack and tossed me a red and white cardboard and plastic cylinder, then joined me at the table. I held it to my chest and smiled. "Ah, the good stuff." I poured a liberal amount in my cup and stirred it with my finger, ignoring the minor burns I received for my efforts.

Gabby sat quietly, observing me while I finished my first cup of coffee, and again halfway through another cup. Finally, I decided to break the ice. "So, kid, did that vamp hurt you at all?"

She shook her head. "Naw, he was too busy with all that

nuclear stuff." She looked down at the table and chewed her lip. "Sam couldn't resist him, though. That *pendejo* said I had to go with him, or else he'd make Sam kill himself." She stopped and pushed around some sugar crystals that I'd spilled. "I'm sorry about your friend. He was a really nice man."

I looked into my cup and swirled it around a bit. "Yeah, he was."

"So what's the plan?" She propped her feet up on the table, then leaned back in the chair and crossed her arms. "I mean, besides scaring old ladies who don't know when to shut up."

I smirked at her. "She deserved it."

"Yeah, she did." She locked her fingers behind her head. "Still doesn't tell me what we do next."

I swirled my coffee again to mix the last few dregs of sugar and that heavenly nectar into a uniform, syrupy liquid that I tossed back in a single swallow. "Well, now I get you all back to the Facility. And hopefully in one piece."

"And then?"

"Then..." I paused and thought about it. "Then I'm going fishing."

[38]

WIFE

We spent the day prepping for the trip back to the Facility. Camp Bullis was a long ways off, and I now had twenty-plus warm bodies to get there while avoiding any casualties. I figured that once we picked up Colin's crew, we'd have plenty of fighters on hand to help get everyone to safety. But we still had to get them all back to the Facility, which presented a hell of a logistical conundrum.

But no matter how much trouble Piotr had caused for me, he had given me a crazy idea. His Tesla was spotless, and it ran like a top. The research campus had generators that were still in good working order; where they got diesel that wasn't gummed up was anyone's guess, but they worked. Plus, they had solar, so it wasn't that difficult to charge the thing up and use it to zoom around. I started thinking about it, and wondered if it might be possible to round up several electric vehicles that we could use to ferry everyone out of here.

I seemed to recall that most electric cars had ranges of one to two hundred miles on a full charge. The area we were in had been yuppie central, so I was fairly certain we could find more than a few of them in the shopping center parking lots and garages nearby. If we could find some that were still operational, they might get us within walking distance of the Facility; "might" being the operational term. But the real question was whether any of them had survived the EMP from the nuclear attack.

I tasked Bobby and Colin to search the parking garages, and Gabby and I took the parking lots. Soon we'd located and map-marked a half-dozen vehicles that might have still been in working order. I had Colin drive while Bobby pushed and Gabby and I rode shotgun, and six hours later we had them all back at the research campus, charging up off their solar and battery backups. Only those that had been parked in the garages on the lower levels showed any promise. The rest had succumbed to either the EMP or the Texas heat; it was difficult to know which was the more likely culprit. I decided to wait until morning to try them out, figuring that it was best to allow them to reach a maximal charge before testing them to see if they were still operational.

Time was running out, though. With the wolves gone, it was clear that the local nos' we'd run into at the theater wasn't keeping the dead out of the area any longer. Whether he'd cut bait and run, or decided to have a little fun at our expense—well, that was anyone's guess. What was clear was that deaders were massing at the fences in a few key points, and all our activity hadn't done much to help the situation. In a few days, the fences would be down, and we'd be overrun.

Yet, even by stuffing people into cars like circus clowns, we were short at least a half-dozen seats. We had four vehicles that could potentially operate, including the Tesla. That'd get us maybe twenty bodies, tops. Plus, the more people we loaded the cars down with, the shorter their range. We could end up having to hole everyone up at Canyon Lake, and then make the rest of the way on foot.

No rest for the weary, I thought as I looked at the maps and wondered how I was going to get my people safely all the way to the Facility.

———

IT WAS TOO much to think about at the moment, so later that evening I set it off to the side and buried Sam. Bobby helped with the digging, and Gabby and some of the settlers who had known him showed up to say a few words. Despite the moans and sounds of the dead in the distance, it was a nice ceremony. After that, all I wanted to do was forget about things for a few hours. I stayed up late drinking cheap bourbon, playing cards and talking shit with Colin.

"You know, we still have that bet going on," he said as he dealt the cards out on the table. "By my count, you have me beat four to two."

"Eleven to two."

"What, you're counting the explosion? Fine, then I get credit for the vamp."

I snorted. "Seriously? I did all the heavy lifting there, as I recall."

He shook his head. "Actually, your girlfriend did all the heavy lifting. I just finished the job." He must've noticed the look on my face, because the smile on his vanished. "Sorry, didn't mean to bring her up. I know it must be a sore subject right about now."

I ignored him like it was no big deal. It was a big deal, and he and I both knew it, but the guy code said you didn't talk about deep, serious shit, and especially not during a card game. Alcohol could temporarily suspend the guy code rules, but neither of us were drunk enough for an exception at the moment.

I looked at my cards, pursed my lips, and gave a small wave of my hand. "S'okay, don't sweat it." I looked at my cards again. "Hmph. Well, I've been kicking your ass at poker all night, so I guess I can let you take credit for ganking the vamp." I sipped my bourbon and set my cards face down on the table.

Colin looked at me, looked at his hand, and looked at me again. "Why do I get the feeling you're about to show another winning hand?"

I resisted the urge to grin and maintained my best poker face. "Does that mean you call?"

"I think that means I fold." He tossed his cards on the table, face-side down, and stood up. "At least the bourbon makes losing a little easier." He downed the rest of his glass and grimaced. "Wow, that's bad."

I laughed. "Score stands five to three then. I'll concede the 'thropes that were caught in the explosion."

"Five to three? Where'd you pick up the fifth one?"

"If you're taking credit for the vamp, that means I get credit for Van."

"You're a piece of work, Sullivan," he said as he yawned and stretched. "Alright, we have a long haul ahead, so I'm going to sack out. Remember, tomorrow's a new day—there's plenty of road between here and the castle, and plenty of time to even the score."

"Hope you're not too attached to that big pig sticker of yours. From the way things are going, it has my name written all over it."

He laughed as he walked off. "Keep dreaming, buddy. Keep dreaming."

After he left, I checked his last hand; he'd had a full house.

I didn't take pity well. *You need to get your shit together, Sully,* I thought as I headed off to the couch.

———

I DOZED off sometime before midnight, and woke not long after with the feeling that someone was watching me in my sleep.

"Hi, Scratch." It was Kara's voice.

I cracked my eyes open and searched the room, finding her sitting across from me in the dark. I sat up on the couch and rubbed the sleep from my eyes. She'd discarded the lab coat, heels, and pencil skirt, and was wearing jeans, hiking boots, and a long-sleeved t-shirt. Her hair was pulled back in a ponytail, and her hands were folded in her lap.

I cleared my throat. "Are you—still you?"

She sat as still as a stone, without breath or heartbeat. It was creepy as all hell, and I started to reach for my pistol just as she took a single breath and spoke. "Sorry, I often forget to breathe these days. Piotr told me that I needed to teach myself to do it without thinking about it, so I could blend in and avoid frightening people off." She rubbed her hands on her jeans and slapped her knees lightly. "In answer to your question... I just don't know yet."

I just sat there watching her and waiting for more, when I realized she was covering her mouth with her hand whenever she spoke. It was silly, because it was her movements that gave her away; the lack of breathing, her unnaturally quick gestures, and how *still* she could be when she wasn't speaking. It was uncanny, it was revolting—and yet, it was still her.

She took another, awkward breath and continued. "When they—took me, Piotr tried to put me under his control. I couldn't be broken that way, so he started killing people. After he killed a little girl, I gave in and let him—well, I let him have his way with me. He said it was more enjoyable if I cooperated. One night not long after that, he bit me, and the feelings it gave me... I can't describe it. It was like he knew me, knew everything about me, just as soon as he'd bitten me. Little did I know, that connection would only make it easier for him to control me with his mind."

She wriggled around in her seat, and after failing to get comfortable, she stood up and paced the room. "All I wanted was to save these people. I didn't want to cooperate, and I didn't want to help them build the gateway, or whatever it was he was trying to accomplish here. At first, I tried to resist by doing little things to sabotage the project. A few lines of bad code here, a deleted line of code there—whatever I thought I could get away with. I actually thought that I could cause a meltdown, and that even if I killed everyone, it'd be better than the alternative."

"But he knew what you were doing." It was a statement, not a question.

"Yes, damn it! Every time he fed from me, I became less human, and more one of Them, and the more influence he gained over me. He could see inside my mind, he knew my thoughts, and soon there was nothing I could hide from him. After I was completely under his control, he'd spend hours picking through my memories, sifting them like wheat, playing with them. Let me tell you, there's no rape like someone raping your mind. I couldn't wash enough to get clean after that." She paused and took another deep breath, letting out a sigh before she continued. "And then, he made me feed."

She walked to a window and looked out on the grounds below. "She was a child, no more than ten or eleven. He brought her to me in the middle of the night, after I'd been working for hours, and I was so hungry. I nearly killed her, Scratch; I couldn't stop feeding. He had to beat me off her to keep me from killing her, and not because he cared about that child, but because he said it didn't make sense to waste cattle needlessly. Cattle, he called her!

"After I came to my senses I tried to cry, but you know what? Vampires can't cry. Funny, huh? No blood tears, no real tears, nothing." She rubbed her face and chuckled mirthlessly. "After that, I fought him harder, and eventually figured out that I could resist his will, but only at the cost of a great deal of mental pain. But I was able to do it, so I stopped working for him. That's when he told me that you were coming for me, and that the only way he'd let you live was if I would complete the project."

"You could have held out, Kara—"

"No Scratch, I couldn't. Ultimately, you were the one thing I wasn't willing to sacrifice. After I understood what he was trying to accomplish here, and what that might mean for humanity, I was willing to sacrifice everyone and everything else. Janie and the rest of them, the kids, myself. Everything and everyone but you."

I decided to change tack. "Kara, maybe there's a way to change you back. There's this scientist I met, and she knows about how these things work. Maybe she can fix you, and turn you back to the way you were before."

She shook her head, which was creepy because of how fast she moved when she wasn't paying attention. "I'll never be human again, Scratch. Piotr was eight hundred years old, and he knew just about everything there was to know about the undead. He said there was no cure for vampirism, no way to go back to my former life."

"Maybe he lied."

She "gruffled" at me, an affectation of hers that was a cross between a growl and a huff. I'd always found it to be endearing, but this time, her heart wasn't in it. "No, Scratch, I don't think so." She sat and hung her head, and cried in tearless sobs. I got up the courage to stand, and I walked over to her and put my arm around her shoulders, holding her close. She leaned into me, sobbing on my shoulder, and then suddenly she shoved me away with a sharp, vicious palm-heel that sent me sprawling.

"No! You can't be that close to me. I—I can't control it, not when I can feel your heart beating and sense the blood pulsing under your skin." She gathered herself together, sighed an inhuman sigh, and stood. "Sorry if I hurt you, but I'm dangerous to you right now. To everyone, in fact."

I rubbed my chest and stood. "Nothing wounded but my pride. And my broken cowboy heart."

Her head tilted in sympathy. "Oh darlin', please, just don't." She walked up to me, and softly cupped my chin in one cold, undead hand.

"I promise you, my love, that if I can find a way to be with you again, I will. But for now, I can't be around for fear that I'll hurt the one person I can't bear to lose." She dropped her hand and turned to go.

How's that for bitter freaking irony? I thought as she started to walk away. Then my conscience overrode my self-pity, and I remembered that I had a duty to protect the innocent.

"Wait. Kara, how will you survive?"

She cracked a crooked grin, and I caught a flash of incisor as she spoke. "Punter blood's as warm as any, yeah?" She winked at me. "Stay true to yourself, Scratch, and don't wait for me if you can't."

I decided that I could live with that answer—or part of it, anyway. I gulped and nodded. "Be seeing you."

She nodded back. "Someday, Scratch. Maybe someday."

And then she was gone, in the span of a heartbeat. The love of my life was gone, and I didn't have a clue what I was going to do next.

Now Colin and Janie are headed back to the castle house with all the rest of the settlers, and Gabby, Bobby, and I are hoofing it on foot. Colin says they'll look for more cars near the castle, and charge them by scavenging for more solar panels and a bigger power convertor. Then we'll ferry everyone in as many trips as it takes to get us all to the Facility. But it'll be a slow process, and I'm nearly certain there'll be trouble along the way.

To be honest, though, I'm kind of looking forward to it. I have a lot of anger issues these days, and the only thing that seems to sort it out for me is killing Them. It's only a temporary solution, and one that I find I have to repeat. I'm looking forward to getting a lot of therapy on the way to Camp Bullis.

Incidentally, Van and Piotr look real good, tied up with barbed wire on the front gates of the research facility. As a parting gift I carved a warning into their chests, one I borrowed from the Scottish regiments:

Nemo me impune lacessit.

In Texan, that roughly translates to, "Mess with me, and die."

This concludes Counteraction: Werewolf Apocalypse... but the story continues in Gabby's Run: Paranormal Apocalypse and Extinction: Undead Apocalypse!
Look for them at all major online booksellers.

And be sure to get your two FREE ebooks at
http://MDMassey.com

ABOUT THE AUTHOR

M.D. Massey has been a soldier, an emergency room technician, a fitness trainer, a truck driver, a martial arts instructor, a cook, a consultant, a web designer, and a security professional. He also spent six weeks in law school before deciding that, if he was going to lie for a living, he'd do it honestly as a fiction writer. M.D. lives in Austin, Texas with his family and a huge American Bulldog who keeps him company while he writes the sort of books he likes to read.

Find out more and get two FREE ebooks at:
http://MDMassey.com

www.ingramcontent.com/pod-product-compliance
Lightning Source LLC
Chambersburg PA
CBHW060130130626
46556CB00006B/2300